Pages of Promise

COASTAL HOPE

JESSICA ASHLEY

B.A.D.
PUBLISHING

B.A.D.
PUBLISHING

PAGES OF PROMISE
A Coastal Hope Novel
By Jessica Ashley

Edited by Love Kissed Books, LLC
Edited by HEA Author Services

Proofread by Dawn Y
Cover Design by Covers by Christian
Photographer: Wander
Model: Jack

Pages of Promise

———

A wounded veteran who walks by faith. A traumatized woman struggling with hers.

Running from secrets that could bury her, Eliza Pierce has traveled cross-country for her fresh start. But a threatening letter left in her mailbox less than a week later throws her back into the flames of her past.

Former Army Ranger Lance Knight may have been discharged from duty, but that doesn't mean he's any less a soldier. As the owner of a private security firm, he's fought plenty of battles stateside.

When someone makes an attempt on Eliza's life, it's Lance she turns to. And despite a first impression that left both of them wanting nothing to do with the other, he agrees to help…even if it means trading his own life for hers.

If you are looking for a sizzling (but not spicy!) romantic suspense, with a protective Christian hero, a small town that protects their own, and a team of wounded veterans turned private security officers, then Pages of Promise is for you!

A Note from the Author

After spending quite a few years chasing a love I wasn't sure existed, I found my husband, Nathan, on a dating website of all places. It was my last resort, given that I was in the Army and working absolutely crazy hours.

We've been married thirteen years now, and have been blessed with three beautiful children. He was my first true love, and to this day, I'm still not entirely sure why God allowed me to have such a life after I spent so many years running from Him.

God also blessed me with the passion for telling stories. And after spending nearly the last decade writing romance novels for the secular world, I began to feel the pull toward Christian romance.

It's been a scary jump—after all, I've built a career writing in other genres—but with this leap of faith came such a beautiful understanding of what true love really is.

Of how two people can find each other in the darkest of moments, and—guided by the light of God—their faith can grow even when things are bleak.

Pages of Promise is a love story that I have poured my heart and soul into. I have prayed for guidance, done my best to ignore the voices of doubt, and now I am beyond proud of the story I have told.

Eliza and Lance are close to my heart, because just as Lance wants to guide Eliza, it was my husband who pulled me back into the light when we first met. It was him who brought me back into church when I'd been left disheartened by others I'd been to.

And it was he who helped me see that God doesn't let you down—ever.

Over the last year, I have grown substantially in my faith, and now spend my mornings reading the Bible chapter by chapter, letting His word guide me through my day-to-day.

I've come to understand—thanks to our amazing pastor—that we cannot heal ourselves, but God can. And He will. All we have to do is let Him into our heart.

And every single day I wake up, I am beyond grateful for the gift of forgiveness and the Holy Spirit.

I hope, that this story brings you closer to Him, and that you realize you are loved, even when you feel as though you are alone.

-Jessica

To all those who feel unworthy.
You are worthy.
You are loved.
And when the struggle gets to be too much to carry, just remember Joshua 1:9.

CHAPTER 1
Eliza

I have this recurring nightmare where I'm lying on a set of train tracks in the dark. I can feel the chill of the steel beneath my body as a light breeze blows across my face. The deep booming of the train horn is deafening as the lights grow brighter and brighter the closer it comes.

Even as the vibrations grow stronger, I do not move.

Owls hoot, and coyotes yip, seemingly warning me to get up. To get away.

But I don't.

I just lie there. Waiting for an end to a life that I don't feel I ever really lived. My therapist believed it was because I felt as though I had no control over my life. No real purpose besides being arm candy to my husband. Then again, she also thinks my divorce was strictly to gain that control. Likely because, as it turns out, she's one of the nine other women he was having an affair with.

Truth be told, my marriage was little more than a shell long before I learned about his infidelity. Mean fists and a meaner tongue stole away plenty of years before that particular embarrassment came. What's sad, though, is it wasn't until I learned he'd been cheating that I found the courage to leave. I was more concerned with what the public saw than what went on behind closed doors.

You're not there anymore, Eliza, I remind myself.

For the first time in ten years, I'm free.

For the first time in my entire *life*, I'm free.

Whatever that means.

I shove the past where it belongs and focus on what's right in front of me. The sign for Hope Springs is straight ahead. The population number is worn down so much that I can barely make it out, though I know from my research it's in the vicinity of seven-thousand.

The complete opposite of where I'm coming from, which is perfect. I want nothing to do with who I was before. It's a fresh start for me, baby. A brand-new Eliza.

As I sit here on the side of the road in the early morning, no one passes. The road has been relatively vacant for the past fifteen miles, so I remain right where I am a bit longer, staring at the sign ahead and the sand dunes all along my left where ocean meets land. To my right, a parking area with two cars allows visitors the chance to move across the highway and head down to the water.

The idea is tempting, but if the pictures of my new home are anything like those the realtor sent, I'll be sitting beachside momentarily.

"Okay, old girl. We've got a few more miles, right?" I gently pat the dash of my beat-up old car just before turning the key, breathing a sigh of relief when the engine rumbles back to life. The guy I bought this beat-up old car from hadn't believed it would make it all the way across the country, but here I am.

Grinning, I roll the window down and take a deep breath. Salty sea air fills my lungs, and I grin. I've lived near a beach my entire life, and yet, I already can't wait to get my toes in the sand as though it's my first time.

Because here, in Hope Springs, Maine, I am getting my fresh start.

No cheating husband.

No abuse.

No pitied onlookers who knew it all and chose to do nothing to help.

Just me. My computer. And blissful silence.

With a smile still lingering on my face, I guide my car back onto the road and head into town. Main Street looks exactly like it did in the pictures I found on the internet. Weathered, aged buildings line the street, a mixture of brick and wood that are beyond charming. The place might as well be the cover of a Small Coastal Town USA magazine. If such a thing existed.

People stroll down the sidewalks, smiling and chatting happily, completely unaware that I'm driving in for what is the first—and hopefully last—time.

As I drive, I make note of the buildings and business locations so, when I head out later, I'm not completely lost.

The hardware store where Felix Bishop—the plumber who will install my new water heater works—is absolutely adorable with a freshly painted sign and bright yellow and white awning.

The small movie theatre is playing a movie that has been out for nearly a year in LA, yet there are a few people standing in line to buy tickets.

Through the picture windows of the diner, I can make out happy people dining together.

A gorgeous white church with a single steeple is the only building on Main Street that sits on the side of the ocean. *Man, I bet the view off the back is stunning.*

I turn the corner and pass a school with a playground full of small children. From the research I did, I know it's one of the rare schools that house all grades, K-12. And with an average class size of twelve, it makes perfect sense.

After following the road past the school and over a small hill, I finally get the first look at the out-of-service lighthouse that will serve as my new home. Its tall tower is wrapped with faded red and white stripes, and the light may have gone out years ago, but I was able to pay cash for it, thanks to the divorce settlement.

Which makes it all mine. Honestly, aside from this car, it's the first and only thing I've ever owned completely. Even the clothes on my back once came with stipulations.

"Smile, Eliza."

"Look like a woman worthy of being on my arm, Eliza."

"Befriend that woman, Eliza."

Shaking my head to clear memories I'm determined to

keep in the past, I focus fully on what's ahead of me as I pull down the gravel drive, put the car in Park, and turn off the engine.

I grip the steering wheel tightly and close my eyes, breathing in the salty sea air again through my open window. As I do, I imagine myself stepping outside with a fresh cup of steaming coffee and a good book. "Welcome home, Eliza," I whisper to myself then climb out and stare out at the ocean view that should have cost me a fortune but thankfully didn't.

A rickety fence and a small sand dune are all that separates me from a gorgeous beach and an even more stunning ocean. How cool will it be to sit right on the porch and stare out as storms roll into the harbor?

Peace. That's what I'll find here. In *my* home. Not Erick's, not a foster home, not an orphanage. Mine. And I know exactly what I'm doing first.

After locking the car, I rush toward the sagging iron fence then push the gate open and descend worn wooden steps. As soon as I've reached the bottom, I slip out of my shoes and slide my toes into the sand.

It's cold. Nearly freezing in the February weather, but I can't be bothered to care. Because there is no one here to tell me how foolish it is to walk barefoot in the sand. No one to tell me all the hazards waiting for me for simply enjoying the way it feels.

"There are worms in the sand, Eliza."

"Junkies leave their needles on the beach, Eliza."

Nothing Erick said to me will ever matter again. None

of the things he told me I could never do, or the behaviors he expected out of me, will stand even a second longer. From here on out, I will do what I want. When I want.

As soon as I've brushed as much sand from my feet as I can, I slip back into my flats and climb up the stairs toward my house. I unlock my car and grab my purse from the passenger seat, then make my way up onto my porch.

The front door is aged, some of the wood splintering, but some sanding and a fresh coat of paint will have it gleaming once more. I stretch up, gently tapping my fingers on top of the doorjamb as I look for the key the realtor left. As soon as my fingers close in on it, I pull it down and slip it into the lock.

Why does unlocking a door feel so good? The moment I hear the lock disengage, I nearly do a happy dance.

And the simple fact that it would have horrified my ex has me shaking my hips happily as I push the door open. With each move I make toward my new destiny, I feel like I gain back time lost in a marriage that tore me apart.

Stale air greets me, and dust particles dance in the air, thanks to the light breeze carrying through from outside. All of the furniture is covered in dusty white sheets, but as I flick the switch on the wall to my left, I'm elated to discover the light fixtures are in working condition.

The floor is old wood, but I know all it needs is a good cleaning to gleam like it once did. A metal spiral staircase encircles the interior, but I don't head up just yet, opting to inspect the small kitchen instead. It's a far cry from an entertainer's space, but given that I want to avoid all people for the foreseeable future, it's perfect.

Aged wooden countertops can be sanded and sealed, and the sink may be coated with dust, but it's a good size for just me. The appliances are long gone, but I already have new ones on the way to be delivered along with my furniture later this afternoon.

I turn and head for the staircase, following it up to a single bathroom and bedroom. Just off the bedroom, a balcony waits for new iron railing, but I still risk stepping out to stare out at the ocean.

Forget the front porch. This is where I'll take my morning coffee.

Nearly squealing with excitement, I race back downstairs and start pulling the sheets off the wooden furniture that is likely older than I am. A rocking chair, splintering coffee table, and a couch with torn and dusty cushions set atop a cracked wooden frame.

Still, I smile. Because, even in its current state, this tiny lighthouse feels more like home than the four-thousand-square-foot house I lived in with my ex-husband ever did.

"Okay, Eliza, this is it. Time for a fresh—"

Someone knocks at the door, so I cross over and pull it open. I'm expecting my realtor, or possibly the moving company here early, so when I'm greeted by a too-handsome-for-his-own-good man wearing a tight white t-shirt and dark jeans, I'm instantly put on edge.

All humor vanishes, and I'm left with this twisting in my gut that is part attraction and all nerves.

His hair, a light auburn, is longer on top and short on the sides, and a neatly trimmed auburn beard has threads of gold woven into it. Freckles give his face character while also managing to somehow make him look even more masculine.

Or, perhaps, that's the light coat of dirt on his tanned arms and the toolbelt around his waist that does that particular trick.

"Can I help you?" I demand, realizing with complete mortification that I've been staring.

"I'm actually here to help you." He smiles and holds out a hand. "I'm Lance, and I believe I'm supposed to be installing a hot water heater out here today? That is if you're Eliza Pierce."

I study his hand with the intensity of someone trying to diffuse a bomb but don't take it. Slowly, he lowers it. "No, Felix Bishop with Hope Hardware is supposed to be coming."

The man smiles, and the part of me that isn't dead inside warms. Which, of course, is aggravating. Haven't I had enough of handsome men? Men who come in and charm you then turn out to be literal walking nightmares?

"Felix had to watch his granddaughter today," Lance replies. "He sent me over to get it installed for you, Ms. Pierce. However, if you'd prefer him, I'm sure he can get out here tomorrow."

"Tomorrow? There's no hot water."

"Hence my visit."

I swallow hard, contemplating just how much I'll hate

not getting a shower tonight. I did my research on Felix since he was the one I was expecting. The aged hardware store owner and local plumber checked out completely. But I know nothing about this man.

I scan his hands for a ring, but there isn't one. Which makes me even more uncomfortable.

"Why don't you call and check in with Felix?" Lance questions. "Put your mind at ease that I am who I say I am."

"Yeah, I should do that." *Except, I don't have a cell phone.* "Never mind, I don't need to do that."

He arches a brow. "Are you sure?"

"Yes." I force a half-smile, but based on how I'm feeling inside, I imagine it reflects just how uncomfortable I am. Why did I not get a new cell phone? Of course, I know the answer to that. Money. "Go ahead and do it. I can show you where it needs to go."

"That would be great, thanks."

Stepping aside, I make space for him to come in and instantly regret not just pointing and giving directions. The man takes up space in a way you only ever read about. Even movies can't quite do it justice when showing the presence some people simply have.

And Lance—whatever his last name is—has a presence about him. An authority that unnerves me. "I need to go out to my car," I blurt. "The water heater is just back that way." I point in the general direction.

Lance nods. "No problem. I can manage." He smiles again and heads through the small living area until he reaches a back room and disappears inside. As soon as he's out of view, I head out onto the front porch and take a deep, steadying breath.

You're fine, I tell myself. *Erick is halfway across the country and has no idea where you are.*

The mantra is something I've repeated to myself over and over again for the past few weeks, ever since our divorce was finalized. Yet, right now, it doesn't seem to do much to quell my nerves.

Lance comes back out of the house and heads straight for his truck—a white Chevy—parked just behind my car. He reaches into the back and pulls out a box that seems far too small for a water heater before setting it on the ground and retrieving a toolbox.

"What is that?" I ask, pointing to the box.

"A tankless water heater," he replies. "Felix said it's what you ordered?"

Feeling foolish, I breathe a sigh of relief. What did I think was in the box? *Come on, Eliza. Get it together.* "Yes. That's what I wanted." I cross my arms over my chest and step back as he passes, keeping a wide berth between us.

"Great. Do you mind grabbing my toolbox for me?" Without waiting for a response from me, he lifts the box and heads inside.

I stare at it for a few moments, trying to decide what to do. I really don't want to go back into the house with him, but the sooner he gets it installed, the sooner he can leave.

Which is also what I want.

Ugh. With a groan, I head over and lift the heavy toolbox, then head back into the laundry room. There's no old tank, just a spot where it once sat along with a bunch of fresh copper piping that looks like it's only been in there a few days.

He flashes another grin at me. "Thanks."

"Seems like I'm paying you to install, not have me carry things for you." Despite my tone, his smile brightens.

"Doesn't hurt to shave a few minutes off the install time, does it?" he asks as he pulls out a knife and starts opening the top of the water heater box. Not only is he thoughtful, but the muscles in his arms flex with each movement, and my attraction for him begins to grow.

Which, of course, agitates me even more. He just had to be attractive, didn't he? I cross my arms. "So, you work for the hardware store?"

He unboxes the new water heater—a grey box with connection points out the bottom. "No. I ran into Felix at the diner when I went in for breakfast, and he asked for help. I wasn't doing anything this afternoon, so I stepped up."

I stiffen. "I'm sorry, but are you a licensed plumber?"

Lance stops and looks up at me. "As it so happens, I am. I just don't do plumbing as my day job anymore."

"So, you're out of practice yet feeling the need to—what—fill a nice-guy quota for the month?" My anger is misplaced, I know that, and still, I can't stop it. He's not supposed to be here. But here he is. On his knees in my laundry room.

Lance cocks his head to the side and studies me. "All

right, Big City, how about you fill me in on just what I've done to offend you in the mere minutes since we met?"

"No offense," I reply coldly. "But you're not the man I hired for the job. Not only that, but you're also not even a practicing plumber." The moment the words are out of my mouth, I feel like an idiot. But I refuse to be charmed by any more men. They can keep their smiles and bright eyes to themselves.

"Practicing plumber?" He laughs. "I'm not a doctor, Ms. Pierce. And installing a water heater is hardly surgery. I don't need to be actively practicing in order to do the job properly. And, if it makes you feel any better, I just installed one of these last week for Mrs. McGinley down at the library."

"Since I do not know Mrs. McGinley, nor can I follow up on your claims, it doesn't make me feel better."

Lance cocks his head to the side once again—like he's sizing me up. I step back. Despite my tone, he doesn't look angry. Not like Erick would have. Honestly, Lance looks… confused?

"Again, I will ask, if you would prefer Felix to do the work, I can gladly have him come over tomorrow, once he's done watching his granddaughter."

I should say yes. Should insist on it.

But the idea of a hot shower calls to me.

"No. Just do the job." I turn on my heel and march out onto the porch, all the while feeling angry at him and furious with myself because he didn't actually do anything to deserve my attitude. Not all men are Erick. I'm not so jaded that I don't see it.

An aged minivan pulls into the drive, and a woman wearing a brightly colored floral sundress climbs out. Her flaming red hair is a dead giveaway, and I find myself smiling as I cross down to greet her. Birdie has been an absolute delight to work with, even though, as soon as she found out I was newly single, she insisted on setting me up with her brother, who she swears would be perfect for me.

Thankfully, I sidestepped that by reminding her I just got out of a nasty divorce.

"Mrs. Eliza Pierce," she says with a bright smile.

"No *Mrs.* anymore," I reply. "Just Eliza. It's nice to finally meet you in person."

"You too. Get in here!" The realtor I've spent the last few months going back and forth with wraps her arms around me and pulls me in for a hug.

I pull back as quickly as I can without being rude.

"You are just as beautiful as your pictures. Maybe even more so." She beams. "Are you sure you don't want to meet my brother?" Before I can respond, though, she throws her head back and laughs. "I'm just kidding, I know you're in the process of moving on. We'll table it for now."

"I—"

"Well?" she interrupts. "What do you think? Is it everything I told you it would be?"

The woman is a whirlwind. "Yes. Complete with a not-plumber installing my water heater."

Her smile fades just a bit. "What do you mean?"

"A man named Lance is in there. He said he doesn't work for the hardware store but was doing the man you recommended a favor?"

That smile broadens. "Ahh yes. I heard Felix is on grandfather duty today. Lance is good people. He moved here about seven years ago, I think? Came from Boston."

"Boston."

"Yes. Handsome as God makes them, isn't he?" She wiggles her brows like I'm supposed to giggle and flush with color like some sort of schoolgirl.

"Arrogant, too," I reply.

"Really?" Her brows draw together. "I've never gotten that from him." She looks past me toward the porch and smiles brightly. "Hey, Lance! I see you've met Ms. Eliza Pierce."

"Something like that." Just the sound of his voice has me on edge. His tone is calm. Gentle. But it carries an edge and washes over me like warm rain. I don't care for it. Not even a little.

I force a smile and turn toward him. "Taking a break already?" I ask, venom lacing my words.

"Hardly," he replies. "It's done. Pleasure meeting you, Ms. Pierce." He shifts his attention to Birdie. "Tell that husband of yours I'm up for some fishing next week."

"Will do. See ya, Lance." She waves him off then turns back to me. "What exactly happened between you two?"

"Nothing. He showed up and wasn't what I expected, then informed me he wasn't a practicing plumber. I voiced concerns; he dismissed them."

"Practicing plumber. Is that a thing?" she asks. "Never mind. Come on, let's go see your new home!"

CHAPTER 2

Lance

That first impression could have gone better. Though, for the life of me, I can't quite figure out what I did wrong. Could be as simple as her not caring for the fact I showed up instead of Felix, but I can't shake the feeling there's something more. She'd looked almost—afraid. Once she realized she didn't recognize me.

Eliza Pierce. The woman is beautiful, there's no denying that. But it wasn't even her physical appearance that had me awestruck from the moment she opened the door.

It was her eyes that captivated me. A crystal blue, they carry darkness that I've only ever seen in the victims I've helped as a security officer or soldiers who come back from war. The "I've been broken, and I'm doing everything I can to remain standing" look. It's one I had after that IED sent me packing.

Though, I get the impression Eliza Pierce has spent time on a very different type of battlefield than I am used to. Ex, perhaps? Toxic family?

Realizing I've been staring at the outside of her house for longer than is socially acceptable, I turn the key in the ignition, my mind still focused on Eliza because I have this feeling that my interactions with her are far from over.

Is it just that I hope they're not? That I'll get to see her again? Maybe exchange an actual pleasant greeting at some point?

Or is it something else?

Shaking it off, I put my truck in reverse, and back out of her drive to make the five-minute commute back to Hope Hardware. Hope Springs has been home to me for the past seven years. I came here, ready for a break from the life I'd built after a career-ending injury had me medically retired from the Army. It wasn't long after arriving that I decided I had no interest in returning to Boston. A few weeks later, I'd managed to move the security firm I started with some other veterans to this small coastal town and haven't looked back since.

While the small town of Hope Springs doesn't have a lot of need for a skillset like mine, we manage to run the business side of things from here as well as handle client issues that arise, and host a few safe houses on the edge of town. Plus, we're only about three hours outside of Boston, making it easy to drive up and deal with problems that occur.

All in all, it works. And I wouldn't want to be anywhere else.

After parking on the curb in front of Hope's Hardware, I climb out and head inside the small store. A few of the usuals are browsing aisles while the owner, Felix, sits behind the counter, a baby monitor in front of him.

Through it, I can hear the sound of rain from the noise maker in his granddaughter's nursery. He looks up and smiles at me. "How did it go?"

"It's installed," I tell him. "Though you might be getting a complaint from our newest resident."

Felix's expression turns to full-on amusement. Likely because he thinks I'm kidding given that I've never had a single person complain about anything I've helped with. "And why is that?"

"She was not happy you weren't the one installing it. Honestly, I think my very presence agitated her."

He chuckles and focuses on someone behind me. "Find what you were looking for, Mr. Leroy?"

"Yes," an older man nearing his eighties sets a handful of screws on the counter. "Lance, you get a good look at the newcomer, then?" he asks. "Or did I overhear wrong? I am getting old, you know."

"Age is nothing but a number, Sir," I reply with a grin. "And yes, I did."

He scoffs. "All these big city folks coming in and buying up our land. Downright angering if you ask me."

"Not too long ago, I was one of those big city folks," I remind him with a grin.

He chokes out a laugh. "And I didn't like you then, either. You turned out all right, though." He offers Felix some cash then takes the offered bag. "See you at church?" he asks me.

"I'll be there. Trying not to look like I came from a big city."

He throws his head back and laughs then begins whistling and leaves the hardware store with a smile. The moment he's out of earshot, Felix turns back to me. "So, she was angry I wasn't there?"

I nod. "Not sure why. Aside from the fact that she doesn't consider me a practicing plumber."

His brow furrows. "A practicing what?"

I run my hand over the back of my neck. "Plumber. Anyway, it's installed, and if she does call and complain, then just remind her that, because of me, she gets to shower and wash dishes tonight." I glance around to see if anyone is within earshot. "What do you know about her?"

"Ahh, find someone who interests you?" He arches a brow.

"Not in the way you're thinking," I reply. "What do you know about her? Anything?" I ask again.

"Not much. Birdie said that she just got out of a nasty divorce and is looking to settle someplace quiet so she can reset."

"Which makes her initial distrust in me understandable."

"Birdie seems to like her. But the woman kept most of

her personal life under wraps. Aside from the divorce that is."

Which means she's guarded and her reaction to me was likely a result of the sudden change. "Gotcha. Thanks." I tap a hand on the counter. "I'm headed into the office now. Need anything else?"

"Nope. Lilly is bringing me lunch in a bit when she checks on Sarah." He points at the baby monitor. "She's napping now, thankfully. Kid did not want to go to sleep."

I laugh. "Well, you're doing amazing, Grandpa. Give me a call if you need anything else."

"Will do, thanks, Lance."

"Anytime."

I get in the car and make my way back to my office, which is situated just above the town's one and only bakery. Just down the street from the diner, *Icing* has been a Hope Springs staple since the very beginning, originally owned by a married couple and then passed down to their granddaughter.

Even as I make my way around the back of the building and up the stairs leading to my office, I can smell the delicate aroma of freshly baked pastries and brewed coffee.

"About time you got in."

I grin at one of my partners, Elijah Breeth, another ex-Army Ranger who nearly lost his life thanks to an IED that left him with scars over most of his torso. He also has limited hearing in his right ear, but that in no way makes him any less effective as a security officer.

The man is wicked smart and deadly if he needs to be. And he knows his way around a computer better than anyone I know.

"I texted you. Had a water heater install at the old lighthouse." I toss the jacket I've yet to put on today onto the back of my chair.

Elijah arches a dark brow. "Which means you got a look at the new girl."

Gotta love small towns. Everyone old enough to talk will be chatting about Eliza for days to come. At least until something else happens to shift their attention. With Valentine's Day coming up? That distraction is likely right around the corner. Something about love in the air makes people act more foolish than normal.

"I did. What did you find out about her?" When he doesn't immediately respond, I shake my head. "We both know you look into everyone who moves into town, so get on with it."

Elijah chuckles. "It's my job to know things, Lance-A-Lot." He holds up his notepad. "Twenty-nine years old. Born in Ojai, California. No living family—her parents abandoned her when she was seven then died of a drug overdose a few years later. After they left her, she bounced around to various foster homes until she turned eighteen. Then, she moved to Los Angeles, met and married a big-time lawyer out there when she was twenty, and is recently divorced. Wrote a couple children's books, but aside from that, no career to speak of."

The more I learn about her, the more our interaction makes sense. The woman is guarded, untrusting. And sounds like she has the past experiences to back up both.

"Sounds like she'll probably be keeping to herself."

"My thoughts exactly." He whistles. "She's a looker, though. Downright gorgeous."

The bite of jealousy catches me off guard. I take a seat and stare out the window at the ocean across the street. *What is it I'm supposed to do for her?* The feeling in my chest, the desire to help, is stronger than I've ever felt. Even now I can feel the tightness. Like a warning that there's something not quite right.

But why?

I've always trusted my God-given instincts. Honestly, it's that trust that kept me alive during all of my deployments. I just can't figure out why they're popping up now. Eliza Pierce made it clear she wants nothing to do with me. She's new to town, divorced, so what could I possibly help her with?

"Lance?"

"Huh?"

"You daydreaming about your wedding?" he jokes.

I shake my head. "Eliza is gorgeous," I agree. "And standoffish. Ripped me a new one over not being what she considers a practicing plumber."

"That's a thing?"

"Apparently in her world, it is." I shake my head. In my line of work, I've met a lot of beautiful women—movie stars, models, professional athletes—yet it's this woman who has me rattled.

Why?

"She got under your skin," Elijah comments. Calling it like he sees it as always.

"No. She didn't. I just have a lot on my mind." *God, please guide me. Am I misreading the way I feel?* Even as I send up the silent plea, I feel the weight increase. Truth is Eliza Pierce did get under my skin. I just can't seem to figure out why.

"Well? Care to share with the class?"

I chuckle. "Not much to share. I met her; she didn't like me; I installed a water heater and left."

"She didn't like you?" He feigns shock. "A woman who didn't blush at the sight of our very own White Knight?"

I grab the stress ball from my desk and throw it at him. Elijah laughs as he catches it and launches it back toward me. "Do you have updates on our current clients?" I ask. "Or anything mildly useful?"

Elijah rolls his eyes and laughs as he clicks something on his computer and begins rattling off a list of updates.

New system installed at the Benedict's summer home fourteen miles up the coast.

A brand-new camera installed at an art gallery in downtown Boston…the list goes on, and even as I try to focus, my attention is once again pulled to our newcomer. I can't help but wonder what type of man would let a woman like that go.

What was it about her divorce that made it so nasty?

What happened in her marriage to put that dark look in her eyes?

And, just what does God have planned for me in regard to this beautiful stranger?

Is it possible it's all just in my head?

CHAPTER 3
Eliza

The moving truck is *still* not here.

I stare outside, willing it to appear in the driveway. They'd said they could be delayed depending on the weather—we were having an abnormally stormy season back in California—but even as I promised myself I would have patience, I'm so ready to have all of my things.

I wish I had a phone. Then I could call. Check in.

"They'll get here when they get here, Eliza," I say aloud then shift my attention back to the view before me.

Desperate for a change of scenery, I take a deep breath then head out the door and into the salty air.

Dusk has fallen, painting the ocean in bright purples and golds. Beauty that I can appreciate as I reach the bottom of an old wooden staircase and remove my shoes. The moment my feet hit the sand, the tension drains away.

As though every muscle in my body reacts to the way it feels against my bare feet.

And for the second time today, I find myself wondering how I went so long without putting my toes in the sand. Wrapping my cardigan more tightly around me, I start walking down the shoreline. Seashells sprinkle in the sand, crisp whites, soft browns, I even pass a few sand dollars. Bending, I pick a small white shell off the ground and study it.

When I was young, back before my parents left, I used to sneak away whenever they were on one of their benders. I'd take a bus to the beach and spend my day collecting shells. Honestly, they were the one thing I wish I could have kept after my parents abandoned me.

But at the very first foster home I went to, the woman who'd taken me in threw them out. Not long after that, I was moved again, but I'll never forget the look on her face when she told me they were gone.

She'd smiled.

Grinned like tossing those things that were so precious to me made her happier than she had been in years.

I take a deep breath and remind myself that I'm here to move on.

Not relive the past.

I stop walking and face the ocean, then close my eyes and force myself to focus on the sound of the waves crashing against the shore. Here, I will heal. Here, I will find my center again.

"Ms. Pierce."

Serenity destroyed, I open my eyes to find none other than my not-plumber standing in front of me, wearing basketball shorts, a sweat-soaked blue t-shirt, and running shoes. He's a sight to behold, sure. A picturesque representation of beautiful masculinity.

But I am uninterested.

Or, at least, that's what I plan to continue telling myself. The reality of it is that I've been unable to get him off my mind since he left. Battling with guilt that I'd been so rude, and agitation because he'd been there in the first place.

Keep things professional, Eliza. I don't want friends and I certainly don't want another man in my life. "Mr.—I'm sorry, I didn't get your last name."

"Knight," he replies. "But you can call me Lance."

"Out for a run, Mr. Knight?" I ask, purposely choosing to keep things formal. The last thing I want is to give this man any ideas whatsoever when it comes to me.

He grins. One of those lopsided grins that send your blood buzzing.

"What gave it away?" he asks.

His easy demeanor makes me uncomfortable, but I try not to let it show. In my experience, men who come across as kind and genuine are only waiting for a moment alone to show you what they're really like. Snakes waiting in their hole until you're close enough. Then they strike and drag you down into their darkness.

"The smell," I reply cooly.

His grin spreads. "My apologies, I thought the breeze

would tame the stench down. Maybe next time I'll shower both before and after a run."

I force a smile. "Well, as riveting as discussing your personal hygiene is, I need to get back to my house." I turn.

"Wait."

Stopping, I take a deep breath before turning back around and crossing my arms. "Yes?"

"I'm afraid we got off on the wrong foot, though I'm not entirely sure how." He runs a hand through his auburn hair.

I bet it's soft. It looks soft.

"I didn't get off on any foot with you, Mr. Knight. You came and installed a water heater; that was it."

"Did I do something to offend you?"

"No."

"Then is it my base existence that bothers you?"

"You don't bother me, Mr. Knight. I—" Closing my eyes, I try to take a deep breath. "I am tired, and my things didn't get in today like they were supposed to, and I just want some peace and quiet. Okay?"

He studies me, and I get the feeling that the man misses nothing. Finally, though, he nods. "Then I hope you have a great night, Ms. Pierce. Please let me know if there's anything I can do to help." Without waiting for a response, he turns and begins jogging down the beach.

I watch, unable to help myself. Running on sand is no easy feat, yet he moves smoothly, his feet barely making a sound as they hit the ground.

Worried he'll stop and turn around to see me staring, I head the other way, passing by my steps and heading toward the town. There's just enough light that I can see the sidewalk clearly as I make my way down toward Main Street.

Though, as soon as I reach the main part of town, the lights are on, and the sun is down.

It doesn't bother me, though, because I've never been afraid of the dark.

I learned at a very young age the worst monsters don't hide in the shadows. No, that would be too predictable. Instead, they like to live in the spotlight. No one expects them to be there. Makes preying on the weak entirely too easy because they don't see it coming.

Pain shoots up through my foot, and I hiss through clenched teeth, lifting my leg and nearly falling over in the process. The bit of blood on the bottom of my foot thanks to a treacherous rock on the sidewalk reminds me that I never put on shoes.

How did I forget to put on shoes?

"You all right?"

I turn, half-expecting to see Lance. Instead, an older man wearing a suit and tie stands in the doorway of the little church. "Yeah, sorry. Stepped on a rock."

He comes into view and smiles softly. Kind grey eyes with lines on either side study my injured foot. "I have a first aid kit just inside."

I study the front of the church then look to him and back at it. I haven't been in a church since the divorce.

Erick made me go every single Sunday. We sat there, in the front pew, as he held my hand and pretended to be the world's most perfect man.

I'd never given a lot of thought to God before, but after everything Erick put me through, what little faith I had was gone. It's hard to believe that you are loved when everyone who has ever been in your life left you out in the cold.

"If you keep walking on it, you're likely to get sand in the wound, and that won't be pleasant at all. Take it from someone who's had it happen a time or two."

"Okay. A bandage would be great."

"That I can do." He smiles and offers me his arm. I take it, hopping and feeling like an absolute idiot.

Warmth envelopes me as soon as we get into the sanctuary. After guiding me to a pew toward the front, he helps me sit. I stare up at the crucifix on the wall and the altar with two flickering candles.

"I'll be right back," he tells me, then heads through a door off to the side.

I continue staring straight ahead at the stained glass window that undoubtedly overlooks the ocean. Colorful flowers in sconces decorate the walls on either side of the altar while a podium—the same gleaming dark wood as the floor—holds a large bible.

My thoughts drift to the worn bible that remains in a box in the back of the moving truck. It was a gift from my third foster parents. They were the only ones who actually made me feel welcome, but they'd been forced to give me back when the wife had been diagnosed with early-onset dementia.

I haven't had the heart to get rid of it, and it's the one thing I've carried with me from childhood. Even if I haven't opened it the entire time I've had it.

The door opens again and the man comes back out carrying a red case with a first-aid symbol on it. "Now, I'm no doctor, but we can call Doc if need be. He usually works late." He takes a seat on the pew beside me and reaches down to lift my foot.

"Doc?"

"Our resident doctor," he replies with a wink. He visibly winces when he gets a look at my foot. "Ouch. How long have you been walking?"

"A while," I admit. "Lost track of time."

He tears open a white package and wipes it on the bottom of my foot. I jolt as pain shoots up through my foot again. "I'm sorry, there's no way around that, I'm afraid." Though, even as he says it, he waves his hand to try and get some air moving on it. "Are you Eliza Pierce by chance?"

"I am."

"Word travels fast in a small town," he replies. "I hear you bought the old lighthouse."

"I did."

"It's a neat place. I knew the original owner," he says. "Before it got passed down to his nephew. Never met him since he wasn't from here." After reaching into the container again, he applies some cream and places a bandage over the injury.

My gaze finds the crucifix again.

"Do you go to church?" he asks.

"Not anymore," I reply. "Sorry, that was rude."

"Not rude at all," he says as he wraps a bit of gauze around my foot, covering the bandage. "Our church isn't much, but it's home."

"It's pretty," I tell him truthfully. "And a lot more welcoming than any of the other churches I've been in."

He chuckles. "Well, I'm glad to hear it." Gently, he sets my foot on the pew behind him, keeping it elevated as he packages up the supplies. "So what sent you out walking without shoes this close to dark?"

"I got distracted," I reply.

"This town will do that to you," he replies softly. "But is everything okay?"

"It's fine. Thanks for bandaging up my foot. I really appreciate it." I start to stand, but the moment I put weight on the sole of my foot, I hiss.

"It's going to be tender for a few days, more than likely," he says. "If you don't mind waiting, my wife will be here in a few minutes to pick me up, and we can drop you off. Our daughter just got engaged, and it's her celebration dinner tonight."

His happiness is infectious, and I find myself smiling. "Congratulations to her."

"Thanks. Her fiancé is a good man. Which is the best thing a dad can hope for." He stands.

"You really don't have to drive me."

"I really don't mind."

"I'd hate for you to be late to your daughter's dinner, Mr.—"

"Pastor Redding," he replies. "And we won't be."

"Pastor." How did I miss it before? Of course he's the pastor. Who else would be here this late? Kicking myself all over again for my comment about not going to church anymore, I try to stand again. "I'm sorry for the inconvenience, I—"

"Easy," he says with a chuckle. "Please, sit, Eliza."

I do as he says, mainly because I'm not sure I could even make it to the door right now. "I really am sorry about my comment earlier. About not going to church anymore. It was rude."

"It was not," he says again. "Though, can I ask you why?"

"Why what?"

"Why don't you go to church anymore? And please, be honest. No judgment here, I can assure you."

Something about the man puts me at ease, soothing the nerves that have been frayed since I saw Lance Knight on the beach. "I don't know if I believe anymore."

"No?" he questions. "Why not?"

"I've seen too much." My throat burns, and I toy with the bottom of my cardigan. "It's just hard to believe that God would let some things happen."

The pastor doesn't respond, doesn't preach to me. He

simply listens to the words as I say them, his expression remaining completely neutral.

"My ex was a Sunday morning man, and to be honest, he was one of the worst people I've ever met. He did things that—" I close my eyes then open them again and laugh uncomfortably. "I'm sorry. Here I am, a complete stranger, pouring my heart out to you, and all you were doing was being nice."

"Eliza, please do not apologize." He leans back against the pew and offers me a kind smile. "Listen, I want to extend an offer for church this Sunday." Before I can respond, he continues. "I know that one visit likely won't be enough to change your mind, but I'd love for you to come."

I take a deep breath, trying to decide whether or not I should take him up on his offer.

"You don't have to answer me now, I just want you to know it's there. And as far as pouring out your heart to me, that's what I'm here for. If you ever need someone to listen, please feel free to come see me. Nothing we speak about gets shared outside of my office, and sometimes, simply having someone to talk to makes all the difference."

"Given my last therapist slept with my husband, I— And there I go again." Shaking my head, I laugh nervously. "Oversharing once again."

He laughs. "It's quite all right."

The doors to the church open, and a woman with greying hair strolls in, a wide smile on her face. "Hey there, handsome." Her gaze finds mine. "Eliza Pierce, I presume?"

"How did you—small town," I add.

"Exactly. I run the bakery in town." She holds out a hand. "Kyra Redding."

I take her offered hand. "Nice to meet you."

Her gaze lands on my foot, and she releases my hand. "What happened?"

"I was out for a barefoot stroll in the dark and stepped on a rock. Your husband was kind enough to lend me some first-aid."

"Yikes. Are you okay?"

"I'll be fine, thanks."

"I said we'd drop her off at home on our way to Kassandra's engagement dinner."

"Oh, of course!" The woman gently touches my shoulder. I flinch, hating myself for the reaction. Thankfully, I don't think either of them notice it. "Come on, hun, let's get you home."

"Thanks so much. I am so mortified I left the house without shoes. It's just... the beach is right there, and then I ran into La—Mr. Knight, and—" I start rambling again. What is happening to me? Neither of these people asked for my life story, yet here I am. Pouring it out anyway.

First impressions are clearly not my strong suit.

"Lance? Oh, yes, he loves his dusk runs. Goes nearly every night. Nice guy. If you ever need anything done handiwork-wise—he's your man."

Nice guy. He'd certainly seemed that way. But people said the same thing about Erick before, too.

"Good to know."

They guide me out the front door and over to the parking lot off the side of the church before helping me into the backseat of a sedan.

The pastor gets behind the wheel, his wife in the passenger side, and they hold hands as he pulls out of the lot.

The genuine expression of affection makes me yearn for a version of myself where I truly believed such a love existed for me. But that naïve dream went out the window the first time Erick split my lip open.

And I know I'll never again be able to trust enough to let myself fall for anyone else.

CHAPTER 4

Eliza

S omething scrapes against wood, ripping me from sleep. I sit up, narrowing my gaze as my eyes try to adjust to the dark. Heart racing, I scan the room for any sign that I'm not alone. I reach for the old lamp and flick it on, illuminating the living room in a light glow.

With no moving truck, I'd had nowhere to sleep but the dusty old couch with only an emergency blanket I keep in my car. After rubbing my eyes, I get to my feet. My left foot still aches thanks to the rock last night, but I manage to limp forward a bit, looking for the sound of the noise.

Something scrapes again, and this time, I realize it's outside.

The wind. It's just the wind.

I sit back down on the couch and take a deep breath, trying to steady my panicked nerves. As soon as I'm no longer shaking, I get to my feet again and do a quick wobble-walk through the house—just to be sure. It's empty, just as I expected it to be, but there's still this sneaking feeling that someone is watching me.

Moving slowly, I make my way over to the window and peer out through the curtain, but I see nothing but a sea of darkness.

Your mind is playing tricks on you, I assure myself, but even as I really do believe it, I know there will be no more sleep for me. After firing up my laptop, I check the time, noting that it's just now five-thirty in the morning.

With no internet, I have no idea what time the diner opens, but given that it's a small town, and nearly six, I opt to give it a try. It's not like it'll hurt to get some driving in. Especially if it's in the pursuit of coffee and food.

In response to the thought, my stomach growls. Dinner last night consisted of a granola bar from the bottom of my purse, so it's no wonder I'm starving. I dress as quickly as I can then splash some cold water on my face and run my travel brush through my hair.

The shoes make it easier to walk on my injured foot, offering some padding, thankfully, but I still pop two ibuprofen in my mouth and swallow it down with a glass of water.

Once I am mildly presentable, I head outside to the car, scanning the dark around me as I do. As soon as I'm inside, I lock the doors, check the back seat, and take a deep breath.

It's been over a decade since I've been alone.

And honestly, it's making me feel absolutely pathetic, especially given that the first half of my life was spent without anyone besides myself to count on. Is that what made me such an easy target for Erick? Who am I kidding, of course, that's what made me an easy target.

I pull out of the drive and make my way through town.

There are no cars on the road, though I do spot a few men and women out for an early morning jog. The image of Lance swims into my mind, and my stomach twists into knots.

He's a snake, I remind myself. Another Erick just waiting to take advantage of me while I'm vulnerable. Something that will *never* happen.

The diner light is on, but the open sign is yet to be illuminated. Still, I park my car and limp up to the front door to check the hours of operation sign. Six a.m. Not too much longer now. I consider heading back toward my car, but before I can, the door opens, and a woman with dark hair sticks her head out. "You okay?"

"Yeah. Sorry. Just waiting for you to open."

The woman smiles. "You must be Eliza. Come on in." She moves aside, and I step into the warmth of the diner. After flipping the closed sign to open, she gestures for me to sit at a booth off to the right.

I limp over, grateful it's close.

"Are you okay?"

"Had an unfortunate interaction with a rock last night," I reply with an embarrassed laugh.

"Yikes. I hope it feels better soon. I'm Lilly. Can I get you some coffee?"

"Yes, please. That would be amazing."

"You got it." She grins and steps away from the table, heading around behind the counter. Alone, I let my gaze wander. Tables and booths cover most of the floor space with enough space between them that it doesn't feel over-crowded. The floor is gleaming wood, the bar top a light walnut color.

Glass display cases house cookies, pies, and an assort-ment of donuts while a stainless-steel coffee machine sits on the back counter. Double doors lead into a kitchen where there's a single window for orders.

The place looks exactly like one would expect an eighties diner to look, and it brings a small smile to my face. It's peaceful, serene, and exactly what I need to start the day. Especially after the wake-up I had.

Lilly returns with a mug of steaming coffee and a small porcelain bowl of Creamers. "Thank you," I reply.

"You're welcome. Are you hungry?" She offers me a menu.

"Yes, please. I skipped dinner last night."

Lilly laughs. "Been there." A baby cries, and she glances over as a handsome man carrying an infant wrapped in pink walks down the stairs. "Awww, baby, what's wrong?"

"She must have had a bad dream." He offers her to Lilly, and she begins cooing to the child. His gaze meets mine, and he smiles. "First customer of the day makes you lucky," he replies.

I smile awkwardly. "Let's hope so. I could use some luck."

"Can't we all." He chuckles and offers me his hand. "I'm Alex. Lilly's husband."

"It's nice to meet you." I shake his offered hand quickly then pull mine back.

"This is Sarah," Lilly says as she crosses over to the table. The infant is a spitting image of her mother, her short hair a beautiful obsidian.

"Hi, Sarah," I say with a smile even as I inwardly wince. I wanted children and very nearly got my wish, but then it was all ripped away. I swallow hard, grief burning in my heart. "Do you own this place?" I question, desperate for a change in subject.

"We do," Alex replies as he moves back behind the counter.

"It's lovely."

"Thanks." Lilly keeps the child on her hip as she makes her way into the kitchen, emerging a few minutes later with a diaper bag. "I'm going to run her to Dad's. Be back soon." She kisses Alex noisily then smiles at me on her way out.

I turn my attention to the menu, studying breakfast choices that range from French toast to pancakes, biscuits to omelets and benedicts. Since I spent our entire marriage watching my figure and having everything I ate or drank controlled by Erick, I settle for a stack of pancakes, two eggs over easy, hashbrowns, and extra crispy bacon.

But before I can order, the bell above the door dings, and none other than my not-plumber strolls in with two other men who look like they just stepped out of a Men's

Fitness magazine. Tall, built, and handsome, their presence completely consumes the space. But it's Lance who draws my eye even now.

He wears dark jeans, a brown jacket, and a baseball cap. "Morning, Alex!" he calls out.

Alex smiles and waves back, and just before they start my direction, I turn quickly, hoping he'll simply move by and not notice me.

Unfortunately, being the first customer doesn't make me as lucky as Alex claimed.

Because Lance absolutely stops at my table, his friends with him. Every one of them is intimidating, but it's the way my insides twist when I see Lance that throws me off yet again. Only, this time, I realize exactly what it is.

I *want* to like him. He seems to be everything everyone says he is. Kind. Helpful. But so was Erick, and thankfully, the trusting side of me still seems to have enough sense to be wary.

"Morning, Ms. Pierce," he greets.

"Morning," I greet.

"Aww, the infamous Ms. Pierce," a man with light brown hair and eyes nearly the same color says.

Before I can respond, Lance gestures to me. "Ms. Eliza Pierce, I would like you to meet my co-workers. This is Elijah Breeth," Lance says, gesturing to the man who'd spoken. I study him closer now, noting the nasty-looking scar peeking out of the top of his t-shirt and the wide grin on his face. "And this is Michael Anderson," he says, introducing the second man with him. His baseball cap covers most of his hair, but the strands that stick out are nearly black. His eyes are darker than Elijah's but—kind.

"Nice to meet you," Michael says.

"Are you all not-plumbers as well?" I blurt then nearly kick myself. If I wanted distance, cracking a joke is hardly the way to get it.

They laugh. "We heard you gave Lance-A-Lot here a good once-over yesterday," the man he'd called Elijah says.

"Word seems to travel fast in this town," I retort as I try to avoid Lance's gaze. When he's around, I get this knot in my stomach that feels an awful lot like a warning. Like something is trying to warn me that he's not someone I should spend too much time with. Mainly because I can't be trusted around beautiful men.

"That it does," Michael replies. "Let's get to the table. It was great to meet you, Eliza."

"You too." Everyone but Lance leaves. "Can I help you?" I question, forcing myself to meet his gaze.

"What's wrong?"

"I'm trying to enjoy a quiet breakfast," I reply, my tone harsher now.

"No. Something else is off." He studies me with the scrutiny of someone looking at an insect beneath a magnifying glass.

"I'm fine," I tell him. "Just tired. And even if I wasn't, I don't see how it's any of your business."

Lance purses his lips and nods. "Fair enough. Have a good day, Eliza." He turns on his heel and leaves me sitting at the table, though he chooses the one spot where he's facing me, and every now and then I can feel his gaze on me.

————

HOLDING AN ADDRESS SCRAWLED ON A PINK POST-IT NOTE, I stare at the façade for *Icing,* trying to figure out just what kind of joke the postman must be playing on me.

After the intense wake-up this morning, I'd decided to use a portion of my savings I'd set aside for emergencies on a security system. Since the major companies don't service out here, I'd been forced to find someone local.

And the address I'd gotten from the post office worker when I'd gone in there to buy stamps for bills led me here. To Pastor Redding's wife's bakery.

She's behind the counter now, handing someone a delicious-looking muffin, a smile on her face. Even though I'm fairly positive she doesn't install security systems in addition to baking muffins, I opt to head inside anyway. She'd been nothing but kind to me last night, and to be honest, a muffin sounds downright delicious.

"Eliza!" she greets with a wide smile as she comes around the counter. "How's the foot?"

"Better," I reply. "Thanks again so much for your help."

"Absolutely. Anytime. What can I do for you?"

"I think I'm in the wrong place, but one of those muffins sounds great."

"Wrong place?"

"I was looking to have a security system installed, and

the address I got from the man at the post office led me here."

"Ahh yes. Well, you're not in the wrong place, just the wrong entrance." She reaches into the glass casing containing all sorts of delicious-looking baked goods and withdraws a blueberry muffin with berries the size of grapes. My mouth waters just looking at it as she bags it up and hands it over the counter. "On the house."

"No, I can't take this."

"You are going to take it. Consider it a gift since you're really doing me a favor." She turns and pulls a white bakery box from the table behind her then carries it over and hands it out to me. "I needed to deliver this to the guys upstairs and haven't had the chance."

"Guys upstairs?"

"The security office. That's where you're going, right?"

"They're upstairs?"

"They are." She beams at me. "Do you mind taking it up?"

"Not at all." I take the box and set my muffin bag on top. "Thank you so much."

"No problem at all. Come back if they don't get you set right up."

I smile. "Will do, thanks."

"Great. Just head outside and go around the building. The stairs are just on the other side."

I do as she instructed, stepping back out into the chilly morning air and heading around the building. A set of iron stairs on the back leads just upstairs, the sign KNIGHT

SECURITY in bold letters, a chess piece placed strategically beneath the 'K'.

Taking the stairs slowly so I don't anger my already throbbing foot, I reach the top and gently push the door open. It swings, revealing a small waiting area consisting of two chairs and a coffee table with magazines stacked neatly on the top.

A few desks are separated from the waiting area via a short countertop, but no one sits behind any of the computers.

"Hello?"

"Be there in a second!" a man calls out.

As I wait, I make my way over to a wall with photographs. Men in military uniforms smile back from behind the glass. Most of the photos seem candid, but there's one of a man kneeling and speaking to a group of children that catches my eye. I can only make out his profile, but the children are all smiling as they hang onto every word he speaks.

He looks familiar—and then it hits me.

KNIGHT SECURITY.

Lance Knight.

"You have got to be kidding me," I mutter.

"I'm not sure what the joke is, but I'd love to be in on it."

I stiffen then turn to face him. Lance stands a few feet away, arms crossed. For the first time since we met, he looks honestly agitated. And it only takes about a second too long to realize it's because I was looking at the image of him and the children when I spoke. "I didn't realize this was your place; that's why I said that."

"You didn't realize I owned a company with my last name as the header?"

"No," I reply. "I didn't put two and two together until I saw the picture."

He purses his lips and nods. "Makes sense. What can I do for you, Ms. Pierce?" His tone is sharper than it has been since we met, and for some reason, the fact that he dropped the over-the-top nice guy tone actually puts me slightly at ease.

But only slightly.

"Nothing. I changed my mind. Mrs. Redding sent these up." I set the box down and grab my muffin.

"You changed your mind about what?"

"Why I came here. I don't need help." Having Lance monitor my security system seems a bit too close for comfort given that I can't share a room with the man without feeling ridiculously flustered.

"Ms. Pierce, you came into my security office, looking for help. So let me help you." He gestures toward the desk closest to the door. "If I can't, I can at least guide you to someone who can."

I hesitate only for a moment before crossing the office and taking a seat in the chair he gestures to as he sits behind the desk.

"What happened to your leg? You were limping," he adds.

"Stepped on a rock last night."

He arches a brow. "A rock?"

"Yes."

"Sounds painful."

"It was."

He nods, and we fall into uncomfortable silence. Would it be weird if I sprinted toward the door right now? Because that's exactly what I'm considering.

"So, Ms. Pierce, what can I do for you?"

"I was considering having a security system put on the lighthouse and wanted to know how much they run." I sit up straight, trying not to feel completely mortified at the idea that this guy is likely out of my price range.

What if he knows it?

What if he only invited me to sit so he could laugh me out of the office? Would certainly put me in my place, given the way I've treated him.

"I don't really think I need one though, now that I've thought about it."

Lance reaches into the small bookcase right beside his desk and withdraws a white binder. He sets it between us and opens it to a piece of paper set in plastic with a list of systems and prices. "These are all of the systems we offer. Most of them are for corporate offices or larger facilities, but these here"—he points to the top five—"are for residential. The top is the most basic. A control panel plus door and window sensors. It will run you eighteen hundred dollars, which includes a year of twenty-four-seven monitoring."

"Who monitors it? The police department?"

He shakes his head. "We do. We respond if there's an incident and, if required, will contact the police on your behalf."

"You're not cops."

"Not exactly. But we're all highly trained and very good at what we do."

I study the paper again, scanning the prices all the way from the top to the bottom. While the smallest package he pointed out was eighteen hundred dollars, I dang near gasp when I get a look at the fifty-thousand-dollar package all the way at the bottom.

And just beneath that is a private bodyguard hourly rate.

"Is there really a need for all of this here? Hope Springs seems like a relatively safe place."

"It is safe," he replies. "We do most of our work in Boston, though we have a good number of basic systems here."

Eighteen hundred is a good amount more than I'd considered spending, and honestly, given the safety rating of this small town, I don't imagine I'd need it. But that feeling this morning when I wasn't sure I was alone—I really don't want to go through that. Having a monitored system would definitely make me feel better, even if it is a bit overboard.

"How long is the contract?" I ask.

"A year. After the first year is over, if you want to renew, the monitoring for consecutive years using the same equipment you purchased is six hundred dollars."

I breathe deeply. Six hundred I can handle.

As for the eighteen—that's going to make a dent. "How quickly can you get it installed?"

"Well, if you want a licensed and practicing electrician to put it in, it'll be about a week." He flashes me a grin. "But if you're okay with us doing it, we could have it up and running as soon as tomorrow morning."

"I assume you install most of these yourself?"

"All of them," he replies. "Elijah—you met him this morning—handles most of the actual installation since the system is his baby. I will go over it with you whenever it's in, show you how to set up and disarm and all that." He closes the binder and leans back in his chair. "Can I ask why you need it?"

I meet his gaze. "I'm a single woman living alone, Mr. Knight. Is that not reason enough?"

"Sure it is, but I get the sense there's more to the story."

"Even if there were, you wouldn't need to know it."

"I do if there's potential danger. We can make sure we plan for it if there is, tweak the system to fit your exact needs."

"Sounds expensive."

"Doesn't have to be," he replies.

I genuinely consider giving him a shorter version than I gave Pastor Redding last night, but since I've learned how fast word travels and I don't want everyone knowing my business, I decide against it. The likelihood of Erick following me here is minuscule. He got what he wanted. Freedom and nearly every cent. "I'm not expecting anything," I tell him. "I'm living alone, on the outskirts of town, and just want to make sure I have all my bases covered."

His gaze holds mine for a while, and I honestly wonder if he's going to press further. Thankfully, he doesn't. "Okay. Well, I can get you my card, and you can think about it and give me a call—"

"Okay. I will." I take the card he offers and push to my feet. "Thank you for your time, Mr. Knight."

"Anytime." He starts to walk me toward the door, but I move ahead, walking as fast as my slight limp will allow.

CHAPTER 5

Lance

I haven't been able to get Eliza out of my head ever since she showed up at the office this afternoon. She'd looked genuinely shocked to find me there, something I'd found amusing at first, given that my name is on the door. But then I'd noted the circles beneath her eyes and the way she studied everything around her.

The woman is running scared. But from who? Her ex?

A fist slams into my jaw, and I stumble backward as stinging pain shoots through the side of my face.

"You're distracted," Michael says as he bounces on the balls of his feet, boxing gloves held out in front of him.

"And you're taking advantage," I reply, rubbing my jaw. "That was a mean right hook."

He shrugs. "Payback for the bloody nose you gave me last week."

I pull my gloves off and cross over to the bottle of water waiting at the side of the training ring. The gym is

small and Michael's other job when he's not working security for me. He'd been a fantastic boxer before joining the
military, and once he got out, it had been his way of
retaining his edge.

Frankly, I appreciate it because it gives me a place to go
when I'm not at the office or home. Boxing also happened
to be the best type of therapy for me once I got out. I'd
dealt—still deal—with severe PTSD from the incident
overseas that nearly claimed my life and did take the lives
of most of my men.

After Michael got out and joined me back here in Hope
Springs, he opened this place and convinced me to give it a
try. It did for me what two years of therapy and meds
hadn't been able to do, and after Michael and I took to the
ring for the first time, I'd been so exhausted I'd gotten my
first unmedicated full night's sleep in years.

"So, tell me what's going on?" he says as he pulls his
gloves off and tosses them to the side.

"I'm not sure." I climb out of the ring then take a seat in
a chair and drink deeply.

Michael sits down beside me. "This wouldn't have
anything to do with a certain blonde, would it?"

"Is it that obvious?"

"Nah, I just know you. Spill. What's going on?"

"I have no clue." Shaking my head, I let out a frustrated
sigh. "I can't get her off my mind."

"Like to torment yourself that much, huh?" When I
continue staring at him, he adds, "I don't know if you

realize this, but she doesn't seem to care much for you, Lance-A-Lot."

I snort. "That's an understatement. You should have seen the look on her face when she realized I owned the security firm."

"That bad, huh?"

"I had just come out of the back room and saw her checking out the photos from our deployments. She muttered 'You have got to be kidding me' once she put two and two together."

"What did you do when you were installing her water heater? Break a favorite vase or something?"

I shake my head. "Nothing. Aside from the clear understanding that she didn't want me there, I can't figure out just what I did to offend her."

"Maybe you remind her of someone she doesn't care for."

"Maybe." I rub the heel of my palm against my chest, trying to loosen the knot that's been there since I first laid eyes on Eliza Pierce. "I can't get this feeling to go away."

"In love already?" Michael bumps me, and I chuckle.

"Hardly. I just feel like I'm supposed to help her. Like God is pushing me toward her. I don't know how else to explain it."

"Maybe He is," Michael replies.

"For what purpose, though?"

He shrugs. "Maybe she's your soulmate," he jokes.

"Not a chance," I reply. "But it's something."

"Do you think she's hiding from someone? Could be you're picking up on her needing help."

"Elijah is still doing some digging."

"As always." Michael lets out a laugh. "Man can't let anyone come into town without knowing everything there is to know."

"Nope," I reply. Elijah has always been computer savvy, but he worked as a profiler and investigator when he'd been in the Army, helping to smoke terrorists out of their foxholes. The man could find a needle in the haystack —even if that needle was transparent and the haystack a literal ticking time bomb.

"Well, if she does need help, she knows where to find us. All you can do in the meantime is pray, Brother."

"Which is exactly what I've been doing. And the weight just keeps getting heavier."

Michael gets to his feet and rolls his shoulders. "I, for one, am grateful for your distraction. Been awhile since I got a good hit in on you."

"I had a good trainer."

"Inflating my ego will not get you a break in the ring, my friend."

I chuckle. "Fair enough."

"Seriously, though, you can't force her to accept your help," Michael replies. "If she decides to have a system installed, that's when we can step up. Until then, I say just pray and give her the space she clearly wants."

"I know that. I doubt she comes back into the office, though. Even though she sat down and let me show her

our systems, she couldn't get out of there fast enough."
With a groan, I push to my feet. "I need to shower and get
to the church. Pastor Redding is asking for some help
fixing one of the pews."

"I can come with you. Never hurts to have an extra pair
of hands."

———

BOSTON IS ALWAYS BUZZING WITH ACTIVITY, AND FRIDAY
nights are anything but an exception. I pull my car into the
driveway of my parent's colonial, grateful to see the lights
on. It's been nearly a year since I saw them last, mainly
because they spend all of their time traveling.

I climb out, grab the flowers I picked up for my mom,
then head for the front door. As always, it opens before I
can reach for the doorknob.

My father smiles widely. "Look what we've got here!
An old man!" he exclaims as he pulls me in and
hugs me.

"If I'm old, that means you're ancient," I joke as I pull
away and stare into eyes the same color as mine. For a man
pushing sixty, Ray Knight doesn't look that much older
than me. Something he credits more to do with his happy
marriage to my mother than the fact that he's a health nut.
Truth be told, I think it's both.

They've been best friends since they met at a beach
party back when they'd been nineteen and never looked
back.

"Yeah, yeah. Get in here. Your mother is making pot roast and mashed potatoes for dinner."

"My favorite." I step into the foyer of the house I grew up in, and am instantly greeted with warmth, and the mouthwatering aroma of dinner cooking on the stove. It doesn't matter how long my parents are gone for, their house always feels like home.

I follow my father into the kitchen, where I see my mother standing, her back to me, in front of the stove as she mashes potatoes.

"Look who I found, Grace."

She looks over her shoulder, smile instant. Abandoning her mashing duties, she crosses over and gives me a big hug. The scent of her familiar perfume hits my lungs, and I breathe deeply, instantly transporting myself back to the years I was a child.

No matter what I've been through.

What I've faced.

Coming home always puts me at ease.

"You look good, honey," she says as she pulls back and pinches my cheek. "Eating right?"

"Always."

"Going to church?"

"Every Sunday," I reply.

"Good."

"How about you guys? How was Peru?"

"It was amazing!" my mother exclaims. "An absolute adventure. Machu Picchu was absolutely breathtaking." She begins mashing her potatoes again.

"How long are you in town for?" I ask. They travel nearly constantly, popping in for holidays and other random weekends here and there.

"A week," my father replies. "We're headed to Italy next."

"Nice."

"Unless there's a reason we should stick around longer?" my mother questions. "Perhaps to meet a certain special someone?"

"What are you getting at, woman?" my father asks.

I laugh. "Mom, there is no one. Not looking for a relationship, just focusing on work right now."

"And robbing me of years with grandkids." She shakes the masher at me. "That's not right, Lance Knight."

"Grace, leave the boy alone. When he finds the right woman, we'll hear about it."

"Thanks, Dad."

"You're welcome." He wraps an arm around my shoulders. "Now, let's get out of here before your mother starts listing out all the single women in your age group she and her friends know."

He guides me out onto the back porch then takes a seat in front of the stone fireplace that is currently host to a crackling fire. I stare at the flames, my thoughts still focused on Eliza—as they have been all day long.

"Something on your mind?"

"What?" I ask, facing my dad.

"You're abnormally quiet. So spill."

"A woman moved to town—"

"Here we go." My father laughs. "Your mother has a sense for these things. I'm coming to your defense, and you do have a woman!"

"No, no woman," I reply. "She doesn't even like me. Though, I'm not entirely sure why." I run a hand through my hair. "I met her when I went to install her water heater. Felix—the guy who owns the hardware store in town—was busy and needed help. Anyway, she's not a fan."

"That what's bugging you?"

"No. It's more than that." I lean forward, resting my elbows on my knees and staring into the fire. "Did you ever get the feeling you were supposed to do something? A tightness in your chest when you felt like you were being pushed in a certain direction?" When my father doesn't immediately respond, I chuckle. "Never mind, I sound insane."

"Not insane," he says. "Just processing. This feeling, it's in regard to this woman?"

"Yes. Like there's a voice in my head telling me that I need to help her. Which absolutely sounds insane." I chuckle. "Am I making any sense at all?"

"You are," he replies with a smile. "Have you prayed about it?"

"I have."

"And?"

"Feeling is still there."

My father chuckles. "Well, son, it sounds like you might have your hands full. All I can tell you is that, if you feel that strongly about it, maybe you need to spend some time trying to get to know her."

I look out over their backyard, my gaze landing on the aged treehouse my dad and I built when I was younger. He refuses to tear it down just in case he needs it for grandkids. I don't have the heart to tell him that he'll likely be getting none from me. At least, not before time tears it down for him. "She wants nothing to do with me."

My father clasps me on the shoulder. "Perhaps it's not quite what it seems. Or, maybe she just needs some time."

"Maybe."

"How is everything else going?" he asks. "Nightmares?"

I've always been able to be open with my parents. When I'd gotten back from my final deployment, I'd made no attempt to hide the night terrors that strangled my every restful moment. Not that I could have if I'd wanted to, anyway. They'd heard me screaming in the middle of the night for those first few weeks when I was back in my old room and recovering.

It had driven my mother to tears. Even my father, whom I'd never seen cry, struggled with knowing what I'd gone through. So as soon as I was able to, I'd gotten help then moved into my own place as soon as I was strong enough to.

"Better," I tell him truthfully. "I doubt they'll ever be gone, but it's not every night anymore, and sometimes I'll go a few weeks without an attack."

"Good." He pats me gently on the arm. "You know if you ever need us, we're here."

"I know, Dad. Thanks. And speaking of, think I can crash here tonight? I need to check in on one of our clients across the city tomorrow morning. If I need to, I can grab a hotel."

"You'll do no such thing." He stands. "Now, let's head inside so I can beat you at chess before dinner."

"Chess takes longer than a few minutes, Dad."

"Not the way you play," he replies with a grin.

CHAPTER 6
Eliza

Something scrapes against the house, and I sit up, heart already racing before my mind can fully comprehend what happened. I rub the sleep from my eyes and throw my legs over the edge of the bed before standing and stretching.

Tomorrow, I'm trimming that bush so I can stop being woken up—something moves in the corner of my room. A shadow that unravels until it's standing at least two feet over me.

I scream and turn, reaching for the bedside lamp at the same time my other hand grips the handle of the steak knife I'd put on the nightstand.

Dim light floods the room, and I back away from the corner where I could swear I just saw something. Whatever it was, it's gone now, so I rush forward and slam my bedroom door closed before flipping the lock and reaching for the landline phone that literally just got installed yesterday.

"9-1-1, what's your emergency?"

"Someone was in my house," I say quickly. Adrenaline pulses through my system as I keep the knife poised in front of me. It shakes, and I take a deep breath to try to steady myself.

"What is the address?"

I rattle it off. "Please send someone. It's the old lighthouse. Please."

"We're contacting the local authorities," she assures me. "What is your name?"

"Eliza," I reply.

"Okay, Eliza, I'm Betty. Do you know if they are still in the house?"

"I don't know. I'm in my room. I saw them in my room." I scan the area where I'd seen the shadow. All that remains is the chair at my writer's desk, my black jacket on the back.

"Can you describe them?"

"No. I didn't get a good look. I was sleeping, and there was a scraping outside, and I woke up; then I saw a shadow."

"Can you tell me if it was a man or a woman?"

"I don't know!" I take a deep breath. "I'm sorry."

"It's okay, ma'am. The police should be there any minute. Can you get downstairs to open the door?"

"I can try."

"Wait until you hear them," she says. "A lot of times,

that will deter whoever is inside."

But the longer I sit here on the phone, the more I wonder if it had just been my mind playing tricks on me. What if I'm wasting everyone's time? "I'm sorry. I—maybe it was a shadow. I was asleep."

"Let the police check on it, Eliza. It's better to be safe," the woman on the other line says.

Listening, I creep closer to the door, my hand shaking. Someone knocks. "I think they're here."

"Okay. Feel free to keep me on the line. If you see anyone who is not the police, I need you to describe them to me, okay?"

"Okay." Swallowing hard, I unlock the door and peer out into the hall. It's empty, nothing but the slight glow from my nightlight. Moving out and down the stairs, I keep my eyes peeled for anything out of the ordinary, all while holding the knife close to me.

When I finally reach the bottom, I all but sprint toward the door and rip it open. A man wearing a brown circular hat and a Sheriff's uniform is standing on the other side. "It's them," I tell Betty."

"Good. Stay safe, Eliza. If you need us, we're here."

"Thanks." The call ends, and I look to the officer. "

"I'm Sheriff Andrew Vick," he greets. "This is Deputy Matthews."

"Eliza Pierce," I reply. Even with the police here, I can't beat back the adrenaline. I *know* I saw someone…right?

"What seems to be the problem, Miss Pierce?"

"I—uh—I thought I saw someone in my bedroom."

He nods. "May we come inside?"

"Yes, please." I move to the side so they can come in. Sheriff Vick is an older man, somewhere in his mid-fifties, while the deputy with him looks to be about my age. "I thought I saw someone and called before I looked through the house. But when I came down, I didn't see anyone." Closing my eyes, I take a deep breath. "I may have just imagined it. I'm so sorry if I wasted your time."

"Let us check on things," the Sheriff says. "Where is the bedroom?"

"Up the stairs and down the hall. It's the only room," I say.

"I'll check it out," Deputy Matthews says as he places his hand on his firearm, though he doesn't draw it.

"Thank you."

"Of course." He heads upstairs, the metal creaking gently with his steps. It makes me feel even more foolish since I hadn't heard anything.

If someone had been up there, I would have heard them come down.

"I'll take a look in the back, are you okay to wait down here?"

"Yes. Thanks." Feeling absolutely foolish, I take a seat on the couch and wait as the two men walk through my house. A few minutes later, the deputy is coming downstairs right as the Sheriff comes into view from the back. "Anything?"

"Not up here," Deputy Matthews says.

"Back there either. Every window and the back door were locked up tight."

"Same upstairs," the deputy says.

"So I imagined it. I'm so sorry I wasted your time." My cheeks heat. "I cannot believe I wasted your time."

"It's not a waste," the Sheriff says. "It's always better to be safe."

"Besides, gave us a chance to take a look in the lighthouse," the deputy says. "This place has always been a bit of a mystery."

"What do you mean?"

"Old man Wallace who owned it was a bit of a shut-in. No one has been in here since he built the place, though many have tried."

"He's the one who built it?"

"Yup. Died about ten years ago, though, and he left it to some distant relative. No one knows who."

"Either way," Sheriff Vick interrupts, "If you think you see someone else, you can always give us a call." He reaches into his pocket and withdraws a business card. "This is the direct line to our emergency and non-emergency lines."

I take it and study the numbers. "Thanks."

"In the meantime, have you considered getting a security system installed? Believe it or not, Hope Springs has one of the best private security teams in the state."

"Oh, I think it's better than that. I'd say the country," the deputy interjects.

And the road leads back to Lance Knight. "I actually went

and spoke with Mr. Knight about a system though I hadn't decided yet."

"Might make you feel better," the Sheriff replies.

As much as I hate to admit it, a security system would make me feel loads better. So, I force a smile and nod. "I think you're right. Thanks again. And I am so sorry for wasting your time."

———

AFTER A NIGHT OF NO SLEEP, I STEP INTO *KNIGHT PRIVATE Security.* The foyer is empty once again, but there's a man —I believe Michael?—sitting at the desk closest to the door. He looks up and offers me a friendly but hesitant smile.

"Ms. Pierce, what can I do for you?"

"I spoke to Mr. Knight about a system, and I wanted to go ahead and see what it would take to get it installed."

"Lance isn't here right now, but I can help you out if you're good with it." He gets to his feet and crosses over then offers me his hand. "Michael Anderson. We met at the diner."

"Yes, I remember. Eliza."

"Good to see you again, Eliza." He gestures to the chair across from his desk, so I take a seat, hating the fact that I'm disappointed Lance isn't here. I want to see him almost as much as I try to avoid him. "So, did you decide on the system?" He types something on the computer then turns his focus to me.

"The basic one. I think that'll be enough. Does it alert when the doors are opened?"

"And windows," he replies. "If there is anyone who tries to get into your house, you'll know, and so will we."

"So you monitor it."

"Yes."

"And if it goes off, do you call or show up?"

"Both. We'll call on our way, and if everything is fine, you'll say your passcode, and we'll turn around."

Having someone on their way last night would have certainly put my mind at ease. "Do you charge if it's a false alarm? If you show up and there's nothing there?"

His dark gaze narrows on me, and he leans back in his chair. "What made you change your mind?"

"What do you mean?"

"Lance said he didn't think you'd be coming back. What changed your mind?"

"I didn't realize he was a mind reader," I snap. "I never said I wasn't coming back. Just that I wanted time to think about it."

"People reader," he replies.

"What?"

"Lance. He's a great people reader. His impression was that you were not interested in working with us. So I want to know; did something happen? I'm asking because we can tailor the system if it did. Find something that fits what will work best for you."

Given that this is a small town, I imagine he'll hear anyway. So, I level my gaze on him. "I don't appreciate having assumptions made about me, Mr. Anderson," I say. "I don't have the fiscal ability to throw money around, so I needed time to think about the system. As for last night, I thought I saw someone in my house."

Michael sits up straighter now, his expression turning deadly serious. "When?"

"Last night. I called the Sheriff and they searched the house, no one was there, but it made me realize that, if I'd had an alarm system, I would have already known if someone was in the house."

"No one was inside?"

"No."

He types something on his computer. "And you wanted the basic system?"

"Yes."

"What about indoor sensors? We can add those."

"No. Just the basic. Thanks." The idea of someone knowing where I am in my house is far more invasion of privacy than I'm looking for. "Knowing if someone gets in is enough."

"Okay. We have everything we need in stock, so I can schedule the installation as soon as this afternoon. Sometime between five and seven. Does that work for you?"

"Yes. That would be great. Thanks."

"Of course. All I need is for you to fill out these forms then make the deposit, and we'll get it all set up for you." He offers me a folder with a small stack of papers inside. Disclaimers, personal information, the typical.

I stare down at them, already trying to convince myself that this is overkill.

Hope Springs is a safe town. Safer than most.

And no one knows I'm here.

So why do I have this horrible sinking feeling in my gut?

CHAPTER 7

Lance

I pull into my garage and climb out just as Michael's bike comes to a stop in my drive. He pulls off his helmet and climbs off, setting it on the seat. Without saying anything, I grab my bag and head inside, knowing he'll follow.

"Good trip?" he asks.

"It was. Secured the contract extension for the Phillips family. They want to go another five years."

"Fantastic."

I reach into my fridge and offer Michael a bottle of tea. He shakes his head, so I open it and drink it down myself. "So what happened while I was gone?"

"What makes you think anything happened?" Michael crosses his arms and leans against the doorway.

"You're here instead of at the office."

"Maybe I just wanted an update on your trip," he replies.

"Then you would have called. Get it out, what happened? I need to change and head out for my run."

"Your girl called the Sheriff last night."

Every muscle in my body goes rigid. "What? What girl?" I ask, even though there's only one he could be referring to. She's the only one he'd give that nickname.

"Who else? Eliza Pierce."

"Is she okay? What happened?"

"She's fine. Thought she saw someone in her bedroom. Called the cops. Sheriff Vick and Ernie Matthews did a walk-through. They didn't see any points of entry. Think she just got spooked."

"How is she?"

"I'm assuming fine. She came into the office today, though, and set up a basic system installation for this afternoon."

"What time?" I'm already mentally clearing everything I had planned for the evening.

"Between five and seven."

"Why so late?" He could have done that install in a matter of two hours.

"I wasn't sure what time you'd be back. Figured it's something you'd want to handle with Elijah. I mean, I'm more than capable of—"

"No, I'll do it."

Michael chuckles. "Figured as much." He pushes off the door. "She seemed freaked. Even when she came in this morning."

"You think someone was in there?"

"Not necessarily. Vick swears it was empty. But it cements the idea that she's running, doesn't it?"

"It does. Though thinking you saw someone in your house would freak anyone out."

"Sure," Michael says. "But if you ask me, it seemed like there was more to it than that."

"Yeah, that's the feeling I get, too." I'm supposed to protect her, this much I know. The "why me" has yet to be seen, but at least one of my questions has been answered. Not everything in Eliza's life is as it seems.

I only hope I can figure out what brought her here before it's too late.

———

"So what's the verdict on the Phillips contract?" Elijah asks as soon as I've stepped back into the office.

"Extended another five years." I take a seat at my desk and check my email, grateful that there is nothing pressing waiting for me.

"Way to close the deal," he says as he rolls his chair over toward my desk.

"Haven't met one I haven't been able to close," I reply.

He laughs. "Except when it comes to Ms. Pierce. Took Michael for that."

I nearly growl as a strange jealousy creeps over me. I know it's irrational, that it has to just be my competitive side. But it's there. Twisting in my gut like a knife. "I'm helping with that install today," I tell him.

He snorts. "That's not going to end well. She hates you."

"It'll be fine. Though, I used to think she despised all men, and now I'm realizing that I seem to be the only one she harbors a murderous rage for."

"It's not you," he tells me. "At least not entirely. Check this out." He rolls away, so I get up and follow, standing behind his desk as he unlocks his computer. A few clicks later and Eliza's face is on the screen. She's smiling, her body draped in a form-fitting golden gown. The sight of her makes me breathless, every inch of her draped in golden silk like the gown was tailor-made for her.

Who knows, maybe it was.

The man that stands beside her wears a suit that likely cost more than the rent for our entire building. Together, they make quite the pair.

"What am I looking at?"

"Eliza Frank. Or, Eliza Pierce, as we know her now."

"Her ex-husband?"

He nods. "The man next to her is Erick Frank. He's a high-profile attorney out of Los Angeles and has recently set his sights on politics. They went through a rather nasty divorce, though his public relations company did an epic job covering up most of it with charity work. He's got an eye on a political seat, so they're working double-time."

"I thought you'd already done a background on her."

"After Michael's meeting with her, I was curious. Wanted to learn more. So, I—"

"Dug deeper," I finish.

"Exactly."

"Any idea why they got divorced?"

"He's a cheat," he replies then opens a few photographs that were saved to a secure file on his hard drive. Images of Erick with various women wrapped around him pop up. It infuriates me, knowing what it must have done to Eliza to figure out the man who'd sworn to love her the rest of his life was sleeping around.

"So she does despise all men."

"Seems to be. Even if she does have a special dislike for you." Elijah closes out and turns to face me. "Why are you so frustrated by her anyway? It's not like you to let someone get under your skin."

Leaning back against the wall, I cross my arms. "I feel like I'm supposed to help her."

"What do you mean?"

"I think God put her in front of me for a reason. I'm just not sure what that reason is yet."

"Love?" Elijah asks with a grin.

I laugh. "Same thing Michael said."

"That's not a no."

"It's a no," I reply. "But it makes me wonder just what happened between them that has her spooked."

"Do you think this guy is going to come after her?" All humor vanishes from his face.

"We have no reason to think that now," I say quickly. "It's possible I'm misreading things." Though, even as I say it, the feeling of unease grows. Something is going on.

Between the feeling in my gut and her call to the Sheriff's department, I'm sure of it.

"How are you planning to find out if that's the case?" Elijah's grin spreads, and I know he's enjoying seeing me so off-kilter. The prior Army Ranger served right alongside me. Together, we've been in the most stressful situations of our lives, yet he still loves to see me squirm.

Truth is I have absolutely no idea how to approach her when she seems intent on verbally slamming me every time I see her. But if God truly does want me to help her, then the last thing I need to do is push her aside.

Prickly people need grace, too. Maybe even more so.

"I guess we'll see how the install goes."

CHAPTER 8
Eliza

"**O**kay, Liza, you got this." I crack my knuckles and stare at the blinking cursor on the screen of my laptop. Somehow, it feels mocking. Like, as it blinks, it's saying, *"Everyone knows you can't do this, Eliza. There are no new words, Eliza. No original stories."*

"Ugh." It's been a decade since I've published anything, and this will be the first book I've written for anyone over the age of five.

I keep staring straight ahead as though imagining the words will make them suddenly appear. It's not as though I have a story block; I know exactly what I want to write. Who my main character is and what her struggles will be.

Mainly because they are my own.

Still, forming the pictures in my mind into words feels like an insurmountable task—a mountain I am not equipped to climb. Running both hands over my face, I groan.

I'm exhausted.

That has to be it. Even after the Sheriff had searched the house, I hadn't been able to fall back asleep. By the time I'd checked the clock, it was nearly four in the morning, so I'd made some coffee and sat on the balcony off my bedroom, staring out at the surf—every light in my house on and the knife beside me.

I stand and stretch, opting for more coffee and some time on my porch to clear my head.

After making a quick cup, slipping into some comfortable shoes, and grabbing the knife I've been carrying with me all day, I step out on the porch and shut the door. The scent of seawater fills my lungs as I slide onto the aged patio chairs and set my steaming mug down.

Freaky wake-up aside, this place is beyond perfect for me. Erick would lose his mind if he were here, though. There aren't enough people to fawn over him and fall at his feet. No photographers waiting to take his photo outside of a courthouse.

And if he knew I was trying to write a book? Hah. He'd fall over laughing just before telling me how foolish it is. *"You'll never make a living doing that,"* he'd say. *"It's a fine hobby, but leave the publishing to professionals."* Two things he's said to me before, whenever I'd brought it up over the course of our marriage.

I'd wanted so badly to do something other than plan charity events or parties enjoyed by people with fake smiles and even worse intentions. I'd wanted to *be* more. I take a sip of my coffee then pull my cardigan tighter around me.

So many years wasted being told I didn't need any more than I was given. Like a teenager receiving an allowance, I was granted responsibilities as Erick saw fit.

Plan this party.

Get a dress for this cocktail party.

Have my suit cleaned.

Remain silent at my side during this event.

I would be lying to myself if I didn't admit that, even now, I struggle with the idea that I am capable of anything besides being someone else's punching bag. But that's what this new start is. My way of pushing past the noise and becoming who I was always meant to be.

And not being able to find the words is definitely not helping my self-esteem in that department.

Gravel crunches as a white truck makes its way up my driveway. I recognize it—and the man driving it—immediately. Lance and Elijah climb out of the truck and head toward me.

"Are you okay?" Lance asks.

"Fine. Why are you here? I thought you were out of town."

"I'm back now."

"Nice to see you again, Ms. Pierce," Elijah greets.

"You, too." I shake his offered hand then pull back and cross my arms to avoid feeling like I need to do the same with Lance.

"I'll grab the boxes," Elijah offers then turns and heads back toward the truck.

"Are you sure you're okay? I heard you had quite a scare last night."

"It was just a trick of the shadows," I tell him. "I over-reacted."

"When it comes to your safety, it's not an overreaction."

"This time, it was," I say. "But I'm hoping your system will keep it from happening again."

"It'll do that," he replies.

He seems off somehow. His tone not nearly as friendly as it has been in the past. Which, of course, should make me happy. But there's part of me that wants to know what put the dark look in his gaze. A bad day? Or has he just decided he doesn't want anything to do with me either?

Elijah offers a metal box to Lance. "Can we head inside?"

"Sure. Sorry." I grab my coffee and open the door, step-ping aside to allow them in. After setting the mug on my counter, I watch both men set their boxes on the couch.

"Can you show us where you thought you saw someone?"

"Why do you need to see it?" I ask Lance.

"We like to do our own preliminary check. We also need to see all the windows and doors so we can make sure every possible entry point is covered."

"Okay." I swallow hard, nerves churning in my belly. "Right this way."

"I'll be right up. Going to grab my toolkit from the

truck." Elijah slips outside as Lance follows me up the creaky stairs.

"Did you hear anyone on the stairs last night?"

"No. That's one of the things that made me realize I must have been imagining it."

He doesn't respond. We reach the top, and Lance follows me down the short hall and into my room. I move to the side then gesture to the area beside the desk.

"That's where I thought I saw him."

"A him?" he asks, tone taking on a dangerous edge.

I retreat inward, wrapping my arms around myself at the anger in his voice. *I'm not that woman anymore,* I remind myself. *And Erick isn't here.* I may not know him well, but my read on Lance is that he's not an abuser. Arrogant? Sure. But I don't actually believe he'd hurt me.

At least, not physically.

"I'm not sure. I thought it was. It was tall. Really tall." I laugh nervously. "Again, I was clearly not fully awake yet."

"The Sheriff said there was no point of entry?"

"Right. Everything was locked up."

He grunts but doesn't say anything as he studies my room.

"Anything else?"

"Show me where you want the control panel," he says. "Do you typically come in the front or back door?"

"The front."

"Then it needs to be near there, close enough you can turn it off in the sixty seconds before it alerts us."

"Okay." I start toward the door, and Lance does the same. My arm bumps into him, and I freeze, the contact sending an unwelcome jolt of desire through me. A second one following when I suck in a breath and whatever he's wearing—aftershave, cologne, body wash—fills my lungs.

"Sorry," he says as he steps back.

"It's fine." My tone is clipped, but I don't apologize for it. In fact, I wish I'd sounded even angrier so it would erase the feeling of absolute need he stirs within me.

As soon as we're downstairs, I sit back behind my computer and stare at the screen while he begins unpacking things from the box he'd carried in.

Neither of us says a word.

———

"ARE YOU WRITING ANOTHER BOOK?"

I look up from the computer at Lance, who has finished installing a sleek control panel on the wall by my door. "How did you—"

"We did a background check," he says.

I stiffen. How much did he learn?

"Saw that you wrote some children's books a while back."

"That seems like an invasion of privacy."

"Maybe. We like to know who we're dealing with. I apologize if it crossed a line with you."

"You seem to always be apologizing."

"Not quite sure how else to deal with you since every-thing I say seems to offend."

I don't respond because doing so would mean lying about the fact that it's not him offending me, but rather my reaction to him that has me angry every time we're around each other. "I am an author," I reply.

"Nice."

"That's all you're going to say?" I demand, my tone sharp. I'm all but frothing at the mouth for him to spout off about how ridiculous it is that I am trying to write anything. Really, I'm looking for any logical reason for me to continue treating him the way I have been. But as he stands here in my living room, installing a security system, I'm finding it really, really difficult.

"What did you want me to say?" he questions, arching a brow.

"I don't know. Mock me? Tell me what a great hobby it is?" My cheeks heat.

"Sounds to me like you've been hanging around with the wrong people," he replies then turns back toward the panel and turns it on. It beeps, and the screen lights up with three blinking dots. "It's connecting."

"What's that supposed to mean?"

Lance turns to face me. "It's searching for local networks—"

"Not that. You said it sounds like I've been hanging around with the wrong people." I nearly growl the words, even more annoyed that he looks completely at ease despite the turmoil burning in me.

"If the people you're speaking to called your chosen career a hobby, then they don't sound like the greatest people."

I can't even argue with him. Which, of course, irritates me because it gives me a fresh appreciation for the not-plumber. And appreciation for a man who looks like him is dangerous territory. My wounded heart may need healing, but I refuse to let another man be the bandage.

"How's the foot?" he asks.

"What?"

"You don't seem to be limping anymore."

In the excitement since last night, I'd forgotten all about the fact that I'd hurt my foot. "It's fine. Healing."

"Glad to hear it. How's the water heater working out?"

"Once again, fine." It infuriates me, the way he's able to switch subjects so quickly. I'm still reeling over him essentially defending my hobby to me and insulting my choice of friends—not far off there—and he's asking about the hot water.

"What is your Wi-Fi password?"

"It's—hang on." I get up from the couch and cross into the kitchen to retrieve the pink sticky note I wrote the internet information on. Then, I offer it to him. "Here."

"Thanks." He touches the panel then types in the password. It beeps as soon as it connects. After offering the note back to me, he presses a button, and a screen pops up with the locations of the sensors and a green checkmark. "You good?" he calls out.

"Just finished." Elijah comes down the hall with the

silver case he'd brought in. "Every window and door's covered."

Lance scrolls through the list, then turns to me. "Looks good. Ready for me to show you?"

"Yes."

He gives me a quick rundown, which includes choosing both a passcode to arm and disarm the system, as well as the way to check and ensure all of the sensors are armed and working. It's surprisingly simple, something I am incredibly grateful for.

"Do you have any questions?" Lance asks as he and Elijah head outside.

"No."

Lance reaches into his pocket and withdraws a card, offering it to me. "My cell number is on there, so if you think there's an issue, call me."

Having a direct line to him should have made me feel better. Instead, it puts too much pressure on the walls I've kept between us since the moment we met. I hand it back. "I don't need it. I have the office number, which—as I understand it—routes to whomever is on call."

Lance looks at the card then back to me. "It's just a card, Eliza. Use the number, or don't. I don't care."

But he does care, I can see it on his face.

And so do I. Which is why I shove it back into his hand. "No. Thanks."

Elijah looks from me to him then back to me. "See you around, Eliza. Let us know if there are any issues." He heads down the stairs, but Lance still doesn't move.

"You really don't want the card."

Yes. Which is why I can't have it. "I really don't. Thanks for everything. Goodbye." Without waiting for a response, I shut the door and lean back against it, breathing deeply as guilt presses down on my shoulders.

But even as guilty as I feel for treating him the way I am, it creates distance. Distance that is crucial to my survival. I cannot fall for another guy. Not now, not ever.

And Lance Knight is exactly the type of man a woman like me would fall for.

CHAPTER 9

Lance

With the town's Valentine's Day dance practically right around the corner, the entirety of Hope Springs looks like Cupid shot arrows in every single direction. Hearts and streamers hang from the windows of local businesses while pink, red, and white tinsel has been spiraled up every single light post on Main Street.

I can even hear the music already thanks to the open doors of the community center where the high school band is practicing for their performance.

While I've never been big on Valentine's Day, I can appreciate the way this town comes together for literally any holiday that will allow a celebration. Even some that are completely made up. We once had a town-wide barbecue in celebration of a new stop sign going in on Main Street.

A potluck for brand-new lifeguard stands on the beach.

If I didn't love the place so much, it would probably strike me as ridiculous.

I step into the diner and am immediately greeted with the sweet aroma of fresh pie and coffee. "Hey, Lance, grab any seat, and I'll be right there." Lilly, one of the owners, offers me a friendly smile before returning to the table she'd been waiting on.

I shrug out of my jacket and slide onto a bench seat. I've no sooner gotten settled than Lilly is back, a smile on her face.

"How's it going?"

"Good, you?"

"Great. Finally sleeping through the night. Hallelujah!" She throws her hand up in the air.

I chuckle. "I hear a side effect of babies is lack of sleep."

"You heard right. Who knows, maybe you'll find out one day." She smiles. "Do you want the usual?"

"Yes, please. With an emphasis on the coffee."

She laughs lightly and shoves her notebook into the apron tied around her waist. "You got it." After she turns and walks away, I shift my gaze out the window and study the dreary-looking afternoon. It started out bright and beautiful, but shortly after I'd finished the install at Eliza's place, a storm had rolled in.

Fitting, given the mood I'd been in by the time I'd finished at her place. Elijah hadn't even messed with me on the drive back to the firm. He'd remained quiet, scrolling through his phone and pretending that I didn't just essentially have a door slammed in my face.

Speaking of…

My attention lands on a gorgeous blonde as she steps out of the bank. Her hair is swept up in a messy bun, and she's wearing black leggings and a long cream sweater that falls to mid-thigh. The sight of her has my blood pumping with desire. It reminds me of the way she'd brushed against me in her room.

The sharp intake of breath as she'd all but frozen in place.

I *know* she feels it, too. How can she not?

How can a woman be so gorgeous and so incredibly unapproachable all at the same time?

Before I can contemplate much further, she crosses the street and walks right into the diner. Every muscle in my body turns rigid; every nerve reacts to her closeness. I keep my attention focused outside as she walks by me, knowing that, if she sees me, she's likely to run.

The gentle scent of her perfume fills my lungs as she takes a seat in the booth right in front of mine.

The woman is as intoxicating as she is frustrating.

"Hey, hun! What can I get for you?" Lilly asks as she crosses over to her.

"A coffee, please."

"You got it." She turns and leaves the table.

As I sit here, staring at what I can see of the back of Eliza's head, I contemplate what I could say that might change her mind about me, even as the logical side of me doesn't actually believe there is anything I can do to make up for whatever reason she has to hate the entire male species.

Protect her. The words hit me like a freight train.

Well, okay then. Before I can think too much about it, I'm grabbing my coffee cup and walking toward her booth. And, without giving her a chance to say no, I slide into the seat across from her.

If looks could kill, the one she gives me over the top of the menu would surely place me six feet under.

"I'm afraid I'm not looking for company tonight, Mr. Knight."

"What exactly did I do to make you despise me, Ms. Pierce?"

She closes the menu. "Nothing in particular. I just don't care much for your type."

"And what type is that? Men in general?"

Her nostrils flare, and the fact that I get some sort of twisted satisfaction out of pressing her buttons should bother me. "People who pressure others into a relationship," she replies, venom lacing every word. "And those who think too highly of themselves."

I don't even touch the first accusation because, from the outside in, I could see how I am pressuring her into some form of relationship—even though it's not the type she's thinking of. "And how would you know I think too highly of myself? Outside of a few instances where I've been installing something for you, we've never had an actual conversation."

"First impressions are lasting, Mr. Knight."

I take a drink of my coffee. "Enlighten me, then. What was your first impression of me?" I don't have to glance over to know that Lilly and her husband Alex are watching from behind the counter.

"I don't want a scene."

"No scene," I reply. "I just want to get to the bottom of whatever it is you can't stand about me so we can move on. I install a water heater for you, and you insult me. You show up at my security firm looking for help and all but run right back out. Then, I install said security system in your house, and you throw my business card back in my face before slamming the door. Did I miss anything?"

"The run on the beach," she replies.

"Oh, yes, can't forget that."

"Definitely not. It's what led to me hurting my foot." Before I can respond, she crosses her arms in her lap. "You want to know what my first impression was? Fine. You have an overinflated ego and fancy yourself some hero type. Which makes sense, given your past and current profession. Plus, you seem to think so highly of yourself that, even after I have rebuked every one of your advances, you still continue trying to make them anyway. A normal man would have backed off after being turned down twice."

"Turned down?" I ask, brow arched. "I don't recall asking you anything."

Her cheeks turn crimson. "Your actions speak louder than words." But her voice is shaky now. I've touched a nerve.

But since I'm on a roll, I don't stop. "In this case, I don't think they do. So, let me lay it out for you. I have no interest in you romantically if that's what you're thinking. Frankly, the fact that you are so high up on your horse that all you can do is look down at the rest of us irritates me. And since we're being honest, yes, I do like helping people. Though, it's not to inflate my ego further, it's because helping others is a calling that God blessed me with. It's something I enjoy doing." I slide out of the booth and take my coffee over to the table. "I need to run," I tell Lilly as I toss a twenty on the table. "Thanks."

"No problem." She eyes me curiously as I leave, closing the door gently behind myself and crossing the street toward the beach. I'm not dressed for a run, but my need to work off some steam is currently overshadowing my choice of wardrobe.

"God, I have no idea what you want me to do here," I say aloud to the crashing waves. "But if I'm supposed to help her, I need a little help."

CHAPTER 10
Eliza

M en.

Arrogant, conceited, know-it-all, mansplaining men.

But my anger deflates before it even fully forms because I *know* he's right. I made up my mind about him before he even opened his mouth, and it has more to do with me and my reaction than anything he's done.

He did install my water heater even though it wasn't his job, which saved me from having the original installer cancel.

He did get a security system installed so I'd feel safer and was nothing but professional the entire time he was there.

The business card had thrown me off, but as the owner of the company, I can understand why he offered it. Truthfully, if Elijah had been the one to offer his number, it wouldn't have bothered me in the least.

Because I don't feel the same way around Elijah as I do Lance.

I accused him of being an egotistical maniac, and the truth is, I don't get that feeling about him at all. Honestly, I think he might be one of the first actually decent men I've ever met.

"You all right?"

I glance up at Lilly and force a smile. "Fine. Thanks."

"It's not my place, but," she starts then slides into the booth that Lance just vacated, "you read Lance wrong."

"I'm starting to think that." I straighten in my seat, embarrassment heating my cheeks.

"Listen, I can see that you're going through something, and I'm not going to force you to hear my side, but I will tell you that Lance Knight is a good man. He helps a lot of people and asks for nothing in return."

I'm instantly reminded of all the amazing things Erick's friends had to say about him.

'He's an amazing lawyer.'

'He helps people selflessly.'

'He would never cheat.'

'He would never hurt a fly.'

I was dragged through the mud during our divorce by every single one of the people who testified against me. Who insisted I was lying. That the bruises on my face just before I finally left him were because I fell down the stairs after drinking myself into a stupor. Erick loved to paint me as a drunk. Something he somehow managed to successfully do despite me rarely indulging in more than two drinks.

"Anyway, I don't mean anything by it, I just like Lance and don't like to see him hurt."

"I get it. I'm sorry that I hurt him. I just—I don't trust easily."

"Girl, I get that." Lilly reaches over and pats my hand. "Now, can I get you something to eat?"

———

AFTER A QUIET DINNER OF STRANGE LOOKS FROM EVERYONE who'd been in the diner when Lance and I got into it, I decide that I need to make things right. I may not be looking for a friendship, and definitely not anything romantic, but that doesn't mean that things can't be cordial. Especially since he'll be monitoring my security system.

So, pride aside, I step out of the café with a takeout container consisting of Lance's usual dinner—according to Lilly—and follow the verbal directions she gave me to his house.

I stop just outside a restored beach house with pale blue siding, a white picket fence, and a large iron door. My stomach twists into knots as I stare at it as though the house may come alive and swallow me whole.

Images of Erick screaming at me. Of his face beet red— his eyes hard and angry—assault me, but I shove them down. Lance is not Erick. And I am not the woman I was when I left LA. So, burying that fear deep down, right alongside my heartbreak, I open the little white gate and make my way down the cobblestone path.

The grass in his front yard is thick and green despite the cold February weather. A decent-sized maple tree stands in one corner, some flowers I don't recognize in the other. It's absolutely gorgeous, and I suddenly realize that I have no idea if he has a wife.

I turn around.

What if she sees me bringing him dinner as a threat? What if she thinks I'm—

"Are you going to stand there all night or eventually make your way up to the door?" The deep baritone washes over me, and the knot in my stomach tightens.

Swallowing hard, I turn around. My mouth dries as I drink in the sight of him leaning against the front door frame, wearing an unbuttoned blue flannel with a white t-shirt underneath and dark jeans. "I didn't want to intrude," I blurt.

"Yet you're standing in my front yard."

"I brought you food." Embarrassment heats my face for the second time, and I take a step closer. "But if you guys have already eaten—"

"You guys?" he questions, brow arched.

"I'm assuming you have a wife or girlfriend."

"So, because I'm not romantically interested in you, I must be in a relationship?"

Anger burns past my embarrassment, and I clench my free hand into a fist. "That is *not* what I meant."

He grins, one of those 'I know exactly what you meant but wanted to embarrass you anyway' grins. It makes my blood boil even as my attraction for him grows. "Why don't you come inside? Unless you'd rather throw that at my house."

"Considering it," I reply, but I make my way toward him anyway. I am here for a reason. To make peace so that I can remain in this town without awkward interactions around every single corner.

Lance steps back into his house and holds the door open as I move inside. I do my best not to inhale the intoxicating scent of whatever musky bodywash he used but fail miserably. The man smells more delicious than the food in this box.

Danger, I remind myself. This man is dangerous to me.

Wood floors gleam beneath my feet as pale blue walls contrast with a dark navy focal wall. Two driftwood crosses flank either side of an impressively sized flat screen mounted to the center of the focal wall. A leather sectional takes up most of the living room, which opens into a gorgeous kitchen that puts even the one in Erick's massive house to shame.

A huge double oven with a gas range sits in the center of white cabinets and is surrounded by granite with hints of blue, copper, and marble.

I nearly drool just staring at it.

My gaze continues around his house until it lands on a wall beside the hall. A folded flag sits in a glass case and is mounted on the wall beneath a framed photograph of a group of men in the desert. They wear military uniforms, and in the very center stands Lance. I recognize him even though he wears dark shades.

Every muscle in my body becomes acutely aware that he's standing relatively close by, and I realize that I've been staring at his house as though he weren't here with me. I clear my throat. "Army?"

"Yes," he replies but doesn't elaborate. "Can I get you some water?"

"No thanks. I'm not staying long." I all but shove the food into his hand, desperate to do something—anything—to put space between us before I spontaneously combust right here in his living room.

"Big plans?" he asks.

"Work."

He takes the food and carries it into the kitchen, setting it on the granite and opening the Styrofoam lid. Lance studies the burger. "Doesn't look poisoned."

"Would it look poisoned even if it was?" I question. "The whole idea is to hide it, isn't it?"

Lance smiles. "So there is a sense of humor buried in there."

"I told you, you don't know me at all."

His smile fades just slightly. "Fair enough." He lifts the burger and takes a bite. As he chews, I let my gaze travel a bit, studying the few photographs on the kitchen counter. One is of Lance and some children in the desert—similar to the one in his office. He's laughing while two small boys hang from his flexed arm and another has his little arms looped around Lance's neck.

Another is of Lance and a handful of kids in front of a Christmas tree. They're holding gifts, their wide smiles infectious.

"From our town's annual Christmas drive," he says. "And that one is from my last deployment."

I look up, and our gazes lock. There's a snap of connection, a jolt of something that threatens to bring part of me back to life.

I bury it.

"I didn't know the town did one."

"Every year," he replies. "We collect toys that we take to shelters in Boston so that kids who otherwise wouldn't get gifts feel the love of Christmas."

"That's very noble."

"It's what's right. And it gives us the chance to spread the gospel and re-introduce the kids to the love of Jesus. Sometimes, it's the first time they're hearing about Him."

"Hmm."

"Are you not a believer?" he asks.

"I didn't say that," I reply. "I came here tonight to call a truce." The subject change is one I know he notices but thankfully doesn't say anything.

"A truce? I didn't realize we were at war."

"We're not. But I've been short with you when you didn't deserve it. I'm still trying to get settled, and thanks to a bush scraping alongside my house, I'm not sleeping well."

"Do you need it trimmed?" he asks. "I can take care of it for you."

"No. It's already done. I did it earlier." I take a deep breath. "Anyway, I've been treating you unfairly, and for that, I'm sorry."

"You don't need to apologize."

"I do," I reply. "I've been taking out my stress on you, and it's not fair. We're not friends, but we don't have to be enemies."

"We can't be friends?"

"No."

"Why not?"

"Because," I reply, frustration lacing my tone. "I don't want friends. I didn't come here for friends."

"Why did you come here? To Hope Springs, I mean."

"For the quiet," I reply honestly. "I want space and distance."

"From who in particular?"

"Everyone," I reply.

"Why is that?"

I glare at him. "None of your business."

He holds up both hands in mock surrender. "Just trying to get to know you better."

I cross my arms. "Why? I've made it clear that I don't want to be friends, and I've treated you horribly. So why do you keep trying to talk to me?"

All humor fades from his handsome face. "Because, Ms. Pierce, I don't believe in coincidences. I believe you are here for a reason, and I can't seem to shake the belief that you and I are going to be friends one day."

"I thought you weren't interested in me."

"I'm not. I said *friends*, Eliza. It's not code for anything."

"In my experience, friendship comes with strings, Mr. Knight. And I am not in any way, shape, or form interested in being someone's puppet ever again." I turn to leave. "Have a good night. Enjoy the burger."

CHAPTER 11

Lance

B y the time Sunday morning rolls around, I'm still at a loss as to how to get Eliza to see I want nothing from her. I've settled on giving her the distance she's asked for, hoping that in some way, as time passes, she'll start to realize that I'm not looking for a relationship outside of friendship and that mine doesn't come with strings.

I've run into her a couple of times over the past few days, but every time I see her, she turns and walks the other direction. The system we installed on her house has been quiet, so that's something, but I still can't shake this feeling that something is wrong when it comes to her.

Very, very wrong.

Dressed in dark jeans, a button-down shirt, and the only pair of boots I own without scuffs, I sit in the middle of a church pew as Pastor Redding releases the congregation. I stand and turn then remain rooted in place as I see a familiar blonde getting up from the back pew. She keeps her gaze cast down at the ground as she leaves, avoiding any and all conversations with anyone.

I offer smiles and greetings all while trying to make my way quickly to the exit. By the time I reach it, I see that Eliza has been cornered by Mrs. McGinley and three of her closest friends. The elderly women surround her, all of them smiling and chatting happily while Eliza smiles uncomfortably, though, unlike with me, with them she actually tries to appear friendly.

Although, I can see the signs of sleepless nights in the dark circles beneath her eyes and the slump of her shoulders. Have there been more phone calls since the other night?

Plastering a smile on my face, I cross the distance between us and stop just before the women. "Morning, ladies."

Mrs. McGinley is the first one to greet me. "Good morning, Lance. How are you?"

"Good. You?"

"Doing much better now that I have warm water again." She gestures to Eliza who is currently doing everything she can not to meet my gaze. "I was just telling this lovely young woman here that she should stop by the library."

"It's the best one in Maine."

"It's the best one in the country," she corrects with a wink. "Okay, ladies. Time for brunch! You're more than welcome to join us if you'd like, Eliza."

"Thanks, but I have things I need to get to," she replies kindly.

"Of course. Next time, then." The older woman smiles before turning, and she and her friends leave.

"You okay?" I ask. "You looked like you'd been bombarded."

"What's your game?" she asks, narrowing her gaze on me.

"What do you mean?"

"Why have you taken an interest in me? Why are you following me?" Her tone is so different from the other night that it momentarily catches me off guard.

"Following you?" I arch a brow. "I come to church every Sunday. Something everyone here will verify. And as for the interest I have in you, I assure you, Ms. Pierce, it's not anything besides the feeling that you were put in my path for a reason."

"And what reason is that?" she snaps. "Reason enough to leave me this?" She reaches into her purse and shoves a piece of paper into my hands.

I open it, every instinct in my body going on full alert. Scrawled in messy handwriting are the words:

Dearest Eliza,
I watch you while you breathe.
Dream of you when I sleep.
And although you never seem to want to look my way, I cannot be dissuaded.

Always yours.

"When did you find this?" I demand, meeting her gaze.

She glares back at me. "Don't act like it's not you. You're screwing with me."

"Why would this be me?" I ask, tone harsher now.

For the first time since Mrs. McGinley and her friends left, Eliza's expression softens. Not a lot but just enough that I sense a crack in her armor.

"Eliza. Where was this?"

"On my dining room table," she replies. "This morning."

Someone was in her house. How was someone in her house?

"You have access to the security system. I just assumed—"

"I would never do something like this."

"You're just always there."

She looks exhausted. Scared, even. And why wouldn't she be?

"This is a small town. Everyone is always there." I study the writing again. "It was written quickly, as though the person was afraid to get caught. Notice the writing? The way the lines are shaky?" I gesture to it, and when she doesn't answer, I meet her gaze. "What?"

"How do you know that?" she asks.

"It's what I do," I reply. "Did anyone follow you here?

Anyone who might want to scare you? Your ex-husband perhaps?"

The armor slips back into place and she stiffens. "No." She rips the note from my hands and shoves it back into her purse. "I'm still not sold that it wasn't you."

"It wasn't me. And since it wasn't me, we need to do a full check of your system and install some cameras."

"How much is that going to run me?" she snaps.

"Eliza—" Before I can tell her I'm not planning to charge her for it, that she might be in very real danger, she interrupts.

"No. I'm not doing it, Lance. The games? They have to stop. There hasn't been anyone in my house when I'm home, which means it was put in there while I was gone. Since you are the only other person that has the code—"

I'm furious now. "Why would I do this? Tell me that, Eliza. What reasoning could I possibly have for trying to scare you like this?"

She closes her eyes and takes a deep breath. "I don't know!" she yells. "But it has to stop! I can't live like this anymore!"

"Like what?"

"Scared." A tear rolls down her cheek, and I yearn to reach forward, but she pulls away and wipes it before I can.

"You don't have to. Let me help. I'll check the system, make sure no one managed to bypass it."

"That happens?"

"It's rare. As in—this would be a first—but I'm not so arrogant that I'll ignore the possibility."

"Okay."

"Why don't you come with me? I can drive you to the office to get the supplies. Then we'll head over to the lighthouse."

"What? No. I'll just go home and wait in the car." She steps into the parking lot and starts to cross toward her car. A car whips out of a spot and slams on the gas.

I have less than a heartbeat to react, but the entire world seems to slow down as I watch the car barreling toward her. "Look out!" I rush forward, grabbing her and pulling her back onto the sidewalk. We both fall backward. Pain shoots through the back of my head as it slams into the concrete when she lands on top of me. The sedan races past the church and disappears around the corner before I can get a plate.

Eliza's body on mine, I can feel every tremble, every ragged breath as she processes what nearly just happened. Within seconds, she's pulled to her feet as those who witnessed what just happened surround us.

Pastor Redding tugs me to my feet. "Lance! Are you all right?" He looks me over. I reach up and touch the back of my head then hiss as fresh pain slices through my head.

My fingers are streaked with blood, though thankfully it's not a lot.

"Fine. Eliza. Are you okay?"

She nods, though her face is white as snow.

"You're bleeding. We need to get you to Doc," Pastor

Redding says as he places a hand on my upper back and guides me around the corner of the church to the neighboring building. Doc is already coming out, his phone in hand.

"What happened?" he demands as he comes around behind and looks at my head.

"Someone tried to run them over!" a woman—Mrs. Yates—yells.

"Stitches?" I ask.

"No, thankfully, it's just a minor cut. We'll get you both inside and looked over, though, just to be safe."

"Her first," I demand, reaching back. Eliza walks forward, following Doc inside while I scan our surroundings. "Call the sheriff," I tell Pastor Redding.

"Already done," he replies. "I'll be in the church if you need me. Praying that they catch whoever that was."

———

AFTER GIVING OUR STATEMENTS TO SHERIFF VICK, I LEAD Eliza upstairs and into my office. The guys are already waiting for me, each of them with furious expressions on their faces. Two ex-military men who have seen the worst —and best—of humanity.

All of them were in my squad. Brothers in every way but blood.

"We got security footage, but the car has no plates, and the driver knew enough to cover his face with a ski mask."

"So, whoever is after her planned this," I say.

"Possibly. Or they just made a rash decision. Running someone down in broad daylight? Outside of a church on Sunday? It's risky," Michael adds.

"Anything on the security system?" I ask Elijah.

"No one tried to access it. In fact, it wasn't turned off until this morning and then was reactivated right after. Just before eight a.m."

"That's when I left for church," Eliza says. "I found the note on my way out the door. I was going to bring it over right after the service."

"So it was left while you were sleeping," I say, shaking my head angrily. "Which makes this at least twice this person has been in your house."

"Twice?" she asks.

"When you called the sheriff."

She pales. "You think he was there? That I really saw something?"

"I do," I reply then turn to Elijah. "Anything on the ex-husband?"

"Aside from him being an absolutely horrendous person?" he questions. "A lot. But he was photographed leaving his church this morning. All the way in LA."

"So it couldn't have been him," I say.

"Wait. You looked into my ex?"

I turn to face a furious Eliza. "I texted Elijah while we were with Doc. He is suspect number one, given your recent divorce."

Her hands clench into fists at her sides, and she glares at me as though she wants to be the one behind the wheel with me in her crosshairs. "You had *no* right." Whirling, she turns and stalks from the office.

"That one is a hothead," Elijah says as he whistles.

"I like her," Michael replies.

"She's going to get herself killed if she doesn't put her pride aside." I head for the door.

"We'll keep digging, but likely, we're going to need Eliza to give us a thread to follow if we're going to catch this guy," Elijah calls out.

"I'll do my best to get one," I call back as I head for my truck.

CHAPTER 12

Eliza

omeone is trying to kill me.

I white-knuckle the steering wheel as I pull into the drive of my lighthouse. A place that should have been my sanctuary. Even now, I see that the red flag on the mailbox is up...and it was down this morning.

My stomach twists into knots.

Swallowing hard, I remain where I am and try to gather my breathing. I could have told them it wasn't Erick. He doesn't care about me. Honestly, he never did. Not enough to risk everything he's building on some ridiculous vengeance plot.

No, I have no idea who would be after me now.

What did I do to deserve this? What horrific travesty did I commit to bring this type of life upon myself? I left one monster to gain another? How is that fair? Tears fill my eyes, but I angrily wipe them away and throw my door open as Lance's truck pulls up right behind me.

Every time I turn around, he's there.

And it *infuriates* me because I know he must have an angle. Some reason for saying he wants to protect me.

"You just put yourself in unnecessary danger," he says as he crosses toward me.

I cross my arms. Overhead, thunder booms. "I came home."

"Where you are being stalked."

"This is my home!" I scream it. Lightning splits the sky, the storm that has been rolling in finally here. "I will not be chased away from another place!"

Lance crosses over toward me, stopping when he's a few feet away. It's then his gaze sweeps the front of my house and he notices the mailbox. "Did you put something in there?"

"No," I growl. "But I was just about to—"

He pushes past me, gently keeping me from stopping him when I try to do so. I know I need his help. That he clearly has an understanding of what might be happening to me. And even without him being with me outside the Church, I know in the pit of my stomach it's not him.

How? I'm not sure, but I do.

Still, accepting his help is not something I'm prepared to do.

Lance opens the box and peers inside. Reaching into his pocket, he withdraws his phone and presses something on the screen. "Hey, I need you at the old lighthouse.

Thanks." He ends the call and closes the mailbox. "Let's go inside."

"Who did you call?"

"I'll tell you inside. Let's go." He reaches behind him and withdraws a firearm tucked at his back.

"What are you doing?"

"Making sure your house is clear. Unlock the door, disarm the system, then get behind me."

"I don't—is this really necessary?"

"Someone just tried to run you down with their car." His tone is clipped, agitated. "They left a package in your mailbox and a note earlier. Yes, this is necessary."

The reminders serve as a sobering moment for me, clearing my fear momentarily and helping me see the logic. I do as he asks, unlocking the door. The system goes off, a steady beeping as I quickly disarm it then move in right behind him.

Lance clears my house like it's his sole mission in life, and by the time he's made sure every nook and cranny is creep-safe, checking all the window and door locks as he goes, we head back into the living room.

By the time we make it back, there's a knock on the door. Lance checks the peephole then pulls the door open and shoves his gun back into the holster at his lower back.

For the second time today, I'm faced with Sheriff Vick. He removes his hat and offers me a piece of paper shielded by a clear evidence bag.

Lance steps up beside me, and together, we read the scrawled writing.

Dearest Eliza,

Why must you make me do these things to you?

I love you, and I will make you see it.

Even if it's the last thing you see.

Yours always.

I shiver and offer the note back to the sheriff.

"What was inside the package?" Lance questions.

The sheriff holds up another bag. Inside are a bunch of flower petals. Lillies by the look of it. My favorite. "These have any meaning to you?" he asks.

"Lillies are my favorite," I reply. I don't have to read Lance's mind to know what he's thinking. Who better to know my favorite flower than my ex-husband?

"You don't have any idea who this might be?" he asks.

I shake my head. "I know my ex and I had a nasty split, but he's far too preoccupied with everything he has going on to be worried about me."

"He has an alibi for this morning, but that doesn't mean he didn't hire anyone," Lance says.

"No. I'm telling you it's not him. Erick has vast political aspirations. He wouldn't risk that just to get back at me."

"Were any threats made during the divorce proceedings?" The sheriff questions.

"No." I shake my head. "I gave him everything except a small lump sum, which barely took a scratch off the money he has to his name. I know it's not him," I insist.

"Then is there anyone else it could be? Jaded ex-lovers, old co-workers, anyone with an axe to grind or a reason to want you running scared?"

I close my eyes and try to think of someone—anyone who might be capable of something like this. "Not that I can think of. I didn't have any old boyfriends, and for the last ten years, I've been unemployed at Erick's request. I had no friends to speak of, and anyone who would have had an issue with me would have been from over a decade ago."

The sheriff scrawls something on a notepad then looks to Lance. "If you guys come up with anything, let me know."

"We will."

"And if anything else happens—"

"I'll call," I interrupt. Outside, the storm rages on, thunder and lightning splitting the sky as rain hammers down. "Thank you."

He nods. "We'll see if we can get any prints off of the note or the petals." After slipping the two plastic bags inside his jacket, he puts his hat back on. "We'll catch this guy," he assures me. "We might not get a lot of action out here in Hope Springs, but I can assure you it hasn't dampened our abilities."

"I've no doubt. Thank you."

He nods. "Lance."

"Thanks, Vick."

The sheriff leaves, and Lance shuts the door behind him before turning to face me and crossing his arms. "What are you leaving out?"

"Nothing." I'd ask him why he's still here, but the truth is I don't want to be alone. Knowing that the alarm hasn't been tripped yet the note was left on my table is even more unnerving.

"Eliza."

"Lance." I glare back at him and something shifts in the air between us. A charged understanding that I need him and we both know it. My irritation deflates as I take a deep breath. Calm, I need calm. "Do you want some tea?" Thankfully, my things are nearly unpacked, so I make my way into the kitchen and fire up the kettle.

"As long as you don't poison it," he replies.

I snort. "I'll try to refrain."

He crosses the room and stares out the window, watching the gloomy afternoon play out. Without his eyes on me, I'm able to study him. The man stands like a fighter, missing nothing. His handsome features remain completely focused, and I've no doubt he's far deadlier than Erick could ever hope to be.

So why do I not feel fear in his presence? Why is it only this burning attraction that puts me on edge?

"What is the reason?"

He turns. "What?"

"You said I was put in your path for a reason. What reason and by whom?"

"God," he replies simply. "As for the reason, I believe it's pretty obvious now."

I can't help myself. I snort. "You believe that God put me in your path?"

"I don't believe it," he says. "I know it."

"And how is that?"

"Because, from the moment I met you, He's been pushing me toward you."

I shake my head. "I don't believe in things like that."

"You were in church today," he replies.

"Because I haven't missed a Sunday in ten years and can't seem to break the habit," I retort.

Instead of looking offended, Lance seems intrigued. "Erick make you go?"

"Yes."

"But you don't believe in God."

"I didn't say that."

"Then what are you saying?" he questions.

"I'm saying that I question whether or not God believes in me."

Lance's brow furrows. "Why do you question that?"

My throat tightens because I know I've already said too much. Emotion claws at me, a voice in my head telling me it's okay to open up. That my secrets are safe with this man. But reality hits too hard, and I'm reminded that he's a complete stranger.

A man I only met because he installed my water heater.

The tea kettle beeps, so I remove the top and add peppermint leaves to the stainless-steel strainer. Then, I pull down two coffee mugs and set them on the counter. "It's almost ready." A chill fills the air, but as I start toward the fireplace, Lance shakes his head.

"I'll do it." Kneeling before the hearth, he retrieves two logs and puts them inside then uses the long lighter I'd left on the mantle to start it. Less than a minute later, the fire crackles, casting the dim room in an orange glow.

I finish prepping the tea then offer him a mug before squeezing some honey in mine. "Honey?"

"Sure."

I give him some as well, and he stirs. Together, we sit at the small round table with only the sound of the fire and a roaring storm to fill the silence. "I didn't mean to offend you," I say.

"You didn't."

"Good."

"But I want to say something," he says. "Something I had to focus on all the times I've been deployed. Then we'll get back to the crisis at hand."

I level my gaze on his, struck by the shadows dancing over his masculine features. The man is stunning. "What's that?"

"God doesn't let you down. People do. Don't lose sight of Him because you're burdened by the actions of others."

His words hit like a punch to the gut, but I shove them aside because letting them in would mean opening a can of worms I'd much rather leave sealed. "I don't know who's after me," I tell him, changing the subject.

Lance takes a sip of his tea. "I need you to make a list. Find me everyone you've had contact with recently."

"Aside from you, the moving company, and a few gas station clerks, there is no one."

"There has to be. Another ex, maybe? Or someone your ex-husband might have hired?"

"I was only ever with Erick. He was the first real relationship I had and the last." Why that embarrasses me now, I'm not sure. But my cheeks heat, and I cast my gaze down to the mug. "I don't even know why you're helping me. I can't afford to pay you any more than I already am." My thoughts drift back to the price sheet he'd shown me back in his office. "I really can't afford you."

"You think I feel like putting a price on your life?" He arches a brow. "Come on, Big City, surely you've met someone with a decent bone in their body before."

I meet his gaze. "All I know is that everything comes with a price. No one does things out of the goodness of their heart. Not these days." To avoid speaking further, I take another drink of hot tea.

"It's a shame you're so jaded. Otherwise, you might realize that not everyone is as twisted as you think."

My throat constricts and I avert my gaze to avoid looking into his. Then, I take a deep breath and shift the subject yet again because I sense a depth I'm not comfortable with. "I've hardly had contact with anyone," I insist. "And no one in my previous life knows where I went. I have no family, no close friends...I was alone." Just speaking the words makes my throat burn with emotion, but I cram it down. I've spent far too many years crying over my life. I'll waste no more tears.

"You didn't leave a mail forwarding address? A way to send you the rest of your belongings? I'm assuming the moving company you hired knew where to find you?"

I deflate. "Yes. But they wouldn't just hand out that address."

Lance leans in closer, and the firelight makes his eyes shine even brighter. "As you stated minutes ago, there are some people who have a price, Miss Pierce. And if your ex is as wealthy as you say, it's quite possible he would pay someone to find you. Even the most novice of PI's could track you through a moving company."

His words echo through my mind, leaving a sick taste in my mouth and rocks in my gut. Would he be so desperate to keep tormenting me that he'd hire someone to kill me? And why? I've kept his secrets. I said nothing outside of the divorce. Even now, I could tell Lance things that would bring Erick's career and political aspirations to a screeching halt.

Am I being hunted because of it?

CHAPTER 13

Lance

The list Eliza gave me consists of a handful of gas stations between here and California, a moving company contact, her tennis coach back in LA, and two women who were outright furious with her for leaving Erick. Insanely enough, they were both having affairs with him at the time. And since their divorce brought that to light, they blame her for his calling it off.

Groaning, I rub both hands over my face then stand to refill my coffee mug for what is probably the fifth time since I got back to the office two hours ago. "God, please give me clarity so I can see what I know I must be missing." The answer comes in the form of knowing, without a doubt, it is no one on the list she gave me.

In all the years I've been working in private security, I've dealt with plenty of stalkers. Everything from a gardener obsessed with the wife of his boss to ex-boyfriends, bosses, co-workers, crazed best friends, and even a teenager with an unhealthy attachment to the mom of his girlfriend. As insanely unique as each of the cases was, they all had one thing in common: motive. No one on her list has any actual motive.

Sure, the women told her how terrible she was for giving up on her marriage, but they don't have any reason to follow her clear across the country to terrify and kill her. Honestly, even though she didn't bother putting him on the list, her ex is still my main suspect. With his money and connections, he could easily have hired someone so that, when the time came, he would have a rock-solid alibi.

Question is, why? Everything Eliza told me was the truth. Aside from a lump sum of two hundred thousand dollars, which was far less than she could have gotten, she walked away clean. She didn't even ask for marital support, even though he likely would have given in if only to keep the limelight off them.

Truth is she may have gotten her freedom, but fiscally, he came out on top.

"Burning the midnight oil?"

I glance up right as Michael takes a seat in the chair across from my desk. "Something like that. What are you doing here so late?"

"The Millers' alarm went off. By the time I got there, they were ripping their seventeen-year-old son a new one for trying to sneak one of his buddies upstairs for some midnight video gaming."

"Teenagers." I shift my attention back to the list.

"No kidding," Michael replies. "What you got going on over there?" he asks curiously.

"The list Eliza gave me." And because, if I stare at it any longer my eyes are going to bleed, I hand it to him for a second look. "I organized it by how much contact she had with them, and most of the people on that list she would have shared nothing more than a half-hearted smile and a wave."

"The 'M' is motive?" Michael asks, flipping the page on my notepad to the names I added after researching both her and Erick.

"Yes."

"Seems to me the ex has the most to gain by offing her."

I ignore the pang his callous word brings. This is a professional relationship. Another client. Emotions have no place here. "Sure. But why wait until after the divorce is final? Why risk everything on a woman who literally took nothing but a small settlement from you?" I move my mouse so the computer screen comes back to life. On it are pictures of both Erick and Eliza—walking together, smiling, hand-in-hand. They made quite a pair, her with her bright hair and kind smile. Him with his perfectly tailored suits and thousand-dollar haircut.

I hate that it makes me feel jealous knowing she loved him enough to marry him yet can hardly stand to be in the same room as me.

Michael whistles. "She is a looker."

"She is." However, even from these pictures, I can pick

up the subtleties.—the hollowness of her smile, the empty expression in her eyes. I click on a picture I'd minimized just because it made me angry enough that I wanted to drive to California and interrogate the man myself. "Look at this, though." Zooming in on a photograph of Eliza at a charity banquet, I focus in on her cheek.

"Is that a bruise?" Michael demands.

"Barely covered by makeup, yes." I lean back in my seat. If I hadn't worked with domestic abuse survivors before, I likely would have missed it. But I know the signs. The tells. And when someone's skin tone is even slightly off, thick makeup is the first thing I look for.

Then, it's the faintest note of purple or yellow.

"Erick was abusing her," I tell Michael.

"Which means his motive could very well be to silence her."

"Exactly." I take a drink of my coffee.

"You have someone watching her place now?"

I nod. "Elijah is."

"Good. I can fly out first thing tomorrow if you want. Go talk to this guy."

"Nah. I want to do it," I tell him. "I have a buddy out in Cali. Ex-Marine who is a homicide detective in L.A. now. I'll have him go over with me."

"Then we'll keep an eye on Eliza."

THE AIRPORT IS FULL OF PEOPLE COMING AND GOING, ALL OF them moving so fast they can't bother to spare a single look or smile at a stranger. Which is why I despise big cities. After staying in Hope Springs for even a few days, I was ready to leave Boston permanently.

There are too many people around. Too many moving pieces. And for a man like me who always feels the need to watch his six, it's a nightmare.

Thankfully, my ride is already waiting for me at the curb by the time I leave Los Angeles Airport. Jaxson Payne leans back against his black SUV, a smile on his face. A large scar runs the length of his jaw before slicing down his throat and disappearing into the collar of his shirt, courtesy of an attack he'd been the victim of when he got home from Afghanistan.

He'd been jumped by a bunch of men outside a bar and nearly killed. Would have been if it weren't for his brother, who just happened to be meeting him that night. The two of them managed to hold their own until someone called the cops.

He's cut his dark hair short on top and has earned a few strands of silver since the last time I saw him.

"Look what the cat drug in," he says with a grin as he pushes off his car and pulls me in for a hug.

"It's been a long time, Jax."

"Too long, my man." He opens the back door, and I slide my suitcase inside then climb into the passenger side as he slips behind the wheel. "Lunch?"

"That would be great."

"Awesome. I know a place." He pulls off the curb. "So, tell me what's going on? You were cryptic on the phone."

"I have a client that I'm pretty sure has a hit out on her courtesy of her ex-husband." Eliza had been furious when I told her what I intended to do. She'd insisted I not go, that her ex has nothing to do with it, but after I called her on the bruises I'd seen in the photographs, she'd conceded —if only to keep me from talking about it further.

I'd expected her to ask to come with me, but she hadn't even brought it up. Which only makes me hate the guy even more. She's afraid of him even if she doesn't want to admit it.

Jaxson briefly glances my way before turning his gaze back to the road. "And the guy lives in LA?"

"He does. High-profile, too, which is why I'd really appreciate you coming with me. I'm betting he lawyers up before I get my first question out."

"Care to share his identity with the class?" he asks.

I grin. "Have to leave something for surprise, don't you think?" Truth be told, I can't imagine he would have an issue even if I told him who her ex is, but I can't risk him backing out at the last minute. So, I keep it to myself.

Besides, it'll be a lot more fun to see the look on his face when he does figure it out.

"So, high-profile ex-husband, and your client moves to the middle of nowhere Maine."

"Pretty much."

"She cute?" he asks.

"Way above you, my friend."

Jaxson throws his head back and laughs then veers into a parking lot. "But not too high above you?"

"Trust me. This woman wants nothing to do with me."

"Yet, she hired you."

"More like she didn't have any other options," I reply. "She thought someone was in her house, hired us to install the system. Someone then managed to get into her house—bypassing the system entirely—and leave her a note."

"Wow."

"After accusing me of being the one harassing her, her attacker tried to run her down in the parking lot of the church. After that, she didn't really feel like she had much of a choice."

"She accused you of harassing her?" He laughs. "Wish I had seen the look on your face when she did that."

"Wasn't one of my best moments, that's for sure."

"Man." He shakes his head. "That's rough."

"Tell me about it." We climb out of the car and head toward the restaurant. My phone vibrates, so I pause and, after checking the readout, tell Jax, "Go on inside, I'll be just a minute."

"Sure thing."

I press the phone to my ear. "What's up, Michael?"

"Make it to the big city in one piece?"

"I did. Everything okay?"

"Your girl is not happy that we're hanging outside her place, but so far, there's been nothing aside from a phone call with some breathing."

"And you couldn't track the call?"

"A burner phone. Whoever is doing this is smart," he replies. "You headed over to deal with her ex?"

"Grabbing a bite. Then yeah. Keep me posted. Let me know if anything changes."

"You know I will." He ends the call, so I shove the phone back into my pocket. Eliza's life is in danger. That much I know. But there's something twisting in my gut that has me worried that we're missing something.

Something that will inevitably mean the difference between life and death.

CHAPTER 14
Eliza

"H ere." I set three bottles of water on the patio table just outside my back door.

Michael and Elijah glance up at me curiously, though Michael flashes a grin that has likely worked on countless women in the past. "Thank you, Eliza."

"Figured if you're going to insist on sitting out here, I might as well make sure you don't die of thirst." I cross my arms. Truth be told, I can't get my mind off Lance and what he's doing.

Has he already met up with Erick? Are they talking right now?

Has my ex already managed to convince Lance it was all my fault? That I'm unhinged and imagining everything?

"We appreciate that," Elijah replies, jolting me back to the here and now.

"Can I have my phone back?" I gesture to where the cordless sits on the table between them.

"Sure thing." He reaches into his pocket and hands me a flip phone.

I stare at it then shift my glare to him. "That's not mine. I don't want a cell phone."

"It's a secure line that your would-be attacker doesn't know anything about."

"But—"

"It's just a precaution," Elijah assures me. "We have your phone tapped so we can track the numbers that come and go. While that's not a big deal for you, if we can keep outgoing calls to a minimum, then it makes our job of combing through the information easier."

"His job," Michael corrects. "I'm your muscle."

Elijah rolls his eyes, and I can't help but smile. Truth be told, both men are equal in height and muscle mass, and I seriously doubt Michael is any more deadly than Elijah.

"I also added our numbers in so you can reach us at any time." Michael grins at me.

"You're a real ladies' man, aren't you?" I ask him.

"I try."

Elijah snorts. "And fail."

The two men completely put me at ease. They're incredibly handsome, smart, strong—just like Lance. So why is it that I don't feel as on edge around them as I do around their boss? Lance's mere presence makes me feel completely and utterly vulnerable. Why?

"When this is all over, you can give it back," Elijah

assures me. "Then you can go back to not having a phone in your pocket like the rest of us."

"Thanks. So, Lance said you are all veterans?"

"We are."

"Did you all know each other in the service? Or is this something that happened afterward?"

"We all served together."

"Army?"

"Rangers," Michael replies.

"Mr. White Knight was our Captain. We both served under him," Elijah says.

"Really?" I ask, honestly surprised. I'd known he was a Ranger, but a Captain?

Elijah snorts. "You seem surprised."

"I guess he just doesn't seem the type."

"Why not?" Michael questions. He's clearly not offended, but my cheeks heat with embarrassment anyway.

"He doesn't seem—"

"Old enough?" Elijah replies.

"Well. yes," I reply with a laugh.

Michael chuckles. "Lance will have to give you his history, but I'll tell you this. There is not a single person on this planet I would rather have watching my back than Lance Knight. When he's in your corner, there's not a thing he won't do for you."

There's a darkness that lingers over both him and Elijah. A heaviness in the air. It makes me wonder just what these men have suffered together. What did Lance do to deserve such loyalty? Is it just being a good leader? Or something more?

"Clearly, you guys like him enough to come work for him even after getting out."

"Being in a warzone changes the way you see the world," Elijah tells me. "Transitioning to civilian life is not an easy task. Being around others who are going through the same thing as you helps the transition go smoother."

"And working in an industry where you are still fighting a battle must be helpful." I mean no judgment, and thankfully they realize that.

"Exactly. We get to use our skills to help people, and that's the very reason we all served in the first place."

"How long have you been doing this?"

"Three years for me," Elijah replies.

"Two for me," Michael adds.

"And Lance?"

"A bit longer," he says after sharing a knowing look with Elijah.

"Has he always taken jobs because he feels that God wants him to?"

The two men narrow their gazes on me. "You don't believe?"

"I didn't say that. Just seems a bit far-fetched to believe that God has taken a personal interest in my safety."

"Lance is the reason we all were able to cling to faith when being shoved in situations more horrific than you can even imagine." Elijah takes a deep breath. "He survived something that would have killed any other man. It should have killed him."

"I wasn't a believer when I met him," Michael confesses with a chuckle. "He didn't pressure me. Didn't beat me over the head with his faith. And, honestly, because he shared it with me without being overbearing, I started to look into it myself. One bullet to the chest was what it took to pull me into the understanding that we're not alone." He points to the spot just above his heart.

"You were shot in the chest?"

"I was. Lance was with me, and he prayed. I prayed. And somehow, I'm still standing. After that, I realized there's not a thing God can't handle."

"That's amazing," I all but breathe. I may not be fully convinced myself, but hearing such a harrowing story warms me toward these men who might as well be brothers. We fall into a silence that has me thinking things I'd rather ignore. So, clearing my throat, I ask, "Do you deal with stalkers often?" I sit down on a chair beside Elijah then turn my gaze out to the sea. I've always enjoyed the way the waves dance. The way they roll back into the ocean before crashing against the sand.

"More than we'd care to," Michael replies.

"How often does it escalate to violence?"

The dark look they share is one I can read easily enough. "Almost always." Elijah rolls his shoulders. "But it's not something you need to worry about. We've got you." He grins, but it doesn't reach his eyes.

"Has anyone ever died?"

Both men exchange another dark look before turning to me. "Yes," Michael replies. "But we weren't involved in the situation until much later. With you, we're starting from the beginning. Before things get too rough."

Before things get too rough. How much worse will things get? I swallow hard and turn back out to the ocean. "It's really beautiful here."

"If there is anything you haven't told us about your ex, now is the time," Michael says, completely ignoring my statement.

I turn back toward them. "I feel like you probably know more about him than I do. Given all your research."

"We can find out nearly anything we need to," Elijah agrees. "But there are some things you need firsthand knowledge to understand."

"Like what?"

"Does he have a violent streak?"

My stomach drops at Michael's question. I never reported the abuse. First, because I'd foolishly believed it was a one-time thing. Then it became a matter of survival. Not just out of fear for what Erick would do but out of pride for myself.

His circle was the only one I ran in, and though none of them saw him hit me, I couldn't believe they never suspected it. I'd been afraid of how they would look at me. Afraid that they would see me as weak.

Pathetic.

How wrong I'd been.

When Lance brought it up last night, I'd nearly lied.

Told him that Erick never hit me. That he was a perfect husband other than his transgressions. But I'm tired of being afraid. Even if telling the truth is embarrassing, I won't cover any longer. "He has a temper," I tell them. "But not enough of one that I think he'd try to kill me."

"If a man will hit his wife, there's not much else he's not capable of." Michael all but growls it.

"Did you ever report the abuse? I didn't find any police reports."

"No," I tell Elijah. "I never reported it." Emotion burns in my throat, so I stand. "I need to grab some coffee. Want a cup?"

"Sure. Thanks."

"Yeah." I push open the door and step inside. It slams shut behind me and locks. I whirl and scream as a man in a black ski mask lunges for me. "Help!"

"Eliza! Can you get to the door?" Michael yells.

"No!" The man lunges for me again, and I scramble back, hitting my hip on the counter. I reach for the knives in my butcher block, but an arm bands around my waist before I can get to them.

"You're mine," a deep voice growls in my ear.

"Help!" I scream.

Something heavy hits the door—a foot maybe?

"Are you near the door?" Michael yells.

A hand slams onto my mouth before I can say anything.

I squirm then slam my foot onto the boot of my attacker. He releases me, and I rush forward, but he grabs my hair and yanks me back. Pain shoots through my scalp, but I still fight. All I have to do is buy time; they'll get in one way or another, won't they?

"Get away from the door!" Michael yells.

A gunshot rings out, and my attacker throws me forward, I slam the side of my head into the edge of my countertop, and pain explodes behind my eyes. He tries to drag me up the stairs, pulling me by my hair.

I let my entire body go limp, a tactic I'd used whenever Erick attacked me.

Another gunshot.

Something slams into my door. It flings open and light floods the room. The attacker throws me forward, and Michael catches me before the stranger flees up the steps.

He gently guides me to the ground then bolts up the stairs after the man. Elijah kneels at my side, gun in his hand.

"Are you okay?"

"My head hurts." I reach up to touch it, but Elijah grabs my hand.

"You're bleeding. Doc is coming. Just hang tight."

"I—he was in the house. How did he get into the house?"

"I don't know," Elijah replies, his expression hard. "But we're going to figure it out."

Sirens sound in the distance, and a few seconds later, the sheriff is pulling up. He and a deputy I don't recognize come racing into the house, guns drawn.

"Michael ran after him," Elijah tells him. He puts his

weapon away and lifts me, carrying me out past the Sheriff.

"Go around back," Sheriff Vick tells the deputy. He looks at me. "Are you okay?"

"I—" I'm not even entirely sure how to answer it, so I don't.

"I'm taking her to Doc," Elijah says. "Have Michael meet us there whenever you catch the guy."

———

"You've got one heck of a concussion, young lady," Doc tells me as he steps back from looking over my eyes. "Your hip isn't fractured, but it's going to be a nasty bruise. Other than that, you're going to be just fine." He gently squeezes my shoulder and smiles.

I don't have the heart to tell him that this is hardly the worst that I've dealt with. That, in comparison to my time with Erick, a concussion and bruised hip might as well be a stubbed toe. I swallow hard, tears burning in the corners of my eyes.

That lighthouse was supposed to be my beacon of refuge.

A safe place.

And now it's been violated by violence. Just like the house I'd shared with Erick.

"Do you want me to let Elijah come back in?" he asks.

I wipe my face. "Not yet. Please. I need a few minutes."

"Not a problem." Doc smiles knowingly and slips from the room. I take a deep breath—then another.

Where am I supposed to go from here? I can't go home. I have no money for a room at the B&B. I could sleep in my car —I did it the first two weeks of my divorce. But can I even stay in Hope Springs once everyone learns about what happened?

I'll be inundated with questions.

Are you okay?

How are you holding up?

Do you need anything?

As though everyone here actually cares about me—a complete stranger.

Someone knocks on the door. "You can come in."

The door opens, and Elijah slips inside, Michael at his side. Both men look furious and frustrated. "You okay?" Elijah asks.

"Fine. Concussion and bruised hip."

"That's not fine," Michael replies.

"Did you catch him?" I climb off the exam table and slip back into my jacket. From the looks on their faces, I know the answer before they speak it.

"He got out upstairs somehow. I'm still not sure how, but he managed to slip past all of us. We scoured your house, searching every single nook and cranny, and didn't find anything except—" He trails off.

"Except what?"

"This." Michael reaches into his pocket and withdraws his phone. After flipping through some images, he turns it around to show me. A picture of a letter that had been placed on my bed fills the screen.

> Eliza,
> You continue to make things difficult for me, so I will do the same.
> Stop making me do things like this.
> You are mine.
> Always yours.

You are mine.

You.

Are.

Mine.

My heart begins to race as I'm shoved back into the living room, his arm banded around my waist, his lips against my ear. I draw a deep breath, then another.

"I'm afraid he also left this." Michael swipes again and I'm greeted with an image of my laptop—shattered and on my bed. My stomach plummets.

I have no extra money to replace it.

Every penny to my name needed to be counted until I finished my book and was able to sell it. In order to replace it, I'd need to eat into the money I set aside to market it, and I can't exactly do that given my budget was virtually nonexistent as it was.

"I'm sorry, Eliza," Michael says.

"It's not your fault." I take a deep breath, trying to calm myself once again.

"It is. It's our job to keep you safe, and somehow, he got in. I swear, we're doing everything we can."

Leveling my gaze on him, I feel the weight of every horrific memory I carry. "Unfortunately, I've learned the hard way that, when someone wants to get to you, there's not a force in this world that can stop them."

CHAPTER 15
Lance

Erick Frank would be an imposing man to anyone who didn't know to look past the thousand-dollar suit to the worm underneath. Brown eyes that might as well be those of a rat smile back at me as he shakes my hand.

"What can I do for you, Mr.—"

"Knight," I reply. "Lance Knight of Knight Security out of Maine."

"Mr. Knight." He releases my hand and shifts his gaze to Jax. "And my assistant tells me you're with the L.A.P.D."

"Detective Jaxson Payne," he replies, shaking his hand.

"So, what does a security officer from Maine and a detective from the L.A.P.D. need from me?" He sits down behind an impressive mahogany desk. To the left of it sits a framed photograph of a brunette smiling widely. Rebeccah

Andrews—his newest flame according to the research I did on the plane.

Anger burns me from the inside. The ink on their divorce papers is likely not even dry, and he's already replaced her. Though I'm not sure why I'm surprised. Men like him are only after appearances. Being a broken-hearted man fresh out of a divorce probably doesn't look good for numbers.

But a man who had a rough divorce and still managed to find love? Isn't that sweet?

"We have reason to believe your ex-wife is the target of a hitman." I keep it blunt mainly because I imagine a man like him is used to people beating around the bush, and I wanted to see his expression.

Jaxson coughs, likely to cover his own surprise at my bluntness.

The attorney's eyes widen in shock. It looks real enough, but I'm not buying the worry lines creasing his forehead. "Eliza?"

"Yes," I reply.

"Is she okay? What happened?" He leans closer over the desk.

"She's fine. Can you tell me how you and Miss Pierce left things after your divorce?"

The attorney mask slips into place. "Is this an inter-rogation?"

"If it was, Frank, we would be down at the station," Jaxson replies. "We're simply trying to gauge the situation. See if anyone around you would be angry enough to try and run your ex-wife down with a car."

"Someone tried to run Liza over?"

The nickname makes my blood boil. He abused her— likely more times than we can even imagine over the time they were together, cheated on her, left her next to nothing in the divorce, and still has the audacity to call her by a pet name. "Yes. They've also left her notes and have recently started harassing her with phone calls."

"That is horrible." Erick shakes his head, "What can I do to help?"

"Answer the question," I reply.

His gaze darkens with anger for just a moment before the worried ex-husband mask slips back into place. "They ended amicably given the circumstances. Eliza was troubled," he says sadly.

"Troubled how?" Jaxson asks.

"She'd been seeing a therapist. Her past was something we were never able to get through. Her parents both abandoned her," he says. "Trust was not something that came easily. She accused me of cheating on her. Even believed I'd slept with her therapist." He shakes his head slowly, and anyone else would have likely believed the production. It's quite convincing.

But I see it for what it is.

A theatrical show.

"You didn't cheat?" I ask.

"No. Of course not. I loved Liza. She was everything to me."

"Yet you seem to have moved on rather quickly." Jaxson points to the photograph.

Erick's mask slips for a brief moment. "Liza and I had been having trouble for years. After the divorce, I was heartbroken, and Rebeccah came out of nowhere. But that doesn't mean I loved Liza any less. We met when we were young, and I ignored a lot of red flags." He leans in. "Did anyone actually see her nearly get run down? It's possible she is imagining it. She suffered from delusions before."

It takes every ounce of willpower I have not to leap from my chair and strangle the man. My temper is something I have always struggled with, and he is pressing on every single trigger I have. "Given that it was me who pulled her out of the way, I can assure you it was no delusion."

Erick's expression shifts so quickly that I barely notice the change. *Lawyers.* "I wish I could be of more help, Mr. Knight, but I haven't spoken to her since our final divorce hearing. I urged her to get help, though. To check herself in somewhere so she could work through her past trauma. The drinking had become a problem and—"

"Drinking?" Jaxson interrupts.

Erick nods. "It started with a glass of wine a night. And eventually, it escalated. I cannot tell you how many nights I had to carry her to bed because she passed out."

"Can you think of anyone who would want to hurt her?" I ask, trying to move the conversation along because, if he continues spouting off things I believe to be lies, I'm going to lose the fight with my control.

He shakes his head. "Liza had her problems, but she didn't have any enemies."

"What about the women she accused of having an affair with you?" Jaxson questions.

Something slides over his expression, and he mutters something under his breath. "They all knew about her issues because they were all close. That's what made it so hard. The divorce was over quickly because Liza knew that she had no proof, and I convinced her not to allow herself to be dragged through the mud. She never said anything to anyone about her accusations, I'm surprised she said anything to you about them."

"Accusations of infidelity also wouldn't have looked good on someone who has their eyes set on a career in politics," I say.

"No," Erick agrees, jaw tight. "They wouldn't have."

Jaxson clears his throat. "So there is no one you can think of?"

"Not that I know of."

"We'd still like a list of those who had any kind of run-in with her. Even if it seemed mild." I reach into my pocket and withdraw a business card then offer it to him.

He takes it and studies the white card for a moment before slipping it into his jacket pocket. "Sure thing. I can get you that this afternoon."

"Thank you, Mr. Frank. You've been a great help." Jaxson stands, and I follow.

"Is Liza doing okay?" Erick questions as he gets to his feet.

"Better than she was," I tell him. "Even considering the threat against her life."

The insult lands, and Erick's anger is palatable. "Good. Please tell her I've been thinking about her. Eliza is always on my mind."

─────

"That could have gone better," Jaxson says as soon as we've climbed into his car.

"It could have, but then I wouldn't have the information I need."

"You got something out of that? Because I was in that same meeting, and all I heard was a bunch of bull."

"This is why I would make a better cop." I grin his way, and Jaxson rolls his eyes.

"Sure. But then you'd have to actually follow the law, and that would hinder quite a bit of what you do."

"Fair point." While we don't actually break the law, we've been known to stretch it a time or two in order to get answers. "Erick did everything he could to paint Eliza as the problem."

"You mean she's not an alcoholic on the verge of a psychotic break?" Jaxson pulls off the curb and heads toward the freeway.

"Hardly. But the fact that he felt the need to discredit her tells me that he has reason to fear she'll come out with whatever information he believes she has."

"Which gives him motive."

"Exactly. Eliza seems sure that he's not the one after her, though."

"Could just be her hoping that he's not," Jaxson says.

"That's my thought too. Even as much as she despises him for what he put her through, it's not uncommon for someone in her position to continue defending her abuser despite him no longer being in her life."

"Old habits die hard," Jaxson surmises.

"Yes, they do." My phone vibrates, so I pull it out and press it to my ear after seeing Elijah's name pop up on the screen. "What's up?"

"There was an incident."

I can feel the blood drain from my face as my stomach turns to granite. "What kind of incident?"

"Her stalker was in the house. Attacked her when she went inside."

Every muscle in my body goes rigid. "Is she okay?" I ask, terrified of what the answer might be. Why did I insist on coming out here? Why didn't I send Michael when he offered?

"She's okay. A concussion and a bruised hip."

"How did he get to her?" I demand. "Were you not watching the house?" Even as I ask it, though, I know they were. Michael and Elijah are no slackers. If there was anything that could have prevented it, they would have.

"He got inside somehow. We cleared the house when we got there, checked that everything was locked up tight, then waited on the front porch. Right by the door while

Eliza was inside. She'd been out with us and went in for coffee where he was waiting for her."

"Did you catch him?"

"No. He got out. One of the upstairs windows I know was locked when we got there was unlocked. The guy managed to climb out and slip past me and the sheriff."

I swallow hard. Whoever this is, is smart. Calculated. Capable. Scaling down the side of a lighthouse is not something many can do without getting caught. "Did she get a good look at him?"

"No. He was wearing a ski mask. I promise you, Lance, we checked that house. And Elijah checked all the sensors. None of them were tripped. I don't know how this guy is doing it, but he might as well be a ghost."

"She's okay?"

"Holding up."

Minor relief ebbs the fear for a moment, though the helplessness I feel being clear across the country is unsettling. This woman is getting under my skin. More than I've been prepared for. "Take her to grab some things from her place; then get her settled into my guest room."

"And if she doesn't want to do that?"

"Don't give her a choice. I'll be back in a few hours." I end the call.

"Everything okay?" Jaxson asks.

I nod. "Stalker somehow got into her house without unlocking a single window or door. Attacked her when she went inside for coffee."

"What? How the—"

"I don't know."

"Is she okay?"

"Concussion and bruised hip."

Jaxson mutters something under his breath. "You know, I've got some vacation days and no active case at the moment. Want me to come with? Might help to have an extra set of eyes."

"I may just take you up on that," I tell him. "But not yet." Turning my attention out the window, I go over everything we know so far, looking for anything I may have missed.

But even as I try to focus, all I can see is Eliza's face as she fell on top of me outside of that church.

She'd been terrified.

If this guy can sneak past two former Army Rangers and a top-of-the-line security system undetected, how am I going to catch him in time?

CHAPTER 16

Eliza

L ance's house without him in it feels like an empty shell.

It shouldn't. After all, it's just a house, and I've only been here one other time. In truth, I should be uncomfortable and completely irritated that I'd been given practically no choice but to temporarily move into his guest bedroom.

I may not have wanted to go home, but this is the exact opposite of the space I needed from the security officer who is somehow managing to sneak past every wall I have erected. I should have insisted I not come here. That I could stay home and one of them could bunk on the couch, yet I barely put up any fight at all. Instead, I'd agreed then been silent as they'd taken me home, and after clearing it not once—but twice—shadowed me while I packed a bag.

Elijah is in the living room on his laptop right now, scouring zeroes and ones for some proof of a breach against my security system. According to him, Michael is watching my house, waiting to see if the guy tries to get in again.

It felt so surreal, being in that place and knowing I was compelled to leave.

Neither Elijah nor Michael will tell me whether Lance has any new leads after being in California, and he's not answering his phone. Granted, it's probably because he's on a plane, but I still can't help but be agitated.

This is my life we're talking about.

My home.

And since I've been forced out of the latter, I'd really rather catch this creep before I lose the former, too.

With my knees drawn up to my chest, I lean my head back against the padded headboard of the bed in Lance's guest room and breathe deeply. I'd told Elijah I needed a nap, but truthfully, I just needed time to be alone. Time to process the fact that, the one time I make a decision for myself and move across the country, I end up in the crosshairs of yet another sadistic man.

What does that mean for me? Why am I being shoved back into another life-or-death situation? The only difference now is that this time I don't know the identity of the monster beneath my bed.

Muted voices carry down the hall toward me, but even without them, I would have known the second Lance arrived. The air seems to shift when he's near, and the churning in my stomach eases just slightly. As though his presence alone makes me feel safe.

I hate it.

Heart in my throat, I get up and make my way out into the hall. I'm just stepping into the living room when Lance —back to me—closes the front door.

Elijah is gone, his laptop and gear all packed up, too.

Lance turns to face me, and we stare at each other.

The exhaustion on his face is the first thing I note. There's a darkness in his eyes that wasn't there before, and his mouth is flattened into a tight line. "Are you all right?" he asks, setting his bag down and crossing over to me.

My throat constricts. "Doc says I'm fine."

Lance reaches up and gently brushes my hair behind my ear. "But are *you* okay?" When his gaze is on me, I get the sense that Lance sees so much more than I try to let him. Almost as though he can see straight through me to the deepest recesses of my soul.

The desire to lean into him, to wrap my arms around his waist, is so strong that I force myself to take a step back. "I'm fine."

Lance drops his hand. "I'm sorry I left. I should have been there."

"There's nothing you could have done," I insist.

"Still." He shakes his head, his expression defeated.

"You don't think it's Erick, do you?"

Lance breaks the eye contact first and starts toward the kitchen. "Why do you say that?"

"Because if you thought it was him, you would look a lot more relieved." I join him in the kitchen, though I don't cross the island separating it from the living room.

Lance reaches into his refrigerator and withdraws a bottle of water. "Why did you marry him?"

"What?" I stiffen, taken aback by his question. Anyone who spends five minutes in Erick's presence is typically charmed by him. But the look on Lance's face—his tone— speaks to someone who is anything but.

"Why did you marry Erick? What did you see in him?"

"I don't see how that's any of your business."

Lance's expression is hard. Annoyed. He drinks some of the water then places it on the counter and crosses his arms. "It's my business because someone is trying to kill you, Eliza. And it's my job to find them."

As much as I want to ignore the question, I want this nightmare to be over even more. I take a deep breath and pinch the bridge of my nose. "I was nineteen when we met," I tell him. "Erick was gorgeous, a smooth talker, and larger than life. I'd thought—'Hey, here's a man who can give my future children a life I never had.' Clearly, it backfired."

"Why stay with him as long as you did? You were married nearly ten years. Seems a decade is long enough to realize just what type of man you've tied yourself to."

I swallow hard, embarrassment and anger at war with each other. The tenth degree is infuriating, sure, but it's the embarrassment that has me withdrawing. I cross my arms in an attempt to calm myself. "I wish I could tell you it's because I was afraid to leave. And honestly, a part of it was that. But I was all alone. I have no family, had no friends… there was no one besides Erick and those in his circle."

"You felt trapped."

"Yes. It wasn't until right before I left him that I realized he'd surrounded me with his people. My friends were his. They loved him and merely tolerated me. Even the therapist he told me I needed was someone hand-picked by him."

"Abusers will do that. They aim to control."

"The abuse wasn't all the time. That's how I rationalized it." A tear slips down my cheek, and I quickly brush it away.

"He said he tried to push you into rehab."

I can feel the blood drain from my face. "*Excuse* me?"

"He said alcohol had become a crutch. That it started with a glass of wine a night then escalated to him having to carry you to bed every night."

The rage that burns through me at the accusation is enough to have me needing to take a step back in order to collect myself. "I was an athlete in high school. Was in my first year of college, thanks to a scholarship I got playing softball. He'd convinced me to drop out, but I *never*—and I mean never—had an issue with alcohol. I barely drink anything. And only ever when we were at an event."

"According to him, you drank like a fish, and your accusations of his unfaithfulness were all due to trust issues you gained after being abandoned by both of your parents."

The air leaves my lungs like I've been sucker punched. All of this comes as a surprise given we barely spoke about the infidelity during the divorce proceedings—and only ever in private. "He said that? Seriously?"

"Granted, I accused him of cheating beforehand, but yes. He did."

I turn away and try to reign in my emotions. Somehow, it feels like I'm being betrayed all over again. Like Erick already won but feels the need to kick me while I'm down. After a deep breath, I turn back to Lance. "I am not an alcoholic, Mr. Knight. I did not imagine Erick's infidelity, nor did I make accusations without proof. I merely realized it would be better for me—mentally—to move on without the drama and extra media attention a cheating scandal would likely bring."

He offers me a nod. "How bad was the abuse?" When I don't immediately answer, Lance moves in closer and stops a foot in front of me. "I don't want you to relive this, Eliza, but I need to know. We tried to find medical records, but—"

"You won't. He had a doctor friend he played golf with. Anytime I had any injury, he'd take me straight to him, and we'd spin a story about how I fell."

"How bad?" Lance all but growls the question.

"A broken rib once. Broken arm. Bruises. He pushed me down the stairs once, and I fractured my hip."

Lance blows out a deep breath and clenches his hands into fists. I can see the war on his face—a battle over what though, I'm not sure. "It's entirely possible he is behind this. And as of now, he's still suspect number one. I need that doctor's name."

Embarrassment heats my cheeks again. "He's not—"

"Eliza. Someone is trying to kill you. Stop protecting that monster, and let me do what I do best."

I close my eyes to fight off tears. He's going to uncover everything anyway. I'd rather him hear it from me. "I had a miscarriage due to the abuse. Three years into our marriage. The time I fell down the stairs. I was still in the first trimester, but I lost the baby." I cannot bring myself to open my eyes, to look into eyes I know will be full of pity.

Then fingers gently caress my cheek. Warmth spreads through me at his touch, and I open my eyes to find Lance standing directly in front of me. He wipes my tears away, his gaze soft and gentle.

"I am so sorry, Eliza. I know it doesn't make anything better, but I am so absolutely sorry for everything you suffered at his hands."

"The only person who knows about it is the doctor. Dr. Jon Reynolds. He's out of Los Angeles." I swallow hard, knowing I should pull away but unable to move. The miscarriage was the darkest moment of my life. Even given the abandonment I suffered when I was a child and the abuse from Erick, losing that baby felt like I'd lost my chance at being happy. Like the one bright spot in my life had been ripped away.

I haven't spoken about it since.

Not to Erick.

Not to the therapist he made me see.

Not to anyone.

Until Lance.

His gaze drops to my mouth, and I get the faintest feeling like he's going to kiss me. But then, he drops his hand and steps back. "I'll have Elijah get me contact info, and we'll set up a video chat. Same thing with your therapist."

"Janet?" I nearly choke on her name.

"She's another on my list."

"Why? Why would she hurt me?"

"Because Erick mentioned her. It means he's likely going to warn her that we might be contacting her, which also means she'll be working off of a script. I want to get her to break it."

CHAPTER 17

Lance

Even two days after Eliza told me the severity of the abuse she suffered, I'm still furious. I've prayed for the ability to release it and apologized to God for the violent thoughts I've had ever since. I can think of a dozen things I'd love to do to Erick, despite knowing that, in the end, vengeance belongs to God, not me.

Still—

Taking a deep breath, I raise my fist to knock on the door to my guest room. Eliza has barely spoken since the night I got back, spending all of her time either in the guest room or wrapped in her own thoughts. There's been no movement at her house, and the stalker has made no attempt to contact her home phone.

So far, it's been relatively uneventful. Only those who spend a lot of time in this profession know that quiet is even more troubling. It means whoever is after her is taking their time. Being meticulous in their planning makes it less likely they'll slip up and make a mistake.

She answers the door wearing a pair of leggings and an oversized cream sweater. Her blonde hair is loose around her face, falling in waves that look silky smooth. I yearn to run my fingers through them, to hold her and make everything that's ever caused her even the mildest pain to disappear.

But I can't.

She's not mine to hold. And trying to change that would be a mistake neither of us can afford.

"Is everything okay?" she questions.

"I'm going to go out for a run on the beach and wanted to know if you were up for getting out of the house. If not, Elijah can come sit with you until I get back."

For a moment, I feel like she's going to say no, but then she nods. "Getting out could be good for me. Can you give me a few minutes to change?"

"Absolutely." I offer her a smile before heading back into the kitchen and sending a text to Elijah to let him know he's not needed.

I get a thumbs up in return.

After setting my phone down on the counter, I turn my attention out the bay window off my kitchen. It's overcast today, darkening the waves in the distance. It's supposed to start raining this evening and not let up for three days. considering I haven't run since before my trip to California, this seems like a great chance to get out and burn off some steam.

PAGES OF PROMISE   167

Steam that is a direct result of the desire I feel for a woman I'm only supposed to protect.

It's not like she even particularly cares for me, and yet I can't get her off my mind.

The door to the guest room opens, and Eliza steps out wearing the same leggings but an off-the-shoulder t-shirt, the bright blue strap of the tank top underneath nearly the same shade as her eyes. I'm struck with need at the sight of her. The woman undoes me, twisting me into knots and making me want things I have no business wanting.

She's been broken by the men in her life. First, her father abandoned her, then all the horrific things Erick did to her. The last thing she needs is me trying to take what's between us a step further.

Keep it together, Knight.

"Ready?" I ask, grateful my tone doesn't betray me. *God, please give me strength.*

"Yes. Though, I haven't been for a run in—I don't even know how long."

I grin. "I'll go slow."

To my absolute delight, she smiles back. "How gentlemanly of you."

We make our way outside and into the gloomy afternoon. She takes a minute to roll her shoulders then begins jogging down the sidewalk. I fall into step beside her, an easy pace, as we head down the path and onto the beach. With the weather being what it is, there aren't many people out and about, though I do spot Mr. Daniels—our local pharmacist—taking his dog, Bruno, for a walk.

He waves and offers a friendly smile, though his gaze is firmly on the woman beside me. No doubt, the entire town will think we're an item by dinner time.

Word travels fast in a small town. Which is yet another reason I'm struggling with the identity of Eliza's stalker. We're an hour away from the nearest hotel, and there's no one new checked into the local B&B. Someone would have noticed a stranger, and so far, there's no word out of the ordinary.

Sheriff Vick has scouted all nearby campsites as well as had local police check the hotels in bordering towns—but nothing.

Boston is only a three-hour drive, so it's possible whoever this guy is, he's hiding out there and making the drive, but something tells me he's closer. I just wish I knew where. The idea that it could be a local has crossed my mind, and I have Elijah looking into everyone who fits the height and weight of the man who attacked Eliza, but so far, we've got nothing.

I spare a glance at Eliza, noting the pink in her cheeks and the way her gaze is focused firmly overhead. I've been deployed all over the world. To active war zones and some places no one will ever know about.

I've seen good men die.

Bad men bleed out right in front of me as they begged for mercy.

Your soul cannot suffer moments like that and remain unscathed. Which is why I recognize the darkness in Eliza. She may never have been a soldier, but she's still a warrior.

A survivor.

I stop jogging and face out toward the ocean. Eliza does the same, crossing her arms as she comes to stand beside me. "I can't get over how beautiful it is out here," she says.

"You are the strongest woman I've ever met." The words are out of my mouth before I can stop them.

She turns to me. "Excuse me?"

"It's easy to think that we're defined by the things that have happened to us. The things that we've done." I shift my attention from the ocean to her. "But you aren't. And even when you feel alone, you're not."

"Because I have you watching my every move." She tries to play it off, a defense mechanism I've noticed she uses whenever conversations get too deep.

"No. At least, not entirely." I sigh, trying to decide if I should say exactly what's on my mind and knowing within the same second that I need to be as open as possible. "God is in your story, Eliza. He's always there for you, even when it feels like He's not."

She shifts her attention away from me. "You have no idea what I've seen, Lance. If you did, you'd struggle with your belief, too."

"No," I tell her. "I may not know everything you've seen, but I can tell you that I have witnessed the ugliest of humanity. The evil. The monsters masquerading as men. But I've also seen survivors. I've seen beauty erupt in the midst of war. Humans coming together to help one another in the face of tragedy."

"Why let the horrors take place at all? Why allow bad

things to happen to good people? If God is truly as powerful and wonderful as you think, then how come He doesn't step in and stop it before it happens?"

It's a question I've heard many soldiers ask after being overseas, and not one I've ever had the answer to. Until now. It may not even be the right one, but the words come to mind so easily, so clearly, it's as though they're being spoken into my ear. "When the darkness settles in and we're stuck in the worst moments of our lives, that pain gives us a chance to remember that this isn't our final home. We're meant for somewhere perfect. Somewhere there is no pain, no hurt. Honestly, it's in those times I lean on Him the most. I pray for guidance. For understanding."

"Do you ever get it? The understanding."

The doubt on her face is clear, but I also see something else behind her crystal gaze. "Sometimes," I reply. "Other times, I walk whatever path I feel pulled toward and hope it's the right one."

She crosses her arms again and faces back out toward the ocean. "I wish I had your faith. The unwavering belief that there's a greater purpose to everything we face."

"Maybe you will one day," I reply then nudge her shoulder with mine.

She smiles softly at me, but before she can respond, a red dot appears on her chest. My heart hammers, adrenaline propelling me into action. I throw myself in front of her, spinning and taking her to the ground seconds before a bullet hits the sand.

Keeping her beneath me, I scan the area for some cover but find none. We're completely exposed out here.

"Run!" I roar, ripping her to her feet and shoving her in front of me.

Another shot fires, hitting the sand. The gun must be muzzled because I can barely hear it.

"Go, Eliza!"

Another bullet barely misses me. I try to discern the location of our shooter but see nothing but tall grass. I run, sprinting through the sand. A bullet slams into my shoulder, tearing through my flesh as it sears me. I stumble forward, barely staying on my feet as I cover the wound with my hand and bite back a groan. Any noise would draw Eliza's attention back to me, and those mere seconds could mean the difference between life and death.

Heart racing, I barely manage to make it around the corner before another bullet whizzes past me. Finally, the shooting stops, and I sprint through my open door. Eliza slams and locks the door then turns to me, eyes wide.

"You're bleeding!"

I ignore her, pushing to my feet and rushing for the firearm I keep hidden in the kitchen. I grab it with my good arm, grateful that I am a great shot, no matter which hand is holding the gun. "Grab the phone, and call Michael."

She doesn't hesitate.

"Put it on speaker."

Again, she does as she's told, and seconds later, I can

hear the ringing. I check the windows, keeping out of view as I peek out to make sure we weren't followed.

Michael answers, "What's up?"

"Sniper," I tell him. "On the ridge by the lighthouse. I've been hit, send Doc."

"On it."

The call ends, so I lean back against the wall, my firearm still in my hand. "Stay out of sight of the windows," I tell her. "Stay behind the counter."

"You're going to bleed out," she says as she ignores my order and rushes over with a towel that she presses to my wound, winding the fabric over my arm. "We need to get you to a hospital."

I shake my head, the adrenaline waning enough that a fresh wave of pain shoots through my body. "Doc is on his way."

"Doc?"

"He lives right down the road. With any luck—" Someone knocks. I push to my feet, hissing through the pain, and check the peephole before opening the door and ushering the good doctor inside.

"What happened?" he demands as he grabs my good arm and tugs me down into a chair. Eliza clicks the lock and crosses over to stand by me, her eyes wide, both arms wrapped around herself.

"Got shot."

"I can see that. How?"

"Sniper," I tell him. As a retired Army medic, he's seen plenty of gunshot wounds, and most of the time when we have a run-in with a dangerous situation in our line of work, he's who we call. "Michael is on it."

My gaze lands on Eliza again. She's pale, her body shaking just slightly.

And then the front window shatters.

CHAPTER 18
Eliza

For the second time today, Lance hits me like a linebacker, taking me to the ground and covering me with his body. The air is knocked from my lungs, his heavy weight pressing down on me. Doc is right there, too, dodging out of the way as glass rains down on us. A scream echoes through the house, and it takes my throat burning for me to realize that it's coming from me.

Will this ever stop?

The fight I seem destined to live over and over again?

"Stay down," Lance whispers in my ear as he gets to his feet. I roll over so I can watch him crawl over broken glass toward a red brick in the center of his living room. "You good, Doc?"

"All good over here," he says as he crouches low and crosses to me. "Are you okay?" He looks me over, and I wince when his finger touches my cheek.

"I'm okay."

"You won't need stitches; it's just a cut." He smiles reassuringly, but I can see the worry in his grey gaze. Reaching into his pocket, he dials 911 and rattles off Lance's address as he asks for an ambulance.

My gaze remains on Lance. His shirt is saturated with blood; how much more he can lose, I'm not sure.

But it can't be much. I'm not even sure how he's still on his feet.

"Is it a bomb?" Doc asks as he sets down his phone.

"Bomb?" I choke out. It's then I realize Lance is kneeling over something on the floor.

"No. Just a brick with a note."

"Good. Then it can wait. You can't." Doc grabs his medical bag from the floor where it fell and rushes over toward Lance, who looks even paler now than he did a few minutes ago. He hisses through clenched teeth as Doc pulls his hand away and grips the neck of his shirt.

He shreds the fabric away, revealing a blood-smeared, muscled torso. Scars mar the muscled expanse of his chest, old, puckered wounds that resemble what I imagine the one on his shoulder will look like once it heals.

How many times has he been shot?

How many times has he nearly died?

"Can you come here?" Doc asks me. "Just stay low. I could use an extra pair of hands."

"She needs to stay down," Lance insists even as his head falls back against the couch.

"She needs you to stay alive," Doc retorts. "Come, dear. Just stay low."

I swallow hard then do as Doc said, crawling on the ground and doing my best to avoid the glass, though tiny shards still eat into my palms and knees. As soon as I'm beside Lance, Doc grabs one of my hands and presses it against the towel.

"Maintain pressure here, I'm going to get a quick wrap on. Just enough to hold until the ambulance gets here."

"It looks worse than it is," Lance jokes, but his eyes begin to close.

"Lance! Wake up." I shake him.

He opens his eyes, but his gaze is unfocused. "I've had worse. Just a flesh wound."

"It's not the flesh wound that's the problem," Doc says. "It's the amount of blood you've lost." He slaps a gauze patch on the back then moves around to the front. At his command, I pull back, and he repeats the process with the front before wrapping a brown bandage around his shoulder as best he can.

In the distance, I hear ambulances. I reach out and take Lance's hand, clinging to it tightly.

"Sorry I took you outside," Lance says.

"You took a bullet for me."

"I'd do it again."

Our gazes hold, and in this moment, it feels like there is so much left to say. I despised this man when we first met. Treated him like actual garbage, and yet he saved my life today, nearly losing his in the process.

And as the seconds tick by and blood continues to stain

the bandage, I realize that he could very well still lose it if help doesn't arrive in time.

Please, God. If You're listening, please save him.

The door opens, and Michael rushes in, Elijah by his side.

"You better not die on us, Knight," Michael says as he drops down to the floor.

"You get him?" Lance asks.

Both men shake their heads. "He was gone by the time we got there. Found these, though." He holds up a bag with spent casings inside. "Here's hoping we get a print."

———

LANCE'S ARM IN A SLING, WE MAKE OUR WAY BACK INTO HIS house the next afternoon. The glass has all been picked up, and the window boarded, but some of his blood still splatters the floor. According to Elijah, they'd had another emergency at one of their clients' places and couldn't get to it yet.

"This place is a wreck," Lance tries to joke. When I don't immediately respond, he grips my wrist with his good arm. I freeze, every muscle in my body going rigid before I can process that he's not a threat. He releases me instantly.

"I'm sorry," I say.

"Don't apologize," he replies. "I'm sorry. I shouldn't have grabbed you like that. I just didn't want—" He trails off.

Silence falls over us just as it has ever since we arrived at the hospital. Doc insisted they check me out, too, but after that, I spent all my time sitting in Lance's hospital room, waiting for him to wake up after the surgery to repair a small nick in the artery that runs through his shoulder.

The surgeon couldn't believe he hadn't bled out.

My prayer comes back to mind. Pleas for a God I wasn't sure existed to save his life. And I'm beginning to believe He actually heard me. Is it possible?

"Why don't you go shower?" he says. "Michael is watching the perimeter, and Elijah installed a new security system and proximity alarms, no one will get close enough to throw a brick—or anything else—through the window again."

My gaze lands on where the brick had sat, and my mind drifts back to the note that had been attached.

I am losing my patience.
Come home or I will destroy his.
Always yours.

Elijah had been furious when he'd given it to us. Lance hadn't even wanted me to read it at first. According to him, Lance's security camera picked up a masked man throwing the brick, but they hadn't been able to gauge much more than a general build from the footage.

"Eliza?" Lance asks.

"What?" I turn to face him. The color in his cheeks has returned, but I can still see pain from the injury reflected in his gaze.

"Why don't you go shower," he repeats. "I'll be right out here."

I look down at hands still crusted in some places with his blood. Then, I study the floor. "I need to clean this up," I tell him then head to the kitchen for paper towels and a spray cleaner.

"No, just leave it. I can get it later."

"It needs to get cleaned up," I insist as I rummage through his cabinets. We need to get the blood off the floor. Clean it first, then we deal with the aftermath of everything else. Making a crime scene disappear was a specialty of mine, given all the times I had to clean up any sign of my own injury before our typical cleaning crew arrived.

"Eliza." Lance speaks my name softly, and it somehow cuts through my panic. I turn to face him, tears in my eyes.

"I need to clean up the blood."

"No," he replies. "You don't."

I break, crumbling into him. I lean against his chest, and he wraps his good arm around me, holding me against his strong body while I cry. My shoulders shake, my throat burns, but I let out tears I've kept contained for only God knows how long.

All while Lance remains still, stroking my hair.

Finally, I manage to stop long enough to pull back. "I'm sorry. You're the one who got shot, and I'm sobbing."

"It's been a rough couple of days," he says as he

reaches up and brushes some of my tears away. "Even longer for you." His touch warms me, sparking a desire I thought had been snuffed out long ago. And it's because of that desire that I am able to gain the strength to move away from him. "I'll get the mess cleaned up. You just get a shower. Elijah cleared the house before we got here, and there are no windows in there, you'll be fine."

"And you? Are you going to be okay?"

He grins, and it twists my insides. "I've been shot many times before yesterday, and I'm still standing. I'm a hard man to kill."

My thoughts drift back to the scars covering his muscled chest. Marks I could see despite the blood-slicked skin. How much war has he seen? How much damage was inflicted on his body during his time in the service?

"Eliza."

"Yes?" I meet his gaze again.

"Go shower. I'll be fine."

I'm afraid to leave him alone. Afraid that whoever came after me will get through Michael again. But then I look back down at the blood on my hands and decide a shower is absolutely necessary for me to feel at least somewhat normal again.

After grabbing some clothes and stepping into the bathroom, I stand in front of the mirror, hesitating before raising my head and looking at myself. I'm streaked with Lance's blood. It's smeared on my forehead, likely from me brushing the back of my hand over my face without thinking.

Some clings to my hair, easily seen, thanks to the light strands.

All in all, I'm alive, but I look like a hot mess.

I turn on the shower and strip down before climbing beneath the hot spray. It hits my back, and the tears begin to fall again as I focus on the fact that Lance Knight—the not-practicing plumber I despised from day one of being in this town—nearly died.

Because of me.

CHAPTER 19

Lance

The security monitors Elijah installed in my office are showing nothing but an empty street and a clear horizon off the back porch. They monitor the exterior completely along with sensors that will alert me to anyone who comes within ten feet of the house.

And on top of that, we've closed all the blinds so no one can see inside the house.

It still doesn't feel like enough.

As it is, I hadn't even felt comfortable taking a shower without having Elijah monitor the screens remotely. Now, shirt in hand, hair still dripping wet, I'm back in front of them, practically unable to tear myself away.

What if I miss something?

What if I fail her...again?

I glance through the open door to the couch where Eliza sleeps, curled on her side. She fell asleep reading a book that has fallen from her hands and now rests on her chest. Given everything we're dealing with, she looks relatively peaceful.

Images of blood-stained sand flash in my mind, memories I'd rather keep buried for eternity. I shake my head as though that action alone will clear a past that seems even more determined than usual to bury me.

And I know why. The fear I'd felt at the idea of losing Eliza is even greater than what I felt while deployed. The men I served with were my brothers, sure, but Eliza is—we haven't known each other long, but the feelings I've tried so hard to avoid are slamming into me like waves against the shoreline. They're breaking me. Molding me into a man who would do anything just to see a smile on her face.

Pushing to my feet, I ignore the ache in my shoulder at the change in position and head into the living room.

I sit down on the coffee table and reach forward with my good arm to grab the book from her. After setting it gently onto the table beside me, I tug the blanket up over her shoulder and stare at her for a moment.

So much beauty.

But it's even more than that. She's kind, despite everything she's been through. Maybe not with me, especially at the beginning, but I've seen her kindness when she talks to others. She even seems to have a soft spot for both Michael and Elijah.

And when she brought me that dinner from the café, she'd apologized for the way she'd been treating me. It's not something she needed to do, but she did it anyway.

My gaze travels over the curve of her jaw and the full lips I long to taste. Honestly, I don't think I'd fully realized just how much I desired her until I'd been staring up at her as I nearly bled out on the floor.

"I already have one stalker."

I grin as she cracks open an eye and half-smiles up at me. "One is probably a good limit," I reply.

"It's one too many," she replies as she stretches. I shift my gaze away from the way her back arches, the blanket falling from her torso.

Desire pummels me, and I beat it aside. She is not interested in me, that much she has made perfectly clear. And even if she were, getting involved would be a deadly mistake. Especially when whoever is after her clearly has their sights set on me, too.

I get up to put some distance between us, opting instead to take a seat on the armchair as she sits up. "How long was I asleep for?"

"A few hours," I tell her.

Her brow furrows. "What time is it?"

"Nearly two in the morning."

"Have you been up all night?" Her gaze narrows on me. "You showered."

"I did." Then I realize I still don't have my shirt on, and I'm not entirely sure how to ask her for help in getting into it. As it is, I had to nearly cut the one off I was wearing just to get in the shower in the first place. "Haven't been able to sleep," I reply.

"You said Elijah was watching the perimeter."

"He is."

"Then why aren't you sleeping? Lance, you need rest. More now than before." She gets to her feet and walks into the kitchen, and it's all I can do to keep my eyes away from the way she moves.

What is happening to me?

I don't do relationships. Not since my ex-fiancé left me during a deployment. I've been alone ever since, focusing all my energy on work and protecting those who need it rather than putting any effort into finding someone.

Do I want to get married someday? Sure.

But not here. Not her. Not now.

When I find a partner, I want her to feel as drawn to me as I am to her. Otherwise, things get messy. Eliza has made it clear she's not looking for anything romantic. And I'm not a man who does casual attachments.

Eliza comes back into the living room with a glass of water and two white pills, which she offers to me. "I'm assuming you haven't taken your pain meds either?"

"I don't need to."

"It's acetaminophen. And yes, you do if you're going to sleep." She reaches down and lifts my hand, gentle fingers caressing my skin. The warmth of the contact shoots straight through me, stoking the flame of desire. "Please."

"Are you going back to sleep?" I ask.

"I'm planning on trying. But I've already had a nap. You're the one who needs rest."

"A nap isn't enough." I take the pills and swallow them down with water. "You have had an emotional few days."

"Emotional?" she scoffs. "I'd say being shot at and watching you almost die was a bit more than emotional." She takes the glass, and her cheeks flood with color. "I'm sorry. I didn't mean to be rude."

"You don't need to apologize," I tell her truthfully as I stand and follow her into the kitchen. I set my shirt on the counter. "I'll do my best to get some sleep as long as you do, too."

Eliza forces a smile. "I will do my best." She plants both palms on the countertop, leaning against it. "So, tell me something about you."

"What?"

"You took a bullet for me, and I don't know anything about you. Do you still see your parents? Any siblings?"

"My parents have a house in Boston, though they're hardly ever there. As soon as I moved out, my dad sold his company, and they've been traveling the world ever since."

"That sounds nice."

"It is," I reply easily. "As for siblings, I have none. No cousins either as both of my parents were only children."

"Did you have a dog growing up?"

I tilt my head to the side, studying her curiously. "Luna," I say. "A black Labrador."

"I wrote a book about a black lab," she says with a smile.

"Ahh yes. The Adventures of Layla and Kaley."

Her cheeks turn an adorable shade of pink. "You know about that?"

"I heavily research all of my clients. As does Elijah."

She covers her face then laughs lightly. "I guess you all know about it then."

"From what I heard, they were highly successful."

"I wrote them my first year of college. Managed to get picked up by a publisher—beginners' luck, I'm convinced —and they did decent. I still get royalty checks occasionally, though, without consistent promotion, they got buried."

"It's impressive. I don't think I could string two words together, much less write an entire book."

"You manage to do just fine in conversation."

"Sure. But if I tried to sit down it would be an epic failure."

She smiles. "Which is basically what I've been dealing with since I got here. The inability to formulate anything that mildly resembles a good book."

"Are you working on another children's story?"

Eliza shakes her head. "Women's fiction. I wanted to tell a story about survival. About breaking out of the rut you've found yourself trapped in and finding who you are really meant to be."

"Sounds powerful."

"I hope it is."

We fall into an easy silence, my mind on her, and Eliza is likely a million miles away. I clear my throat. "Anyway, favorite color is blue, I love all types of food but am partial to a good pizza, and used to be a licensed plumber."

"I thought you still were one?" she asks with a half-smile.

"Someone pointed out to me that I'm not practicing anymore, so I'm basically useless."

Eliza throws her head back and laughs, a genuine show of joy, and it shortcircuits every nerve in my body. I'm captivated by her, by the light that's steadily growing brighter despite everything she's facing right now. "I did not call you useless."

"Might as well have."

She shakes her head as her laughter fades. "What about your time in the service? Elijah and Michael said you were a Captain, but you look too young to have been an officer."

And just like that, my good mood fades. There aren't many topics I avoid, but the last tour I served is one of them. Typically, I'd change the subject now, but since Eliza has shared her war stories with me, it only seems fair to give her something. "I went in as a lieutenant. I was home-schooled, which allowed me to take college courses starting at a young age. I got my bachelor's right before my nineteenth birthday."

"That's impressive."

"I started taking college courses when I was fifteen. I loved to learn and it was the best way for me to do so. It's actually why I got my plumbing license. When I turned sixteen, I got hired on at my dad's company. As soon as I turned eighteen, I applied for my license just so I could have it."

"That's amazing, Lance."

I shrug. "I decided to join the military for much the same reasons. I wanted to do something that would help people, and learn a few things in the process. I joined when I turned twenty-one, went through Ranger school a year after I graduated basic training, and got deployed shortly after. Did three tours before I was injured so badly they couldn't let me stay in."

Her expression has completely changed since I started speaking, going from mild amusement to hanging on every single word. "What happened to you? If you don't mind me asking. Feel free to tell me no. If anyone understands not wanting to share something, it's me."

Something has shifted between us, allowing Eliza to lower some of the walls around her. And I know that I'll tell her anything she wants to know, no matter how hard it is to talk about, just so she won't pull back from me again.

"We were out responding to a call for help from some civilians pinned down by gunfire. Turns out we were the ones being led into a trap, and an IED went off. Elijah nearly died. Michael was not in much better shape. The others didn't survive, so it was me holding off gunmen while I waited for help to arrive." The memory is still so fresh that I can barely keep my head on straight as I relive it for her. "Right as backup showed up, I stepped out from where I was to help get both Elijah and Michael onto a med truck, and took seven bullets for my trouble." I gesture to my still bare chest and the bullet holes in my upper chest, shoulders, and lower abdomen. Everywhere my Kevlar plate wasn't covering.

"Lance." She breathes my name. An emotion-packed sigh that sets my blood on fire.

"They didn't think I'd survive. Every conscious moment, I prayed. I begged God to keep me around just long enough to make sure Elijah and Michael pulled through. Then, about a week later, I was discharged from the hospital and the Army shortly after that."

There are tears in her eyes as she stares back at me, but still, she doesn't say anything.

"When I got home, I found that my fiancé had left me for her dentist."

"Seriously?" Eliza's expression turns furious. "You were dying, and she *left?*"

"According to the note she left pinned to my apartment door, it was too stressful to be with someone who chose the life I did."

"Lance. I am so sorry."

"Don't be. It was for the best. I couldn't see it then, but I get it now."

"When did you start your security firm?"

"About a year after being stateside. I worked some small jobs here and there, spent some time using my plumber's license. Then, I realized that I wanted to help people. So, Knight Security was born."

"You've had an impressive life," Eliza says.

"It's been an adventure." Our gazes hold, and my breath hitches. I'm unable to look away even though I know I should. My heart pounding, I grip the edges of the countertop to keep from reaching for her.

To prevent myself from crushing her against my body and capturing those plump lips, I close my eyes and breathe deeply. "Can you help me with my shirt? I can't seem to get it over my head."

"Yes, of course." She steps closer and takes the shirt from me then stops just in front of me. Her gaze lands on the cross hanging around my neck. "May I?"

I nod, unable to make myself speak.

Soft fingertips trail over the cool metal then graze against my skin. I close my eyes, trying my best to breathe through the desire currently wreaking havoc on my nervous system.

She touches the bullet hole just above my heart—the one that nearly killed me—and I suck in a breath.

Her touch is paradise.

"I think you might need to sit down. I'm not going to be able to reach high enough."

I open my eyes and meet her gaze. Before I can respond, she steps away and clears her throat.

After sitting down on the couch, Eliza steps up between my thighs and slips the shirt over my injured arm before stretching the fabric to help me get my head in. Then, I slip my good arm through, and she tugs the fabric down before stepping back.

"Now. Sleep." She smiles, but it doesn't reach her eyes. Instead, her gaze drops to my now-covered chest before meeting mine once more.

Is it possible she's feeling what I am?

"Yes, Ms. Pierce," I reply with a half-grin—my attempt

at diffusing the tension between us. "But only if you agree to get some, too."

"Deal."

I'd tried to get her to go to bed earlier in the evening, but she'd insisted that she wasn't tired, only to pass out on the couch. She doesn't want to be alone, which—in this moment—is a feeling I completely understand. "Listen. If you want, we can build a pillow wall, and you can crash in my room. So you're not alone."

She arches a brow. "A pillow wall?"

"For my safety, of course. I hear I'm fairly irresistible." I flash a grin that I hope will disarm her and am delighted with one of her rare unhindered smiles.

"I think I can contain myself."

Chuckling, I turn and head down the hall. "I'm afraid I'll have to insist on that pillow wall, Ms. Pierce."

"If you insist." She moves into my bedroom then pauses in the doorway. I turn to face her, surprised to see that she's looking around the room for what appears to be the first time. "This is a nice room."

"Have you never been in here?"

"No. Why would I?"

"Not a snooper, then, huh?"

Her cheeks flush. "I considered it, but it seemed like an invasion of privacy."

"Well, I appreciate that. And thanks. I wish I could take credit for the decorating, but truth be told, it was my buddy's wife who helped with that."

"Oh?" there's something in her tone that has me fighting a smile.

"She flew in to help. Runs an interior design business out of Boston."

"That was nice of her."

"It's what she does."

"Did you serve with him, too? Your friend."

"No. Everett was never in the service, but he is an amazing contractor. There isn't anyone else I would have trusted. We went to school together."

"That's great. The house is truly stunning."

"Probably nothing like the house you had before moving here." The moment the words are out of my mouth, I want to kick myself in the teeth. "Sorry, that was —I don't know why I said that."

"It's fine." She smiles. "And it's better. Erick's house always felt very sterile. Like I would get yelled at for a single step out of place." She moves farther into my room, and I wish the doors could be opened so she could step out and I could witness the breeze toying with the strands of her hair.

What a beautiful sight it would be to see her standing there, looking out over the ocean from my room.

Her delicate fingers run over the smooth surface of my dresser. "I'd always wanted a home. Big or small, it didn't matter. But after growing up in the foster system, bouncing from house to house, I'd wanted something to call my own. Someplace to decorate." The smile on her face is wishful, and it breaks my heart. "I think that's also why I rushed into marriage. Because I was looking for a family." Her gaze lands on mine, and the air leaves my lungs in a single breath.

"Erick didn't deserve you."

She smiles. "I appreciate that. But I'm starting to think I might be cursed."

I cross over toward her, closing the distance until I'm only a foot away. So close I can see the flecks of gold in her crystal eyes. "You're not cursed. You just haven't met the person God intends for you yet."

She doesn't respond. "I prayed for you."

My heart warms. "What?"

"When you'd been shot." She tilts her face up to mine. "I prayed for what is probably the first time—that I can remember. And you survived."

I smile and reach up to brush some of her hair behind her ear. "Thank you."

Mouth flattened into a tight line, she nods stiffly then looks away.

I long to kiss her. To erase every bad memory she carries and tell her that she is worthy of being cherished. But I sense it would be a mistake to do either right now. So, instead, I turn back toward my bed and start building a pillow wall with one hand and the throw pillows my buddy's wife, Nova, insisted I get for my bed.

"You mean business," Eliza laughs as she begins helping me from the other side of the bed.

"I never kid around about pillow walls or blanket

forts," I reply. "Construction of any kind is serious business."

Eliza laughs again, lighthearted and beautiful as we finish our wall. She climbs beneath the covers on her side, and I remove my sling, then climb in on the other side. We're inches apart, but the scent of her lavender shampoo fills my lungs.

This was a mistake. We're too close.

"He told me I belonged to him." Her tone is low, serious.

"Erick?" I question.

"The man in my house. When he attacked me. He pulled me against him and told me that I belonged to him."

Fury burns through me, and I clench the hand of my uninjured arm into a fist. "You do not belong to him."

"I can hear his voice every time I close my eyes. It won't go away."

I slide my hand beneath the pillow wall, grateful my uninjured side is nearest to hers, and find her hand in the dark. Instead of pulling away, she accepts the touch, threading her fingers through mine and not letting go.

It soothes the anger, just being close to her like this.

"Lance?"

"Yeah?"

"Thanks for installing my water heater."

I smile in the dark. "You're welcome, Ms. Pierce." And as I drift off to sleep, I silently speak my prayer, sending a plea to Heaven.

Dear Heavenly Father, please guide me so that I can protect this woman. Please use me to show her Your love so that she may realize that she was never truly alone. Even when she was at her lowest.

Please, God, no matter what happens to me, save her.

Amen.

CHAPTER 20
Eliza

Barefoot and wearing leggings paired with an oversized navy-blue sweatshirt, I stand in Lance's kitchen, looking out the small window over the sink. It's the only one allowed to be open because it faces the ocean, and there's no place for anyone to get a clear shot—according to Lance.

So I stand here, breathing in the salty air while I sip a cup of steaming coffee. He's in his office on the phone with Michael as they discuss the status of some of their other clients. Regular system upgrades and stuff like that.

Apparently, I'm the only one who's this hands-on at the moment, but it seems like they have a relatively busy company.

The few hours of sleep I got beside Lance were some of the best I've had in—I don't even know how long. Even when I was with Erick, I hadn't slept well. Terrified that I'd open my eyes to find my husband standing over me, furious about something.

I'd forgotten to hang his favorite shirt up.

I'd forgotten to clean out the bathroom sink after he shaved.

Dinner was too dry.

The coffee I brought into his office was too cold.

I close my eyes and take a drink. The image of Lance, shirtless, standing before me, wearing battle scars that nearly stole his life fills my mind. A muscled chest dusted with hair, a silver cross hanging around his neck.

He's beyond gorgeous. A temptation I desperately need to avoid. Don't I have enough problems right now? Why does my heart seem intent on reading into every moment between us?

Even now, the hand he held all night feels like it's missing his fingers threaded through mine. I'm pathetic. Yep. That's exactly what I am.

"There any of that left?"

I jolt at the sound of his voice then turn just in time to see Lance stroll into the kitchen. His arm is out of the sling, and I narrow my gaze at him. "If you put your arm back in the sling."

His crooked grin twists my insides. "I'm supposed to stretch it."

"Not yet, you're not. There are still stitches in there. You were shot yesterday."

Without another word, he turns and retrieves the sling from his office then slips it over his neck and slides his arm into it. "Coffee now? Please take mercy on me, Ms. Pierce."

"Since you asked so nicely and it is your kitchen, after all." Smiling is coming easier to me than it has in a long time, even with the threat against my life. Why? I'm not entirely sure, though I suspect it has a lot to do with the man standing before me. And I haven't figured out what to make of that either.

I pour him a mug then offer it to him. Our fingers brush as he takes it, and a jolt of attraction shoots through me.

Swallowing hard, I pull back and lift my own mug if only to occupy my hands.

"Everything going okay?" I question.

"Seems to be." His phone buzzes, so he pulls it out and checks something. All lightness vanishes from his expression, and he meets my gaze, fury reflected in the depths of his eyes.

"What is it?"

A muscle in his jaw flexes. "Erick is here."

Every single warm feeling I've carried in the last few hours vanishes, leaving me ice cold inside. I haven't seen him since the divorce. I never wanted to see him again. Thoughts my expression must reflect, because Lance is in front of me within seconds, taking the mug from my hand and setting it on the counter before taking my hand in his good one.

"You don't have to see him. Go wait in the bedroom, and I'll deal with him."

I meet his gaze and realize that he would do just that. This man would face down every single one of my demons if only to keep me from having to do it. And he'd do it all just because he felt it was what God wanted him to do. How powerful it must be to have such faith. "No, I'll be fine."

"I won't ever let him hurt you again, understand?" Lance's expression is serious.

Someone knocks on the door, and I close my eyes to take a deep breath.

"Eliza, I promise."

"I know."

"Are you sure about this?"

"Yes."

With a final squeeze of my hand, Lance leaves me to unlock the door and pull it open. From where I stand, I can't see anyone but Lance, but I can feel Erick's presence like an arctic chill seeping into my bones.

"Why are you here?" Lance demands.

"I was told this is where Eliza is staying," Erick says. His voice is razorblades to my soul, and I fight the urge to run and hide. To shrivel back into that person I was when we'd been together. Seen and not heard. Silent but willing to do whatever he wanted.

"That doesn't answer my question," Lance replies.

"I told him he needed to call." *Michael.* His tone betrays his anger.

"She is my ex-wife, and she's in danger. I want to make

sure she's okay," Erick says. "Since this is where I was told I could find her, I know she's here."

Lance glances over his shoulder at me, and I nod, so he opens the door all the way and moves to the side.

Erick's gaze finds mine, his expression one that I can read as easily as words on paper. He's angry that he's here. And that anger has me longing to retreat. But my own fury surfaces when I see who he's brought with him.

My therapist—the woman who had been sleeping with him the entire time she'd been 'treating' me.

And his assistant. Another woman he'd been sleeping with.

Both of them had pretended to be my friends, and both had betrayed me.

"Liza." He rushes forward, and I step back. Lance puts a hand up, stopping him. Erick's anger is palpable. "You will get out of my way."

"If Eliza wants you to touch her, she'll initiate the contact. Given the danger she's in, you have to understand our hesitation."

"I've touched her plenty before," Erick replies. "She never once complained."

I wrap my arms around myself, trying to keep my heart from beating straight out of my chest.

Lance moves in front of me, blocking Erick from getting to me. "Oh, I know all about that, Mr. Frank. And I can't express enough that, should you ever put your hands on her again, I'll make you wish you'd never been born."

"Is that a threat?"

"It's the truth," Lance replies. "You do not touch her without her initiating the contact. Understand?"

"Yes." Erick all but growls the words as his gaze levels on mine. It's one that promises vengeance, and I have to remind myself that he can't touch me again. He can't hurt me. Lance won't let him, and neither will Michael, who looks already prepared to put him to the ground.

"Eliza, it is so good to see you," Janet Striker, the woman who knows everything about me and used every word of it to help Erick manipulate me, steps forward.

"Why are you all here?" I demand. Lance comes to stand beside me while Michael props himself on the edge of the couch. To most, I imagine he looks relaxed, but given all that I've seen, I know he's positioning himself to intervene at a moment's notice.

"Mr. Knight came to see me," Erick explains. "He said someone is trying to kill you."

"We were worried," Sara—his assistant—says.

"I've brought a security detail with me," Erick says. "And given what I heard happened here the other day, I think it's best you come back to LA with me."

"Absolutely not," Michael replies.

Erick doesn't even bother to spare him a glance. "Pack a bag, Liza. Let's get you somewhere safe."

"How does your new fiancée feel about this?" I ask as I cross my arms. As much as I'd tried not to look into him, I'd been unable to fight the urge for long. Which is how I know how quickly he'd moved on.

He doesn't miss a beat. "She understands completely," he replies. "We want to keep you safe."

More like you want to keep me silent. "I'm fine here."

"You nearly died."

"No," I reply. "I didn't."

Erick glares at Lance. "Given the state of his shoulder, I'd say he did. They cannot protect you like I can, Liza. The men I hire are professionals. They deal with death threats and situations like this all the time."

The insults thrown toward Lance, Michael, and Elijah even though he's not here—infuriate me. I clench both hands into fists and take a step forward. "These men *are* professionals, Erick. They have been risking their lives to keep me safe, despite barely knowing me." My strength begins to build. "Not once, in our entire marriage, did I ever feel safe. You were abusive, unfaithful, and made me feel completely and totally unworthy. I chose not to drag your name through the mud during our divorce, and I've no intention of doing so now. But I will not be going back with you. Not now. Not ever."

His fury is palpable, and while Lance has a matching expression on his face, Michael looks almost amused. Janet and Sara are glaring back at me, clearly trying to decide when to jump in and defend their master.

"You are confused, Liza. Have you been taking your medicine?" Janet asks.

I whirl on her. "How *dare* you. There was nothing wrong with me. You kept me medicated so Erick could keep me under his thumb. I should have gone after your license."

"I want you safe," Erick says. His tone surprises me, especially when I turn my gaze back to him and note that the anger is gone. It's Manipulation 101, and even a year ago, it likely would have worked on me. "Let them see it," he says to Sara.

With a final glare at me, she offers the folder in her hands.

Lance takes it with his good hand. "What is this?"

"Threats I have received in the last few months. Specifically, the ones involving Eliza. I thought it would be helpful to provide you with a starting point that wasn't me." He meets my gaze. "I wouldn't send anyone after you."

"No," I agree. "You never were afraid to handle things face to face." The words land, and a muscle in Erick's jaw tightens.

"You really should come with us," Erick tells me. "Let me protect you until we find out who is doing this."

"Ms. Pierce has already made her stance on that particular offer clear," Lance says.

"Liza can respond for herself," Erick snaps back.

"It's *Eliza*. And I already did. Thank you for coming by, Erick, but I am uninterested in your help."

"You're going to get yourself killed," he growls.

"Don't trouble yourself with my well-being. After all, you never cared before. Excuse me." I leave the room, turning and walking down the hall on legs that feel like lead. I shut the door of the guest room behind me and take a deep breath.

Even as I try to block out the thoughts, memories of Erick assault me. Fists, feet, knees. The terror I felt back then is just as fresh as it is now, but the anger is new. I'd never been angry before.

Bitter? Sure.

Depressed? Absolutely.

But I'd never been able to summon anger. I think that's why it was so easy for me to stay. I'd blamed myself for his temper.

Someone knocks on my door. "Eliza? He's gone."

I take a deep breath and open the door to Lance.

His gaze travels over my face. "Are you okay?" Lance is a man who has seen war. He's likely killed and has definitely come close to death more times than once himself. I've no doubt he is deadly. Yet, with me, he's kind. Gentle.

"I'm okay."

"Are you sure?"

I consider his question. "Honestly? No. But I'm better than I would have been before."

"You handled him well."

"I had you and Michael as back up."

"We've got your back!" Michael calls out from the living room.

Lance smiles, and I cannot help but do the same. "You hungry? Michael has graciously offered to get us whatever we want from the diner."

"I could eat," I reply even though my stomach is still in knots.

Together, we make our way back out to the living room. The folder Erick left is on the table, and the scent of his cologne still lingers in the living room.

A reminder of the nightmares I left behind.

CHAPTER 21

Lance

"What do we have?" I ask Elijah as soon as he sits down at my kitchen table right beside Michael. It's been two days since Erick's visit, and Eliza has completely withdrawn. She spends nearly all day in the guest room, surfacing only when she has to.

There are dark circles beneath her eyes, likely from the lack of sleep. I've heard her cry out every night, a whimper here and there, a half-scream that had me bolting into her room, gun-drawn. Even then, she'd apologized and laid back down, turning her back to me while I remained in the doorway, fighting the urge to crawl into bed beside her. I'd spent the rest of the night sleeping in a dining room chair outside her door, just in case.

I steal a glance at her, not surprised that she's staring down at her hands.

"Actually, a few new possibilities," Elijah replies. "The

folder Erick gave us had quite a few threats—not many people like your ex," he adds to Eliza.

She smiles, but it doesn't reach her eyes.

"Who is at the top of your list?" I ask, taking the printout from Elijah. In true Elijah fashion, he's done detailed background checks on every single person who issued a threat to the attorney. It's not shocking that someone of Erick's status would have those who think the world would be easier without him in it, but the sheer number of threats listed here is impressive even for someone like him.

And the threats involving Eliza make my skin crawl.

Graphic depictions of what these monsters would do to the woman beside me make me want to hunt each and every one of them down. I take a deep breath.

"Bryce O'Neal is who I'm favoring at the moment."

"I know that name," Eliza replies. She looks off to the side as she recalls a memory. "Erick put him away for embezzling his clients' money. He was a big financial manager."

"That's right," Elijah replies. "Every one of the messages he sent to Erick involves some mention of you, and—get this—he got out of prison on good behavior just before you moved here."

I study the messages. They aren't overly threatening, and honestly, they read more like updates.

Erick, I've missed Eliza's cooking. It might be the most diffi-cult thing about being in here. Say hi to her for me.

Erick, it looks like I'm getting out of here soon. Say hi to Eliza for me.

Erick, I would like to shake your hand when I get out of here. We have things we should discuss. Say hi to Eliza for me.

And it's the fact that they aren't threatening that makes them a big red flag. They'd likely fly under the radar with some security companies whose focus would be on the immediate threats. But this type of behavior is alarming in every sense of the word.

There's no anger.

Just a personal connection that a lawyer wouldn't typically have with the man he put away. Add to that the cool mentions of Eliza, and you have a recipe for calculated vengeance.

Still, something about it doesn't feel right to me.

If he was looking to hurt Erick, why come after his ex-wife? What about the new girlfriend?

"He mentions missing your cooking; were they friends?" I ask Eliza.

"Erick always toed at a moral line," she replies. "He'd stick his nose in places he thought he might find dirt then use that blackmail to apply pressure when required. He made friends with Bryce and even let him handle some of our investments because he suspected there was something dirty there. When Erick suspected he was skimming, he turned him in to gain favor with the D.A. For a time, Bryce believed they were friends."

"Was he the prosecutor on the case?" Michael questions.

She shakes her head. "He stayed out of it, and to my knowledge, Bryce was never aware that Erick turned him in."

"Did he not testify?" Elijah asks.

"There was never a trial. The moment the police showed up, Bryce cracked. He confessed everything and took a plea deal."

"What did he have to offer?" I ask.

"His partner had embezzled money for some crime boss out of Southern California. I don't know anything other than they wanted him worse than they wanted Bryce."

I meet Elijah and Michael's gazes.

It's a stretch, but if Erick had anything to do with Bryce turning over on a criminal of that magnitude, it's entirely possible that's who may be after her.

"I've been studying the footage outside your house and comparing it against the one traffic camera we have in town as well as the security footage outside the church and the bank on the off chance I catch someone with a similar gait. Nothing so far, but I'll keep you updated. The cameras I placed inside your place haven't caught anything either. The guy is lying low."

"Any word on how Erick got into town without us knowing about it?"

"Private plane with a false name." Michael shakes his head. "He didn't want anyone to know he was here."

"Smart move given he's suspect number one," Elijah says.

"I don't think he's behind it. He was desperate to get Eliza to go back with him." I shake my head. "If it were him, I doubt he would have approached her so openly."

"Unless he was trying to get her so he could silence her. Sorry," Michael adds with a sympathetic look at Eliza.

"No need to apologize," she replies. "I appreciate the honesty."

"That would make sense. He could bring her in then spin some sob story about how he tried to save her but was unable to." I get up and begin to pace, rotating my shoulder to the point of near pain. Thankfully, it's healing quickly, and I'm finally out of the sling.

Though, the ache will remain for weeks to come.

My cell phone begins to ring from the counter. I cross over and stare down at the screen, unease churning my gut. "Unknown number," I say then answer it. "Hello?"

"I want to speak to Eliza."

My body goes rigid, muscles turning to stone. "No."

"You will let me talk to her, or you'll regret it, Lance Knight. Tell me, have your parents decided where they're going next? Or are they planning to remain in Boston for the time being?"

The blood in my veins morphs into ice, and dread coils in my gut. "You won't touch them, or I'll—"

"Let me speak to Eliza, and I won't."

"Who is it?" Michael asks.

"Him," I reply, putting it on speaker and hitting the mute button. "He wants to talk to you," I tell Eliza. "But you don't have to."

"I want to."

"We're right here," I tell her as I set the phone on the table and take my seat.

"I know. Hello?" Eliza answers after hitting the unmute button.

"Eliza." The voice is clearly disguised, low, gravely. Eliza pales.

"Who is this?"

"You know who it is," he replies. "You know me."

"I don't know you, but if you tell me, I can."

"You will know it all in due time. I am curious, though, how is the view off of Lance's patio?"

Her eyes widen, and she looks at me. Michael has his firearm out and is stationed at the front door, Elijah near the back. He peeks out the blinds and mutters something under his breath. Eliza rushes over before I can stop her and pulls back the blinds.

In the distance, orange dances against the night sky.

Fire. The lighthouse is on fire.

"What did you do?" she demands.

"Better get going. I hear heat rises. Won't be long now."

"What won't be long?" she asks.

"I hate that you make me do these things. If you'd just stayed put, I wouldn't have to do this."

"What did you do?" she asks again, her tone panicked.

He laughs, and the call ends.

"It's a trap," Elijah replies.

"Not a doubt in my mind," I say.

"Already called 9-1-1," Michael tells us. "Fire department is on their way."

"You and Elijah head down there, let me know what's happening." As much as I want to go and see for myself, I know that I have to let my team handle this one. Eliza is still target number one with me a close second.

"We can't rule out that he's trying to get us out of here so he can get to you two," Elijah says.

"I can handle things here," I tell him. "Even with one arm, I'm better than most." It's meant to be a joke, and thankfully Elijah takes it as one.

"You're definitely the third-best sharpshooter in this room," he replies.

"I don't know," Michael replies. "We haven't seen Eliza in action."

She doesn't note the joke, though, her gaze trained solely on the orange in the distance. Michael and Elijah slip out the back, disappearing into shadows so if someone is watching the house, they won't be seen.

I move over toward her side and wrap my good arm around her shoulders in an attempt to offer at least some mild comfort.

To my surprise, she leans into me, accepting what I have to offer and resting her head against me.

"I need this to stop," she says softly. "Everything I own was in that house. I've already lost the laptop, and now—"

"We don't know how bad it is," I tell her as I run my hand over her arm. But even as I speak the words, I imagine she probably has lost everything.

Everything but her life.

CHAPTER 22

Eliza

My house is gone.

I stand staring at the charred remnants of the lighthouse, all while fighting the urge to vomit. Everything I had left was in there.

All of my favorite books.

My clothes.

Now, I have almost no money left, no house, and a ton of debris I'll need to find time to clear.

"The fire department said we can go in tomorrow," Lance says as he comes to stand beside me. It's risky, us being out like this. But I was going to go crazy being trapped inside that house much longer.

"It's all gone." There are no tears left in my eyes, and the exhaustion plaguing me has stripped me of my ability to show any emotion at all.

"Maybe not." But we both know Lance is lying. What-ever accelerant was used obliterated everything. Including the cameras. And whoever had done it, cut the internet so nothing was uploaded to the server. "Come on, let's go get some food." He guides me to his truck and opens the door for me to climb inside.

The drive to the diner only takes a few minutes, but it feels as though lifetimes have passed as my mind continues to process everything that has happened to me since I arrived in Hope Springs.

I've had someone break into my house.

Nearly run me down with a car.

Shoot at me.

Throw a brick through the window.

And now, burn my home to the ground.

Lance pulls into a spot outside the diner then comes around to open my door. His gaze travels constantly, head on a swivel, as he watches everything around us. As he ushers me inside, he guides me to a booth all the way in the back, away from all windows, and takes the seat facing the door.

"Hey, guys," Lilly greets, tone serious. "I am so sorry, Eliza. I cannot even imagine what you're going through."

"Thanks," is all I can manage.

"Coffee?"

"Yes, please," Lance replies.

She nods and walks away. Lance reaches across with his uninjured hand and covers mine. "Is there anything I can do?"

"Make all of this go away," I reply then pinch the bridge of my nose. "I'm sorry. I know you are trying."

"I keep failing you." He shakes his head. "But I called in a friend of mine. He's a detective out of LA. Arrived in town this morning."

"Is he the one who went to see Erick with you?"

He nods. "When I was there, he offered to take some time off, but I'd turned him down. Between the shooting and last night, I think it's wise to get help wherever we can find it. He even went and talked to Bryce about an hour ago. Unfortunately, he doesn't think he's the one behind what's going on."

"Why not?"

"For one, he's still in jail, and Jaxson said he doesn't think the guy is smart enough to even realize that Erick turned on him. He believes that Bryce still thinks they're friends."

"So, back to square one." I groan. "Does the Sheriff have any new leads?"

"There were no prints on your laptop, the note he left alongside it, or the bullet casings, and so far, we've got nothing in regard to the fire. We can pick your laptop up today if you'd like."

"They can just toss it. Is that something officers do?" Fresh tears prick the corners of my eyes. I guess I'm not done crying after all. "I don't want to even look at it."

"I know it doesn't feel like it now, but there will be light at the end of this tunnel."

His constant optimism is something I wish I shared. "I'm sure there will be." *Likely when they're lowering my casket into the ground.*

Lilly places two coffees in front of us along with a bowl of cream that she slides to my side. "What can I get you to eat?"

Before we've finished breakfast, Pastor Redding comes into the diner. He strolls over to our table, a serious look on his face. "Eliza, I cannot even tell you how sorry I am for what is happening to you. You are in my prayers, and the entire town is with you."

"Thanks. I appreciate it."

"Of course." He turns to Lance. "I was wondering if the two of you might be able to come by the church after you're finished here? There's something I want to show you both."

Lance looks to me to answer, so I nod.

"Great." Pastor Redding smiles, clearly relieved. "We'll see you soon." He turns on his heel and nods at Lilly before leaving. She disappears into the kitchen almost immediately, and her husband steps out to begin refilling coffee.

Lance takes a drink of coffee then pulls out his wallet.

"I can pay for mine," I say quickly, reaching into my purse.

"No, I've got it this time." He tosses some bills on the table, so I make a note to grab dinner next. I may not have a lot of money to my name, but I don't need him to pity me. "You know, I was thinking something."

"What?"

"The town's Valentine's Day celebration is coming up."

I make a show of looking around me at all the pink, red, and white hearts decorating the diner. "You don't say."

He grins. "The sheriff is working security, given everything that's going on, and I think we should go."

Warmth spreads through my chest as my cheeks heat. "We should go," I say slowly.

"I think we should. Together." He meets my gaze "As friends."

"As friends." It's dangerous, the idea of us going together. I haven't been able to get him out of my head since the moment we met. Even more so now that we're sharing a space.

He arches a brow. "Unless you—"

"Friends is good," I say quickly, warning bells screaming in my head. Everything about Lance screams 'settle down' and 'husband material.' He's good, strong, protective...everything a spouse should be.

But I'm too broken.

The last thing I want to do is lead him on, but he said just friends, right? Innocent friendship.

I stand. "Should we get going?"

"Sure thing." He looks amused by the fact that I am clearly uncomfortable, and I try not to be annoyed by that.

He did make it clear that he's not interested in me romantically. In fact, he was adamant about it, so why am I so worried? And given my lack of interest in any relationship, why does that fact bother me so much?

We pull into a packed church parking lot. Nearly every spot has been taken by someone. People carry boxes full of clothes and other items inside, all of them smiling as they disappear into the church.

"What is going on?" I look to Lance.

"I guess we need to go see." He climbs out, and I join him, not waiting for him to come around and open my door.

The moment we enter the church, I am greeted by what seems like a hundred people chatting happily. There are white tables scattered throughout the atrium, all of them covered with clothes, household items, toiletries, and snacks.

Lilly stands behind the snack table, Mrs. McGinley waves to me from behind the clothing table while a few of the women I recognize from last Sunday handle the other tables. A man I've never met is in deep conversation with Michael, but they both glance over and wave when they see Lance and me.

"What is all of this?" I ask, looking at Lance. "Some kind of drive?"

"Something like that."

Pastor Redding rushes over, his cheeks pink. "Good, you're here. We weren't sure what sizes you needed, so Mrs. McGinley and Lilly guessed. But there are clothes over there, some household items there." He points to the left. "Shoes...we tried to get everything you might need, and while I know it won't replace what you lost—"

"Wait." I hold up a hand. "This is for me?" My chest constricts, and my throat burns with emotion.

"Well, yes."

"Why? I can't pay for any of it."

Pastor Redding wraps an arm around me and squeezes. "You're not going to pay for any of it," he replies. "This town takes care of its own."

"But you all barely know me." A tear slips down my cheek, and I quickly brush it away.

"Doesn't matter. You're one of us."

It all seems too good to be true, and even as I am so beyond grateful, there's a voice in my head telling me that they all want something. That nothing is given without strings attached. Especially of this magnitude.

A man comes in with a stack of boxes, and the pastor releases me. "Take a look around and grab what you think you can use." He rushes over to help.

I turn and head down the nearest hallway that will give me distance from everyone. A place to sit for a moment and gather my thoughts.

I've no sooner leaned back against the wall than Lance is right there beside me. "Are you okay?"

"I don't understand."

"What?"

"Why they would do this? I don't have anything to give in return."

"Eliza, they're not expecting anything."

"Everyone expects something."

Lance moves around to stand in front of me and places both large hands on my arms. "Eliza. Look at me."

Swallowing hard, I tilt my face to look up at him. I'm captivated by the expression he wears, by the complete understanding and lack of pity reflected in his gaze. Never have I met a man like him before. Someone who is willing to sacrifice everything for the good of someone they barely know.

"In my world, people don't do things for free," I say.

He reaches up with his uninjured arm and tucks my hair behind my ear. The touch sets me ablaze with desire, and I fight the urge to lean into him in this moment of weakness. What would his lips taste like?

Would he kiss me gently? Or is there passion in his soul?

"You're not in your world anymore," he says. "You're in mine. And here, we do things for others because it's what God has called us to do."

CHAPTER 23

Lance

Eliza looks about five seconds away from running for the hills.

Straight backed, she stands beside Mrs. McGinley as the woman shows her all the clothes that were donated to help her. T-shirts, sweaters, jeans, pajamas. The town came together and brought what likely equates to a small department store.

Eliza smiles, but it's with hesitation, and I hate that she suffered so much that it ripped away all trust she has in others. *In my world, people don't do things for free.* I've spent enough time in society that I realized within minutes of being here that Hope Springs is not like most towns.

And compared to a big city like LA? It's the exact opposite.

Given her history, I suspect her lack of trust started long before Erick, too. Something that was ingrained in her, likely even before her parents left.

"She's a looker," Jaxson says as he comes to stand beside me. The detective is dressed in jeans and a green sweater. To anyone else, he likely looks casual. But I see the way he studies the room, looking for any sign of danger.

It's one of the reasons I brought him here. Even though he was in a different branch, I'd gotten the chance to see Jaxson in action overseas. He's the best sniper I've ever seen. The man misses nothing. "She is," I agree.

"You care about her."

The fact that he misses nothing is a fantastic quality to have when in battle, but in this moment, it's agitating. "She's a client."

"It's more than that," he replies. "And you know it is."

I sigh and run a hand over the back of my neck. "I'm not sure what I feel. I know that I need to protect her, but I can't see how it could go anywhere beyond that."

"Because she's been divorced?"

I shift my gaze from Eliza to him. "It has nothing to do with her being divorced."

Jaxson shrugs. "Just making sure."

"You know me better than that."

"Fair. What is the problem then?"

"She doesn't trust anyone. Look at her, these people are giving her things out of the goodness of their hearts, and she's watching them like they're going to bite her hand."

"Maybe she's lived in a world of wolves," Jaxson surmises.

"She definitely has." I think of Erick, of the foster homes she bounced around in all through her teen years.

"Maybe you, Mr. Knight, are just what she needs to realize that not everyone she meets has an ulterior motive."

"I've been praying for guidance. For some help choosing my words, and, sure, she doesn't want to rip my head off anymore, but I still sense she's holding back."

"It's only been what—a week and a half—since she came here?"

"About," I reply. When I remind myself of that, I feel like a fool. Yet, even though it hasn't been that long, I feel like I've known her for years. Like a part of my soul recognizes hers. It's hard to remind myself that it's clearly not like that for her.

"Give her some time, my friend, because I've seen the way she watches you, too."

Even as he says it, her gaze darts over to me like it has at least a dozen times in as many minutes. She's constantly looking for me, making sure I'm where she can see me. "She's counting on me to protect her." I brush off his observation because admitting it's something more would likely snap my already strained control.

I wanted to kiss her in that hallway.

And it had taken everything in me to keep my distance.

"You're smarter than that," Jaxson replies.

My phone rings, and I withdraw it. Michael's name flashes across the screen. "What is it?"

"We got something."

"Where?"

"The lighthouse. I'd leave Eliza, though. You should

see this first." He ends the call, and I turn to Jaxon. "Michael found something. Watch Eliza for me. Protect her, Jax."

His expression is serious. "With my life."

———

MICHAEL AND ELIJAH ARE BOTH LEANING AGAINST MICHAEL'S truck when I arrive. Sheriff Vick is there, too, expression grim.

I climb out and join them. "What is it?"

"It's a show-not-tell type of thing," Micheal replies as he nods toward the side of the charred lighthouse. Only a few of the beams remain in place, the rest having been incinerated by whatever was used to start the fire.

Just seeing it infuriates me.

I follow him to the side of the lighthouse, Elijah and the Sheriff right behind us.

Carefully, Michael steps over the rubble, stopping right in what was Eliza's kitchen. "Take a look at that."

It takes me no time at all to note the huge gaping hole in her floor. My blood pounds at the sight of stairs leading down into the ground. "Why were we not aware of this?"

"It wasn't in the original schematics," Elijah says. "And it must have been concealed incredibly well because none of the searches we did revealed it."

"Are the stairs sound?" I question.

"We've already been down," Michael replies.

I waste no more time before pulling out my cell and

turning on the flashlight then descending the steps. They don't go down far, it's maybe fifteen feet before I find myself standing in an old basement. There's a sleeping bag in one corner that is covered in ash, a lantern, a handful of old food wrappers littering the floor, and a bucket that looks like it was used as a toilet.

But the far wall is what really holds my attention.

Charred photographs of Eliza cover the entire wall. Top to bottom. Images of her when she'd been married to Erick that were clearly printed from the internet or cut out of magazines. Images taken with a long-lens camera of her while she'd been on her way here. Sitting in her car and eating, talking to the movers, inside of gas stations. The most recent ones are of her sleeping here. Taken from above like he'd been standing over her.

I lean in and take a look at the only image not dusted with ash.

It's a picture of Eliza and me leaving the diner this morning with the words *Tick Tok* scrawled over the top of it in bright red marker.

Michael points to a set of steep stairs toward the back. They lead up, following part of the structure that is still partially standing. And based on the layout of the house, they would lead right upstairs—into a hallway where we thought hers was the only room. "He was able to move around completely undetected. This is why we couldn't find an entry point."

I stare at the pictures one final time before turning back toward the stairs. "Because he was already here."

I'M STANDING OUTSIDE THE LIGHTHOUSE WHEN MICHAEL pulls up with Eliza and Jaxon. I'd sent him to pick her up since he's a friendly face and she only briefly met the newest member of our team. She's pale, her eyes wide as she climbs out of the truck and heads toward me.

"What's going on? I thought we couldn't go in until tomorrow."

"We're able to go in now," I tell her then take her hand. She doesn't flinch from the contact, and I'm grateful for it, needing to touch her for my own sanity. He'd been living right below her.

Watching.

Waiting.

How many times had he stood over her while she slept? How many times had this person watched her when she thought she was alone? Did he watch her while she showered?

Bile rises in my gut even as rage sears me from the inside out. I shove it away. It'll do nothing but cloud my thinking, and around her, I struggle with clarity as it is.

"What is that?" she asks as soon as we reach the stairs.

"A basement that no one knew existed," I tell her then start down the steps. Thanks to Elijah, there are lanterns down here, so I don't have to pull out my cell phone in order to see. Jaxson moves in right behind us, his expression grim.

Eliza is speechless when we reach the bottom. She

gapes at the wall of photos, staring at pictures of her life from LA and here blended together into one twisted montage. "He was here the whole time?" She whirls on me. "The whole time he was right below me?" Tears fill her eyes as she pales. "No. This can't be happening. How did I not know? How did I not know, Lance?"

I release her hand and cup her face. "Breathe, Eliza."

"The whole time. He was right below me. What if he— what if he saw—"

"Eliza," I say calmly because, if she finishes that sentence it will be cemented in her head forever. "You're not here anymore."

"How did he get in? How did he know about this basement when I didn't even know? Birdie didn't even know, and she sold it to me!" It's then she sees the stairs. "Where did those go? Did they go upstairs? Did he watch me shower? Change?"

She's spiraling, dozens of scenarios going through her mind. I can practically see them playing out on her face. Who can blame her? He was right here. A predator watching while she was at her most vulnerable.

"Eliza." I speak her name more firmly now, hoping it will snap her out of the panic. Thankfully, it does the trick. Her gaze levels on me. Still wide. Still afraid. But focused.

"He was here the whole time," she whispers.

"Yes. But you are no longer here. He can't get to you at my house." I caress her cheek with my thumb, noting the chill on her skin. "I designed and helped build my house, Eliza, and I assure you, I have no basement."

She takes a deep, steadying breath then nods, so I pull her in close, holding her against my chest. Eliza's arms come around my waist, and we remain here, in the damp, ash-covered basement, for far longer than we probably should.

But by the time she pulls away, she's calmer, more collected.

We make our way upstairs to where Michael, Elijah, and the sheriff are waiting. Silent the entire time, Jaxson follows us back up. When I turn to face him, I note the anger on his face, the tautness of his expression.

I imagine he's seen plenty of cases like this, which means he knows what we all do. This has been escalating far faster than we imagined. We've been running on the assumption that it was someone in Erick's circle or someone close to him, but how would anyone know about this basement?

Unless they were from Hope Springs?

"My gut is telling me it's a local," I tell the sheriff.

He sighs and nods in agreement. "I cannot imagine anyone in our town doing something like this."

"They knew about the basement," Eliza adds. "Who would know about it?"

"Could be he got lucky in finding it," Jaxson offers.

"No," Eliza says. "They wouldn't have missed it if it was found by being lucky." Eliza points to me, Michael, and Elijah. Based on their expressions, I know they're thinking the same thing I am. We *did* miss it. And it could have cost Eliza her life.

"He wouldn't have been able to set up while she was in the house, either," Elijah says. "There was a lot down there. Supplies that would have taken a few days to gather and move. Honestly, I'm not sure how he managed to do it without anyone from our town noticing. Everyone sees everything here."

I glance back at the entrance to the stairs, my thoughts drifting to the message scrawled on that polaroid of Eliza and me. "One thing is for certain. We're running out of time."

CHAPTER 24

Eliza

I was never one for horror movies. For one, I don't appreciate being scared. Life is frightening enough at times, so the idea that you want to watch something terrifying doesn't make sense to me. And second, that whole 'the call is coming from inside of the house!' always felt so surreal to me. How did you not know someone was in the house? How did they manage to sneak up on you?

Now, I understand it.

I'd begun to think of my stalker as a shadow. As someone who could slip in and out of my house completely undetected because I'd made him more than flesh and bone in my head. A monster, haunting me.

As it turns out, he is a man.

One who was literally living beneath me for the entire week I've been in Hope Springs and staying in that house.

He heard everything. The screams when nightmares

woke me. The crying late at night as I processed every-thing I'd been through. My conversations with Lance—he was privy to all of it.

The guys eat dinner around me, all of them discussing the case and what to do next. I should be listening, partici-pating in some way, but all I can think about is the fact that he watched me while I slept.

Showered.

And it disgusts me.

"Eliza?"

"Hmm?" I turn to Lance, who sits beside me. Jaxon, who is on my other side, is also watching me intently. Just as Michael and Elijah are.

"Do you want to go with me to talk to Birdie tomor-row?" Lance asks.

"Birdie? Why?"

"She was the realtor who sold you the house."

"But she wouldn't have kept a basement from me. Right? Are you sure she knows anything?"

"I agree that it's unlikely," Lance replies. "But at the moment, she's the only lead we have."

My stomach twists into knots. I cannot imagine the realtor having any knowledge of something like that, but Lance is right in that we have literally nothing else. Lance's cell rings, so he answers. "Hello?" Lance's gaze meets mine, and he pulls the phone down, tapping the screen. "It's Janet."

The knots in my stomach grow tenfold.

"She wants to speak with you, but I can tell her no."

"It's fine." I take a deep breath. "I'll talk to her." Lance puts it on speaker and sets it in front of me. "What do you want, Janet?" My voice is weak, and I hate that.

"Eliza," Janet breathes into the phone. "I am so glad you're okay."

"What do you want?" I repeat.

She sniffles into the line, clearly emotional. "I needed to call you. You didn't leave me a number, so I found Lance's through the security firm, and I'd hoped you were still staying with him."

"Why?"

"Erick is d-d-dead." She sobs, screaming into the phone. "He's dead, Eliza! Murdered!"

My body grows cold in the span of a heartbeat as I stare straight ahead, not seeing or hearing anything else around me. The blood in my ears pounds. Dead? How is he dead? Nothing could touch him. He was stone. Indestructible. Or so it felt.

"Janet, this is Lance Knight."

"This is a private conversation, Mr. Knight. The media is currently unaware of Erick's death, and the police wish to keep it out of the papers for a time." A bit of the emotion fades from her voice.

"You called Eliza on my phone," he reminds her. "And I assure you, I've no intention of taking anything to the papers. What I want to know, though, is how Erick died. You said he was murdered?" His gaze meets mine, but I can't seem to focus.

They sound like they're speaking underwater until

Lance reaches beneath the table and takes my hand. At his touch, it all clears.

My gaze travels around the table. Jaxson has already pulled out his cell and is texting someone while Michael and Elijah listen intently.

"He *was* murdered," she chokes out. "Killed in his house while Rebeccah was at a charity event."

"Erick never missed those," I reply flatly. He was insistent on attending every single one that was held in the area. Even when I'd been sick, I had to go. There was never any option to miss one.

"She claims he was in a meeting."

"Claims?" Lance questions. "You don't believe her?"

"Not in the least," Janet spits out. "Erick was never the same after you left, Eliza. He missed you terribly and spent every moment regretting the way things ended. I think Rebeccah was jealous. They'd been fighting ever since he went out to see you."

"You think she killed him?" I question.

"Yes. But she has an alibi, and the police think it was a home invasion." She chokes on a sob. "Can you please come out? I know Erick's mom would love to see you."

Despite the emotions swirling inside of me, I have to choke on a laugh. "Vicki despises me, Janet. As my therapist, you heard plenty about that." I'd vented to her constantly about the way Erick's mother would come into the house and almost ignore me entirely.

I wasn't good enough for her son. Not to breathe the same air, walk the same halls, and certainly not to be married to him. I was a stain on their good name, according to her.

"She doesn't, though. Not truly. And now that Erick is gone—" Janet begins to sob into the phone. "Please, Eliza, can we let go of the past and just be there for each other now?"

I swallow hard, trying to conjure any pity whatsoever. It's bad, right? To not be sad that someone is gone? "I cannot travel right now, Janet."

"Your life is in danger because of where you are," Janet spits back. "Getting out is probably the best thing for you. What if you're the next one to get shot?"

A bullet would be better than facing all of you. I want to say it, but I choke on the words given that Lance was recently shot. "I am not coming out to L.A."

"Not even for the funeral?" To her credit, she sounds genuinely surprised. Like she expected me to come running, tears streaming down my face.

"No." Guilt weighs heavily on my shoulders. Even after everything, there's a voice in my head that reminds me we were married for nine years and together for a decade. Ten years of my life were spent beside that man, and the idea of being in the same state with him—even for his funeral—has my stomach churning.

"I cannot believe you. You really are self-absorbed, you know that?" All sadness is gone from her tone, leaving nothing but fury. "You never deserved him."

"We're done with this conversation." Lance ends the call, leaving the phone sitting on the table.

Tears prick the corners of my eyes, and I suck in a deep breath to try and loosen the knot in my throat.

Erick is dead.

The man who terrorized me.

The man who nearly killed me.

Is gone. Murdered.

Which makes me wonder—"What if it is someone who is after him?" I ask Lance. "What if they just got to him first?"

"It's the first thing that came to my mind." Lance releases my hand. "You get ahold of anyone?" he asks Jaxon.

"My partner. He said they're looking into it as homicide, back door had been broken into. He was found in the study with a—" He turns to me and stops speaking.

"It's okay," I tell him.

Jaxon nods. "Gunshot wound to the chest. Close range."

"So he saw the attacker." Michael stands and begins to pace.

"Any defensive wounds?" Lance asks.

"None," he replies.

"Which means he either knew his attacker or—"

"Didn't see it coming in time to fight back," I finish then stand and walk into the kitchen. The men continue talking though I tune out their voices, focusing instead on the scene outside Lance's kitchen window.

The ocean is in turmoil thanks to a storm rolling in on the horizon. Dark clouds straight ahead signal that it'll be nasty. The waves crash harder, the white caps taller as they hit the jagged rocks of the cliffside Lance's house is built on.

From here, I can see all the way out into the distance, so I just keep staring.

Processing.

Getting divorced was supposed to be my fresh start. It should have been the happiest time of my life—as it's the first time I would have truly been able to be on my own. Yet in the blink of an eye, I've lost everything.

And now my ex-husband is dead.

"Hey, how are you doing?"

I look over, surprised to see Lance standing beside me. After glancing at the table, I see that we're alone again. "I can't believe he's gone. And I feel guilty for not being more sad about it."

"You shouldn't feel guilty. What happened to him isn't your fault." Lance leans back against his counter and crosses his arms. The muscles of his biceps bulge, and I have to force my gaze away from him. The man is incredible.

Strong.

Kind.

Resilient.

Faithful.

And I have no idea why he's wasting his time on someone like me.

"Why me?" I ask, turning to face him.

"I've told you."

"You told me that you felt like God wanted you to shield me. But why? Why would He put you at risk like this? And for someone like me? Until you got shot, I hadn't prayed in—I have no idea how many years. I only went to church because Erick made me and I was terrified of what he would do if I refused. So why would God ask you to risk your life for me?"

Lance doesn't answer me right away. Instead, he simply stares back at me as though he's processing every word I said, digesting it before he responds. The silence makes me uncomfortable, but I remain where I am.

"I can't pretend to know why God chose me to be the one to protect you, but I can answer your other questions. He loves you, Eliza. Even in the moments where you hid from Him, where you refused to pray, where you sat angry and resentful in a church pew, the Lord never left you."

"No? What about when my parents left me? What about the things that happened to me before I turned eighteen? And what about after? They literally threw me on the street and told me that I was eighteen now, good luck taking care of myself." I wipe my tears away.

"You were never alone, Eliza."

"Then why did those things happen to me? Why couldn't I grow up in a house with people who loved me? Why couldn't I get to marry a man who wanted to treasure me? Why am I not worthy of actual love?"

Lance moves in closer, and the scent of his pine body wash fills my lungs. He cups my face, tilting it so that he can stare into my eyes. "I don't know why those things happened to you. But you are the person you are today because of them. I told you once before that God doesn't let you down. People do. Everyone in this world is human, and as such, we make mistakes. Some people do horrible things, and even though they believe they're getting away with it now, they won't in the long run. I am so sorry for everything you suffered through. You have no idea how badly I want to go back and erase all of it from your memory." His thumbs caress my cheeks.

"Why?" I manage. "I was awful to you when we first met, and you took a bullet for me."

"I'd do it again," he replies, repeating what he'd said when he'd been bleeding out on the floor.

"You make no sense." I try to pull away, but Lance has a firm hold of my face, and when I refocus my gaze on him, my heart begins to pound. The look is so intense, so focused that the entire world melts away around us, leaving only him and me.

"I would do it again," he repeats once more. "And you *are* worthy. One day, you will find a man who treats you exactly as you should be treated. A man who honors God and cherishes you as his wife. He will only ever touch you because he can't stand the distance. Because not touching you—" He brushes his thumb over my lips. "Is pure torment. Anyone would be lucky to have you in their life, Eliza."

Lance's words steal my breath. The voice in my head is screaming at me to run—to put some distance between us because what is happening is dangerous.

But for the first time, there's another feeling. A warmth that envelopes me and silences the doubts. That tells me everything I've gone through has led me to this moment. Right into the arms of this man.

He leans down, and I close my eyes as he presses a kiss to my forehead. His lips are warm, and I am desperate to feel them on mine. Then, he pulls away and leaves the room, disappearing into his office.

Even as I know it's a terrible idea to want him this way.

Even as I'd sworn off all relationships.

I still remain where I am, desire ablaze in my veins, wishing he would come back.

CHAPTER 25

Lance

Eliza beside me, we' walk into Hope Springs' realty office. She's been relatively quiet with me since last night, and I can't tell if she's angry because I got so close or irritated that I walked away.

Either way, I certainly kicked myself all night for not leaning down and tasting lips I've been dreaming about since we first met. I'd come so close. Gotten up in the middle of the night and stood outside her door like a lovesick fool, wishing I'd had the courage to knock.

But every time, I'd reminded myself that we're no closer to catching her stalker, and anything that happens between us makes things even more dangerous for her. So, reminding myself of that, I refocus on the task at hand.

Birdie is one of two real estate agents in the entire town, so the office is relatively small, consisting of two desks and a small sitting area in the far corner.

The only window is in front of the sitting area, so I

guide Eliza away from it and toward Birdie's desk. She smiles as she continues talking into the receiver, chatting happily with someone about the prospect of purchasing a vacation home here in town. "Okay, that would be great. See you then!" She ends the call and stands up, crossing over to pull Eliza into a hug before either of us can stop her.

Eliza awkwardly pats her on the back, and Birdie releases her.

"I am so sorry for what happened. I cannot believe your place burned down! And you'd just moved in." She shakes her head and presses both hands to her heart. "Is there anything I can do to help?"

"You can tell me if you knew there was a basement in that lighthouse," Eliza says.

"A basement?" Birdie looks genuinely confused, her brows drawn together in a tight line. "There was no basement."

"There was." I pull up the images on my cell and show them to her.

Her eyes widen. "Is that a sleeping bag?" She looks up at us, expression a mixture of shock and horror.

"Whoever has been targeting me was living in my house when I moved in."

Birdie shakes her head. "That's impossible. The inspector would have found it when he did his walk-through."

"Obviously he didn't. It wasn't until the fire that we knew it was there." Eliza is angry, rightfully so, but as far as I can tell, Birdie had no idea. She was just as clueless as the rest of us.

"I am so sorry, Eliza. Had I had any idea that there was a basement, I would have told you. I take my job very seriously, and that includes making sure you're happy with your home."

"Do you have contact information for the previous owners?" I question. The lighthouse was in a living trust until the original owner died last year. It went to his beneficiary, but even Elijah couldn't track them down. There is no number, only a name. Randall Fraiser . He has no social media presence; his driver's license is expired, and aside from a dishonorable discharge from the Air Force for drug use, we found no digital footprint.

At least not under that name.

She shakes her head. "I'm afraid we only communicated through email. He signed everything at a title office in Maryland, and they overnighted the paperwork to me."

"Can you get me that email address and the name of that title company?"

"Of course." She rushes around the desk and sits down at her computer. "You don't think he's involved, do you?"

"We're not sure," I reply. "But we're going to track down every lead we can."

She writes the email address onto a sticky note then jots down a phone number and the name of the title office right below it before she offers it to me. "If there's anything else I can do, please let me know."

"We will, thanks."

Eliza turns and leaves the office. After offering Birdie a wave, I do the same, following Eliza out into the early afternoon drizzle, I move her toward the inside of the street so I'm closest to the curb on the off chance her stalker takes a shot.

The storm that rolled in last night was a doozy, thunder and lightning keeping me up most of the evening, and it's supposed to be even worse tonight.

Which likely means I'll be getting no sleep.

Thunder sounds entirely too much like bombs for me to rest during a storm. It reminds me that, while Michael, Elijah, and I got out, there were a lot of good men who didn't.

I shove my hands into my pockets to keep from reaching for Eliza's hand.

"Do you think she was lying?" Eliza asks.

"I'm not sure. It didn't look like it, but I find it hard to believe no one found the basement or the door that led to it from upstairs. She makes a good point about the inspector. He should have found the entrance."

"I was trying to picture what would have been over that spot downstairs, but all I can see is the damage."

"It was in your living room," I tell her. "Right beside your couch. There wasn't anything over the top of it."

"How do you remember that?"

I shrug. "I scope out every room I'm in out of habit. After we found it, I did a walk through to double check it was where I remembered. It was. And I'm honestly not sure how we missed it either. The floor looked seamless, though." I shake my head. It's an oversight I won't make again.

"The boards weren't even squeaky like they are in the movies. You know when you walk over something that is hollow."

I open the door to the diner and step to the side so Eliza can get inside. Without me guiding her, she walks toward the back of the room, right to the booth we'd sat in the other day. I take the seat facing the door, and she sits across from me.

"Things are rarely like they are in the movies."

"Hey, you two." Lilly crosses to the table, a sleeping infant in a carrier strapped to her chest.

"She is gorgeous," Eliza says with a soft smile.

"Thank you," Lilly replies with a smile. "She's teething and therefore wants no one but momma."

"You're her safe space," Eliza replies. I can see the sadness on her face, and my thoughts drift back to the baby she lost when Erick put her in the hospital. I try not to be angry, try to always see the reason behind why things happen.

But the pain she must have felt is not something I can just move past. I hate that she suffered. That she carries those memories as scars. *God, please don't let that ever happen to her again. Please give Eliza the child she desires. Please give her epic love.*

"Can I get you two some coffee?"

"Yes, please," Eliza replies.

"Same. Thanks."

"Anytime."

As soon as Lilly has left the table, I pull out my phone and snap a picture of the sticky note with the Tile Company's information before sending it off to Elijah to investigate. I'm not a hundred percent convinced it will lead somewhere, but in cases like this, where nothing makes sense, sometimes the wildest lead is where we get a bite.

"I just don't understand why the person I bought the place from would be so obsessed. He never even saw me."

"It's possible his obsession started with a google search of you. I worked a case once where someone kept breaking in and the family couldn't figure out who or why. Every lead was cold, but as it turns out the older sister of someone in their son's class saw him in a yearbook and became obsessed. She snapped photos and kept sneaking in to steal locks of his hair while he was sleeping."

"You're kidding." Eliza looks horrified.

"I'm not. We set up nighttime cameras and caught her breaking in. The boy was creeped out at first then decided he was flattered."

She rolls her eyes. "Of course he was."

I chuckle. "The parents of the boy didn't press charges because the girl's mom insisted she would get her help. Which she did. To my knowledge, that girl is now in a long-term relationship where the man is knowingly involved."

Eliza shakes her head. "At least she didn't try to run him down or shoot him."

"Here you go," Lilly breezes over and sets two mugs of

coffee down. "Be right back to take your order." Before I can respond, she's gone again.

Reaching across the table, I cover Eliza's hand with mine. "We'll find him."

She pulls her hand back, and I try not to be bothered by the way she retreats. It's like one step forward, ten steps back with her, and it hurts every time. "So far, we have nothing. I'm not convinced I won't have to go on the run and disappear for a while."

The mere idea of her leaving Hope Springs all but sets me off. I need this woman in my life. In whatever capacity I can have her in.

"Whew. Sorry about that." Lilly, now without the baby in tow, pulls out a notepad. "What can I get you?"

"I'll take a cup of the chicken noodle soup," Eliza orders.

"Burger and fries," I reply.

"You got it." She stuffs the notepad back into her pocket. "So, are you two going to the Valentine's dance?"

Eliza looks at me, then back to Lilly. "Maybe. Haven't decided yet."

It stings, but I let it go. It's entirely possible last night's news changed her mind.

"Well, if you do decide to, let me know. I have a blue dress that will look gorgeous with your eyes." She winks and leaves the table, heading into the kitchen to drop off our ticket.

"If you don't want to go, that's okay," I tell her. "I know it's been a rough couple of days."

"I just need to think about it. There's a part of me that feels wrong doing anything fun with what happened to Erick. And how twisted is that?" She pinches the bridge of her nose. "He would have killed me, but I feel guilty having fun—even though it's not like I'm celebrating the fact that he's gone."

My phone rings before I can answer, so I pull it out of my pocket. "Hey, what's up?" I ask when I see Elijah's name on the screen.

"Where are you two?"

Something in his tone sets my nerves off. "The diner, why?"

"We're on our way. We have something to show you." He ends the call, so I set my phone on the table.

"Elijah is on his way here. Seems they found something."

CHAPTER 26

Eliza

I slide over as soon as the rest of the guys show up. Michael sits next to me while Elijah slides in by Lance, and Jaxson pulls a chair up at the end of the table.

"We've been monitoring the lighthouse and had one of the proximity alarms go off. When we got there, the guy was gone, but the flag on the mailbox was up, and we found this inside." Elijah reaches into his jacket pocket and withdraws a plastic evidence bag with a piece of paper inside.

He offers it to Lance first, who reads over it, expression turning furious. The look on his face when his gaze finally meets mine has me wondering if I shouldn't even read it.

But this is my life we're talking about, so I take the plastic sleeve when he offers it to me. A newspaper clipping has been glued to a piece of paper, the headline reading RESPECTED ATTORNEY MURDERED AT HOME.

Erick's smiling face stares back at me in black and white as he waves outside of a courthouse.

My stomach churns because, even as I haven't read the handwritten note just below the clipping, I have a dozen scenarios running through my head.

> Eliza,
>
> I have tried to explain to you just how important it is you listen to everything I say.
>
> I have left you other letters.
>
> Called.
>
> Yet, you continue to doubt the depth of my affection. I hope your dirty ex-husband being out of the picture will prove to you just how far I am willing to go to get you to come home. We can rebuild together.
>
> We will rebuild together.
>
> And if the one who calls himself your protector continues to come between us, he will be next.
>
> Always Yours.

Bile twists in my gut as I turn the plastic over and see a picture taken of me and Lance on our way into the real estate office. From the graininess of the photo, it was taken from quite a distance, but there's no mistaking who the subject is.

Because a red X has been drawn over his face, and the words, *he's next*, have been scrawled just beneath where it is glued to the paper.

The noise around me begins to fade as the pounding in my ears grows so loud I can hear nothing but the beat of my own heart.

I continue staring at the X and seeing flashes of Lance bleeding out on the floor of his living room. Of him being mowed down by a car.

Burned alive in my lighthouse.

"Eliza."

Blinking rapidly as though to clear a bad dream, I focus on Lance. He's watching me carefully—they all are. "We have to stop this. I have to stop this."

"Eliza—" Lance starts.

"No. He's going to kill you, Lance! Don't you get it?" I'm speaking loudly, and I close my eyes to draw a deep breath and try to re-focus.

"He's not going to stop just because Lance backs off," Jaxson says.

Logically, I know he won't. Whatever twisted obsession he has with me, it's not going to end just because Lance takes a step back. In fact, it'll only get worse and will probably end with me dead.

I don't want to die.

But I can't watch Lance suffer because of me.

"You can't die because of me, Lance." I look around the

table. "None of you can."

"Hey, he's not interested in us. It's clear he knows we're no threat," Michael replies as he holds up both hands in mock surrender. It's meant to lighten the mood, but I can't get the image of Lance dying out of my head.

"I need air." I push at Michael, and he gets out of the seat. Sincerely hoping I'm not followed by one of them, I head out into the dreary afternoon. There's a chill in the air, and I wrap my arms around myself and stare out at Main Street.

Even though it's not something I ever would have done before, I scan the street, looking for anyone out of the ordinary, but see no one aside from an elderly couple walking into the community center.

The door opens behind me, and I know without looking its Lance. My body reacts to his presence like a moth to flame.

"Let's get back to the house, Lilly packed us food to go."

I don't answer, just start walking toward where he parked his truck.

The drive back to Lance's house is done in silence, and even though I carry the food in, I know there's no way I'm eating. So, instead of sitting down and staring at food I won't touch, I walk to the window.

"We really need to keep all the windows closed. Even this one," he says as he steps up beside me.

"I'm not the one he wants dead apparently."

"You're forgetting he tried to run you down with a car and almost put a bullet in you on the beach."

"Maybe he should." The words are out of my mouth before I can stop them.

"What did you just say?"

I turn toward Lance, prepared to apologize until I see the fury on his face. "If I wasn't here anymore, you wouldn't be in danger. This psycho wouldn't be coming after you. He wouldn't be a danger to—"

Lance's mouth slams onto mine. Heat consumes me as I grip his strong shoulders. His lips move against mine, a frenzy that is part anger and all desire.

He deepens the kiss, unleashing passion I didn't realize I possessed.

Nothing has ever compared to this.

The kiss is everything all at once.

Shock.

Fear.

Want.

Need.

And in this moment, when his body is pressed against mine, his hands cradling my face, our mouths molded together, I get the incredible feeling that this is exactly where I am supposed to be. Confirmation that every moment I have suffered through, every bad decision I made led me right here to this man.

He pulls back, breathing ragged, and stares down at me. "Do not ever suggest you should leave this world again."

My heart is pounding, my blood burning with need. "I don't want anything to happen to you."

"It won't." He runs his thumb over my lower lip, and I shiver. "That was probably a mistake, but I needed to know."

"Know what?"

"If you feel the same way I do," he replies then smiles. "I take it you do."

Reality comes crushing down on me. "We can't do this, Lance. He killed Erick. And now he's targeting you because he thinks you're standing in the way. What do you think he will do if anything happens between us?"

Lance gently grips my chin and tilts my face up so I can see him. "Do you feel the same way I do?"

"Lance—"

"No. Leave him out of it. Forget about anything but you and me, Eliza. Do you feel anything for me?"

"I—" I should lie. Should tell him that I don't see him as anything but an acquaintance if only to save his life. But I can't bring myself to utter the words. So, I nod. "I do feel something for you."

"Then that's all that matters." He moves away from me, and I cross over to follow.

"No, it's not. He's going to kill you."

"Many men have tried, and I'm still standing," he replies.

"We have no idea who he is."

"No, but we're one step closer," he replies as he checks his phone.

I'm still breathing heavily, my lips still tingling from the kiss. "What do you mean?"

"Elijah got a hit off a security camera outside the title office in Maryland. He can't make out the guy's face, but the way he walks is a match for the footage we have when he threw the brick through the window."

My blood chills. "The guy who sold me the house is the same one stalking me?"

"So it would seem."

"Which means we have a name but have no idea what he looks like. The photo Elijah found was old—"

"Yes we do." Lance turns his phone around to show me a passport photo that has been zoomed in on.

The man in the image fits the description of so many others. Short brown hair, brown eyes, clean-shaven. He's not smiling but looks relatively—well—normal. I'd expected madness in his gaze, but there is none.

No anger.

No emotion at all, really.

"That's him?"

"It is. Elijah sent the image and name to Sheriff Vick, and Jaxson sent it to the L.A.P.D. with some information about your case back here. That way, if there are links, we can find them."

"If? He confessed to it."

"Could be taking credit where he saw an opportunity. Either way, we can't rule it out. Do you recognize him?"

I shake my head. "I've never seen him before. At least, not close enough to remember. I don't know that I'd recognize him if we crossed paths on the street." Lance pulls his phone away. "Did they find out anything else about him?"

"Not yet. Elijah said his background check came back clean, he has no lines of credit in his name and no bank profile at all. Honestly, it's like he doesn't even exist. The passport was obtained shortly before you bought the house. The house was willed to him by his distant uncle, but as far as we can tell, they had little to no contact. He had no choice but to get the passport in order to sell the place."

"Why target me, though? If he was in Maryland, why come all the way here and live under the floor? If he didn't want to leave the house, why sell it in the first place?"

"I don't know," Lance replies as he sets his phone on the counter and steps up close to me again. He places his hands on my shoulders then runs them down both arms. I used to hate being touched.

Even in the early years before the abuse, I'd shrug away from Erick at the earliest possible moment.

But with Lance, it feels different. His touch brings me comfort, and I ache for more when he stops.

"We have a face and a name, Eliza. That's a lot to go off of. We'll catch him."

"And if you don't? What if you don't find him in time?"

He tilts my chin up. "We will. And then we're going to finish this conversation."

CHAPTER 27

Lance

"We need to talk about you and Eliza."

I glance up as Michael breezes into the room and sets a paper cup of coffee onto my desk. Jaxson and Elijah are watching the house while Eliza sleeps, giving me a chance to come into the office and try to figure out our next steps.

Being around her is clouding my mind, making it impossible to think about anything but the way her lips had tasted. The way she moaned softly as I deepened the kiss.

I'd thought being apart would make it easier; instead. it's just made it harder.

I'm in trouble here.

"What do you mean?"

Michael takes a seat and raises a brow. "Do I really need to spell it out for you?"

"I guess so, given that I have no idea what you're talking about."

"Lance."

"Michael."

We stare at each other a bit longer before I finally cave. "Fine. I'm not entirely sure what's going on."

"But something is."

"Something might be starting."

"Dude." He shakes his head. "You're at the top of a killer's list and making moves on the object of his obsessions. Not really a smart move if you want to stay alive."

"First of all, I'm not 'making moves.' This isn't high school. And second, Eliza is amazing. She's so strong, Michael. Smart. Beautiful. I don't know what's happening to me." Leaning back in my chair I close my eyes and take a deep breath.

"Wait a minute—you're in *love* with her?"

"Whoa, what?" I jerk forward so quickly I nearly give myself whiplash.

"You're in love with Eliza." Michael shakes his head, a sly grin on his face. "I should have known sooner. I'd thought it was infatuation given you never get out. Not that she isn't amazing, you're just not the dating type. Yet here you are, falling in love with a client. You know, we have rules against this sort of thing."

"We do not. And I'm not in love," I shoot back, panic clawing at my chest. Am I, though? Am I in love with Eliza Pierce?

"We do. I wrote them myself. No personal relationship

with an active client." Michael clicks his tongue. "You really should read things before signing them."

I groan and run both hands over my face.

"Hey, don't worry, Elijah probably doesn't remember the rules, either. It can be our secret." He grins at me like a teenager with a secret, and I roll my eyes.

"We need to talk about Randall Fraiser," I say, changing the subject.

"Sure we do." Michael leans in to look at the computer screen. "Haven't been able to find anything new?"

"No. I've been studying the link between him and Eliza, and I can't find anything."

"How did she find the lighthouse? A real estate website?"

"She called Birdie and given her the specifications on what it was she was looking for. The lighthouse went up on the market a week later, and Birdie called to let her know."

"That's a strange coincidence."

"Those were my thoughts," I tell him. "But when we interviewed Birdie, she seemed genuinely upset. Did you know her growing up?"

Michael is the only one of us who was raised here in Hope Springs. He's the reason I came here on vacation all those years ago and ended up staying to put down roots.

"Nah. She didn't move here until after I'd graduated. She's three years younger than I am. I just can't see her as being involved, though. She's always so friendly."

"She is. It could just be coincidence that it came on the market after Eliza called."

"But you don't believe in coincidence."

"I don't." After logging out of my computer, I stand and slip into my jacket before grabbing my coffee and heading for the door, Michael on my heels. The moment I reach for the door, the hairs on the back of my neck stand on end.

It's that hesitation that allows me to hear a faint *click.* "Get down!" I bellow as I whirl and throw myself over Michael.

The front of our office explodes, heat and debris flying everywhere. My shoulder burns, still healing from the shooting, but it's nothing compared to the stinging on the back of my neck or the ringing in my ears.

Everything around me moves in slow motion. Michael gently rolls me off him, and I land on the floor. Pain sears my back, and I must groan because he rolls me onto my side and pushes up. He stumbles but manages to reach for his firearm and cell phone.

I remain where I am, lying on my side, as I stare at smoke billowing from the front of our office. Or, what was.

Michael kneels in front of me and says something, but it's fuzzy. Everything around me is, and I can't hear anything aside from the pounding in my ears.

He looks me over and continues speaking into his phone.

The world around me grows hazy, and I begin to drift,

and the last image I get is of Eliza, lips swollen, staring up at me in my kitchen.

———

Everything aches.

Even though I'd insisted that I was fine, Doc had been even more persistent in forcing me to come in for a full scan. Same thing with Michael, who is currently chatting up a young nurse while she removes his IV.

As we wait for our official discharge papers, I continue scrolling through the pictures Elijah sent me. The front of our office building has been leveled, leaving nothing but twisted beams and rubble. The explosives had been planted right near the door and thankfully weren't very strong. The bakery below lost part of their ceiling, but the fire department showed up before the fire caused by the explosion could spread.

No one besides Michael and I were hurt.

Things could have been so much worse.

The damage to my ears and the concussion I suffered from the blast are the worst injuries I sustained. The leather jacket I'd been wearing shielded my back from being burned, though, according to the Doc, I do have mild burns on the back of my neck.

The jacket won't ever see another chilly afternoon, but that combined with neither of us facing the blast when it happened means Michael and I both will.

I take a deep breath as my heartrate begins to climb. Images race through my mind.

Broken bodies.

Twisted metal.

Flames.

Flashbacks from my time overseas assault me, and for a moment, I'm trapped beneath enemy fire, listening to the moaning sounds of my brothers in arms as they died.

"The hard drives are fine."

I jolt to the present to find Elijah standing beside my bed, a black messenger bag slung over his shoulder.

"You good?" he questions. It still sounds like he's partially underwater, but I nod.

"You got all the sensitive material out?"

"I did," he replies. "And let our clients know there was an incident. We'll keep things covered, but you need to keep your head down for the time being."

"Agreed," Michael chimes in as the nurse leaves the hospital room, cracking the door behind her.

"Maybe let Jaxson take the lead with Eliza for a while. He can take her back to L.A. until—"

"No," I reply quickly.

"Lance—"

"Save it," Michael interjects, interrupting Elijah. "He's not going to walk away from her even if it kills him."

Elijah looks from me to him then back to me and opens his mouth to reply. Before he can, though, the door flies open, and a red-cheeked Eliza rushes inside, a grim Jaxson right behind her.

"You were supposed to stay at the house," I tell her.

"I tried to keep her there." Jaxson shoves his hands into his pockets. "But short of chaining her inside, it wasn't possible."

Eliza rushes to my side but hesitates just before reaching for me. It bothers me, but I don't say anything, nor do I reach for her. This has all gotten too far out of hand, and I can't help but wonder if the emotions I clearly carry for her are clouding my instincts.

"Are you okay?" she asks.

"I am," I reply.

Eliza's eyes fill with tears, but she quickly blinks them away.

"I'm okay, too, just in case anyone was wondering," Michael chimes in.

Eliza smiles with relief. "I am definitely grateful." She turns back to me. "This has to stop, Lance. This is the third time you've nearly died because of me."

"Who's counting?" I ask.

"I am," she replies. "And if we don't find him, he's going to just keep coming."

"Then we keep handling him."

"Until you die?" she snaps. "Until Michael dies? Elijah? Jaxon? Who has to die before you finally see that you can't help me?"

"And just what are you planning to do?" I demand, pushing off the bed. The throbbing in my head increases, but I ignore it.

"We'll be outside," Michael says as he excuses himself.

Jaxson and Elijah follow, shutting the door softly behind them.

Eliza doesn't respond right away, so I cross my arms. "Well?" I ask. "Book a ticket to Fiji? Move to Zimbabwe? What exactly are your big plans?"

She takes a deep breath. "I don't know. But I can't stay here."

"I can protect you. I've done a decent job so far."

"A decent job? You've been nearly run over. Shot. Blown up—that's a decent job?"

"You're still breathing, so I'd say so."

Eyes so wide it's nearly comical, she gapes at me. "How do you figure?"

I step in closer, moving in until she's a breath away from me. "You weren't run down. You weren't shot. You weren't blown up. You, Eliza Pierce, are perfectly safe. Or were before you left my house to come here."

"I may be okay, but what's going to happen when he finally succeeds in taking you out of the picture? What will happen to me then?"

Emotion burns my throat, but I force it back down. "Then Elijah, Michael, and Jaxson will finish the job."

Her anger snaps in the air around us, and she shoves me back with a push. My body aches, and I hiss through clenched teeth, but she's too angry to notice.

"You are an idiot," she growls.

"An idiot? I don't think I've been called that since middle school."

She glares at me. "I don't want anything to happen to

anyone on my behalf, but if something were to happen to you—" Eliza closes her eyes and takes a deep breath. When she opens them again, she's making to move to hide her tears. "Lance, please don't die for me."

I step back in closer, reaching out to cup her face. Her skin is soft beneath my touch, and I yearn to share moments like this that aren't tainted with the idea of death. Moments where it's just her and me. "I make no promises," I reply softly. She starts to pull away, but I quickly cup her other cheek with my free hand, holding her in place. "I don't want to die. But if my death means you live? It's a sacrifice I will make with no hesitation."

"Why? Because you think it's your job? Why would God make you die for me? And don't tell me it's because He loves me." Tears stream down her cheeks. "I haven't done nearly the good you have, so explain to me why He would rather have me in this world than you?" Her question is dripping with anger, her tone bitter on the surface. But underneath, I sense the fear she's struggling so hard to control.

"I don't know that He wants me to die for you. But I do believe you serve a greater purpose. Something you don't even realize yet. And if you die, you can't fulfill it."

"You're wrong."

"No. I'm not." I lean in and press my lips to hers. It's meant to be reassuring, not just to her but to me as well. An assurance that she is alive and so am I. And whatever is between us will continue to grow.

But the moment we meet, my desperation grows

tenfold. I pull her against me, wrapping one arm around her waist and burying my other hand in her hair. I deepen the kiss, and she opens beneath me, the two of us so lost in each other that nothing else matters.

And as we stand here, I come to one stunning realization.

Eliza Pierce is meant to be mine.

Just as I am meant to be hers.

I am her epic love, and she is mine.

I know it.

We just have to survive long enough for me to convince her, too.

CHAPTER 28

Eliza

The last three days have been quiet, which should have thrilled me.

Instead, I have been catching myself jumping at shadows and lying awake all night, staring at the ceiling. Every second of my life has become haunted. How foolish I was to believe I'd escaped the horrors by leaving L.A.

Instead, I walked right into the middle of another nightmare.

The coffee in my hand has grown cold, but I'm barely paying attention to it or the book I've been pretending to read for the last hour while Lance works from his home office.

My mind is still on the explosion and the fact that I seem to be spiraling headfirst into something with him that I'm not quite ready to admit to myself. Even if my heart already seems convinced that Lance is the second chance at the family I'd so desperately wanted.

It angers me to know that, no matter how much I suffer, the naïve little girl inside of me continues to live on. Seeking hope where there is none. Love where it will not be freely given.

Someone knocks at the door, and I jump, splashing the coffee on my shirt.

"It's Elijah," Lance replies as he comes inside. I set my book down, adrenaline still pumping.

"I'm going to go change."

Lance offers me a smile before heading toward the door.

As soon as I'm inside, I lean back against the bedroom door and breathe deeply. *In and out, Eliza. In and out.* The panic attacks are coming more frequently now, though I have somehow managed to hide most of them from Lance.

And the times he's caught me spiraling, I've explained them off as nerves.

At least, the whole not being able to sleep thing has saved me from nightmares.

I shrug into a large sweatshirt then take one final deep breath before making my way out into the living room. Elijah is gone, but a bag of food sits on the table beside a rectangular box. Instantly, the fear is back.

What has been left for me this time? More letters? The charred remains of some poor creature? A head? At this point, the possibilities are frighteningly endless.

Lance steps into the room and stops in his tracks, his

expression going from relaxed to concerned in the span of a heartbeat. "What happened?" he sets the silverware down on the table and rushes toward me, hands gripping my arms.

"What did he leave this time?" I question.

"What do you—" He trails off, glancing behind him at the table. "Oh, no. That's not from him." Lance takes my hand with an understanding smile, and pulls me over to the table. The scent of fried food fills my lungs, but my stomach churns as I stare down at the box. Lance releases my hand and lifts the top, revealing a silver laptop.

I stare down at it.

"It's for you," he says.

"What?" I look up at him. "I don't understand."

"You can't write a book without one. I mean, I guess you could—I hear James Patterson handwrites his manuscripts—but that seems like a lot of work."

"Lance." I'm shocked. Dumfounded. Taken aback. And the kind gesture is like an anvil in my stomach. "I can't accept that."

"Why not?"

"Because it's a computer."

"Yes. And yours was broken."

"But it's a computer," I repeat. "You can't buy me a computer."

Lance crosses his arms. "Why not?"

"Because it's too much."

With a deep breath, he steps back, looking genuinely offended. "First of all, this computer isn't a marriage proposal. In fact, I ordered it right after I found out yours had been broken. So it was before anything. And second, I'm not the only one who chipped in. This is from everyone."

"Everyone," I deadpan because it feels a lot like him trying to force me to accept something that genuinely makes me uncomfortable. *Nothing* comes without strings. And something this expensive likely comes with nice, thick ropes.

"Mrs. McGinley, Lilly, and Alex. Felix from the hardware store—you remember him—he's who you were expecting to install your water heater. Then there's Elijah, Michael, Jaxson, Birdie, Pastor Redding—Sherrif Vick even tossed in a little."

"That doesn't make any sense." I shake my head. "Why—"

"Because sometimes people enjoy doing kind things for others, Eliza. And they do it without expecting anything in return. Everyone here knows you were working on a book. They also—thanks to the small-town charm and their love of the childhood game telephone— know that your laptop was destroyed. Therefore, when given the opportunity, they wanted to help just because it's the kind thing to do."

"This doesn't make any sense. They all barely know me. You all barely know me."

"We know enough."

Lance reaches into the bag and withdraws a burger and a sack of fries then sets it on the table beside the computer.

He repeats the gesture before taking his seat and opening the wrapping on his food.

I'm struck speechless by the kindness of this town as my excitement for continuing my work wars against the rational voice in me screaming that something is wrong with it. That they will expect something.

What? I have no clue.

But something.

"You should eat before your food gets cold."

"I will pay it back."

"No need to. It was a gift, Eliza."

"I will pay it back," I repeat. "It's the only way I can accept it, Lance. Please."

His gaze levels on mine, and even with the emotional turmoil I'm currently feeling, desire is like a punch to the gut. "If you feel like giving me the forty dollars I contributed because it makes you feel better, sure. But I can't promise everyone else will take it."

"Forty dollars?" The computer is a near-exact replica of mine, which I spent over two-thousand dollars on.

"There were quite a few people who wanted to contribute."

A slow smile spreads across my face as I stare down at the computer. The ability to pay it back eases my panic by affording me the opportunity to make things even as soon as I can. "Thank you." I take my seat and bite into my burger.

"No need to thank me," he replies.

I reach across the table and cover his hand with mine.

The touch is warm and so involuntary that I nearly withdraw. "Yes, there is," I reply. "So, Lance Knight, thank you."

———

With a steaming mug of tea beside me, I stare once again at a blinking cursor. But this time, instead of being frustrated, I'm doing it with a smile on my face. It helps that, even though my laptop had been destroyed, the hard drive was not. Elijah had been able to duplicate everything —files and settings—onto this computer.

So, putting myself in the shoes of my character, I begin writing.

One line.

Then another.

My fingers fly across the keyboard, the first chapter playing out in my mind as though it were a movie. And before I know it, I'm hitting the enter key to begin typing chapter two.

I stop and stare at the words, feeling immense satisfaction at the word count on the bottom left of the screen.

I did it.

I wrote a chapter.

And while there's still an entire book to write, this victory is one I would absolutely do a dance for if Lance weren't currently reading his Bible on the couch a few feet away from me.

Knowing he's distracted, I sneak a glance. Brows

drawn together, he's chewing on the end of a pen as he reads words on the thin pages. Other than packing the one I got from my foster mom, it's been years since I touched a Bible.

And seeing how enthralled Lance is makes me curious as to what I would find if I were to crack one open. I start to ask him what he's reading about, but a muted ding from my computer draws my attention.

I shift my focus back and stare at the small window that popped up on the bottom right of the screen. An e-mail icon followed by a random email address I can tell is a fake without actually opening it.

Spam. Gotta love it.

Without thinking, I click on the image and scream.

I shove back from the computer, unsure how Lance got to me so quickly, but before I can even fully register the horror that I am looking at, he's ripped me back and stepped in between me and the computer.

Death.

That's what had been on the screen.

Erick's dead body, a single gunshot wound to his chest. His eyes frozen open as he stared blankly at the camera.

"What does it say?" I choke out, bile rising in my gut. My stomach is lead, my inside burning with the need to expel everything I've consumed today because maybe it will rid me of the memory. "Lance," I demand when he doesn't immediately answer.

"Eliza," he starts, tone sharp. "You see now what I am capable of. The man who claims to be protecting you is not worthy of the air you breathe. I am the one keeping you safe. Me. Erick harmed you. I fixed that. Now, I am offering you one final chance to make things right between us. Lance is keeping you from me, and I am going to remedy that if you don't. The bomb was just phase one. A way to scare him. If I'd wanted him dead, he would be. And, should you not come to me, he *will* be. Always yours." Lance clicks on the trackpad; then the whooshing sound of a sent email fills my mind. "Forwarded it to Elijah." He turns to me, gaze sharp.

Every moment we spend together, his life is at risk.

Every look.

Every breath.

Every single second that ticks by brings this world closer to being without Lance Knight.

I glance to the right and catch sight of Erick's dead body once again. That could be Lance. That *will* be Lance if Randall gets his way.

Vomit fills my mouth, and I sprint toward the bathroom, hitting my knees against the tile just in time to hurl into the toilet. A hand pulls my hair back while another rubs small circles against my back.

I feel weak. Vulnerable. But I can't be bothered to care.

As soon as my stomach is empty, I reach up and flush the toilet then lean back against the wall. Lance offers me a warm washcloth, and I take it, rubbing the cotton over my face.

"I'll give you a few minutes," he says softly then leaves the bathroom, gently shutting the door behind him.

Tears burn in my eyes, and I let them fall, keeping my face covered to somewhat mute my cries. I'm so tired of feeling helpless. Of being weak.

First with Erick and now with Randal—if that is, in fact, who's behind everything.

Why does this keep happening to me? Why can I not seem to find stable ground to stand on?

Tipping my face up, I stare at the ceiling. "God, why me?" I whisper the words, embarrassed and not wanting Lance to hear me. "Why is this happening to me?"

CHAPTER 29

Lance

I continue staring at the image of Erick's dead body until I have memorized every square inch of a home office I have never stepped foot in.

I could close my eyes and give you a full walk-through, including an itemization of everything he had on his desk at the time of his murder. Yet, I still have no clue as to how to find the man responsible.

Elijah has done everything he can, looking into Randall Fraiser's life, but there's nothing. The address his passport was mailed to now belongs to someone else, and every other known avenue we tried to walk down got shut right in our faces.

Somehow, this man has managed to live under the radar in the twenty-first century. Something that makes him even more dangerous than any of the other stalkers we've dealt with. They were easy to find. Family. Friends to talk to. But this guy has no one.

No next of kin.

No friends that we can find.

He's a virtual ghost.

"The email address was a dead end," Elijah says as he closes his laptop.

"I knew it would be," I deadpan, my focus still on the image.

"Dude, no matter how long you stare at that, the guy is still going to be dead."

"There has to be something. Some clue in the image. Otherwise, why send it? He already told her he'd killed Erick."

"Shock and awe," Michael replies as he sets mugs of coffee down on the table.

It was my first thought, too, but I don't buy it. At least, not a hundred percent. "If that were the case, why not send it when he first told her he'd killed Erick?"

"Maybe he was sitting on it for a future torment session," Elijah offers then drinks from his mug.

"Maybe," I say then lean in closer to study the image again. I've zoomed in on every square inch of it, run multiple image scan programs, and found nothing out of the ordinary. It has not been photoshopped or manipulated in any way.

Which means that either it was for shock and awe, or he wanted her to see something in here. Something that only she would notice.

The letters and phone calls have spoken of a man obsessed. So in love that he would kill anyone who harmed her. So why show her a photo of her dead ex-husband days after confessing to the murder?

"I should look at it."

We all turn to see Eliza standing in the doorway. Her golden hair is loose around her face, delicate features that are twisted with pain. Even after all the pain he'd caused her, Erick's death is still haunting for the woman who spent over a decade at his side.

Even if I cannot understand that type of loyalty, I can shield her from suffering anymore. "You don't need to do that," I say.

"I do. If he left something for me to find, then it would stand to reason it would be something I would notice, right?"

"Eliza—"

"Let me do something, Lance. Stop shielding me. I know I was weak before, but I was caught off guard."

I push up from the chair and cross over to her then run both hands over her sleeved arms. "You were not weak."

"I didn't see you vomit," she replies.

"This isn't the first dead body I've seen," I reply. It's something I hate vocalizing, but it's the truth.

Images of twisted metal and broken bodies flash in my mind, and I shove them out.

Her expression softens. "Let me do this."

"It could be helpful," Elijah says.

"She might see something we're missing," Michael offers.

I know they're right, but as I step aside so she can take

my seat in front of the laptop, my stomach feels as though it might as well be full of concrete.

With a deep breath, she takes a seat and leans in closer to the computer. Silence surrounds us as Eliza studies the image, playing a twisted game of *Where's Waldo* with a crime scene photo.

Silently, Michael gets to his feet and heads into the kitchen to prep another cup of coffee, which he sets beside Eliza.

The kindness they show her, the compassion, warms my heart. They might as well be brothers, and they're treating her like their long-lost sister.

"There." She leans back and stretches out a hand, pointing at a small jar on Erick's desk.

"What is that?" I ask.

"Perfume. It's one of the bottles I found in our bathroom, under the counter. It had been stuffed behind some towels and was not mine. He would never leave it sitting so carelessly on his desk."

"Do you know who it belongs to?"

Eliza turns to me and nods. "Janet." Her eyes widen. "Does this mean—do you think he's going after her?"

"It's a possibility," Michael replies. "A bit of a stretch, but then again, she hurt you, too."

"We have to warn her." Eliza jumps up and races into the kitchen. She grabs my cell phone and rushes over for me to unlock the screen.

I turn to Elijah. "Call Jaxson, and have him get someone over to her apartment." I unlock the phone, and

Eliza taps on the number I'd saved when Janet called the last time. "I can do it if you want."

She shakes her head and puts the phone on speaker on the counter between us. "I need to do it." It rings twice before someone answers.

"Hello, Eliza," a raspy, deep voice answers.

Eliza stiffens, and Michael rushes over. "Who is this?" she asks.

"You know who this is."

"Randall?"

The voice chuckles. "You're smart and beautiful. Such a deadly combination, wouldn't you say?"

Her gaze locks on mine. "What have you done to Janet?"

"Nothing she didn't deserve," he replies. "Though, if you get Lance's detective friend to send someone over, she might just pull through."

"Why?" Eliza questions. "Why are you doing this to me?"

"You and I are destined, Eliza. I knew it the first time I saw you that you were meant to be mine. We're sides of the same coin. Both shunned by the world around us. Only I can love you like the queen you are."

I motion for her to keep him speaking while Elijah joins us and gives me a thumbs-up.

"I don't know what you mean. We've never met. How can you know we're two sides of the same coin?"

"You don't have a family. Mine never wanted me, either. Yet you craved that connection. Enough that you married someone so far beneath you it's embarrassing." He spits the word out. "In fact, you're so desperate for affection that you're ruining your second chance by spending time with that private security officer. He can't give you what I can, Eliza. No one can."

"Lance and I are just friends." Her gaze remains on mine, and even though I know she's saying the words to keep me out of Randall's crosshairs, it still stings because I am desperate to be more.

"You lie to me."

"No. It's the truth. He's keeping me safe from—" She trails off.

"You need no one to keep you safe from me!" Randall screams into the phone.

"You tried to run me over with a car."

"I was aiming for *him*," he growls. "I wanted to see you in the sunlight. Watch you smile. And then he got in the way. You looked so frustrated at him standing there that I knew you needed me to do something about it. Even if you didn't realize it. Yet, here you are, spending time with him. Living in his house." He spits the words out furiously.

"If you wanted to see me so badly, why spend all your time under my floor?" Her voice is steady, her tone calm; it's impressive, given the amount of strain I know she's under. Reaching over, I rest a hand on hers only to find it trembling.

"You weren't ready for me yet. You were still reeling over your ex. It's why he needed to be out of the picture. Because he was never going to stop coming for you."

"He came here; that's why you killed him?"

"Yes."

"And Janet?"

"She angered you."

"So your plan is to keep killing people who anger me? Is that it? Lance hasn't made me angry."

"Another lie. Or have you so quickly forgotten how he made you feel the first day you were here? You cried after he left. After the realtor was gone, you curled in a ball and cried. I wanted to come out. To hold you. To tell you that everything was okay now that we were together, but I knew you weren't ready yet."

I squeeze her hand, and Eliza closes her eyes tightly. "I wasn't crying over Lance," she says. "And I didn't know him well enough to be angry then. I was tired. Stressed."

"You were unhappy. And I fixed it."

Elijah holds his phone up in front of my face to show a text from Jaxson.

Jaxson: They're going into Janet's apartment now.

I nod, and he pulls it back, so I hold up one finger for Eliza.

"You could have confronted me," I tell him. "We could have had a conversation about it. Man to man."

Randall growls into the line. "Before all of this is over, I plan to. Goodbye, Eliza. I am always yours." A loud crash fills the phone, and the line goes dead.

Eliza pushes back from the counter, eyes closed, whole body trembling. I cross over and pull her against me as one of the panic attacks she's been trying to keep from me takes over. She begins to shiver, teeth chattering together as she sucks in ragged breath after ragged breath.

I run my hand over her hair, waiting for a break in the storm.

Elijah's phone rings. "Hello? Got it. Thanks." I turn us so I can see him as he sets his phone down. "Janet is alive, but Randall got out the window before they could grab him. Managed to make it down the fire escape and into an alley when they lost him."

"What did he do to her?" I question.

"Same as Erick. Shot her and left her for dead. They found her clutching a kitchen towel to the wound. Eliza calling when she did must have thrown him off. Otherwise, I doubt Janet would be alive." He turns to me. "You saved her life."

"Why leave the bottle on Erick's desk, then? Why would he try to kill her while hoping I would intervene?"

"He wanted you to know it was him," Michael explains. "He likely was counting on you not putting the pieces together until after it was done." He runs a hand through his hair. "This guy is like smoke. We can't get a grasp on him."

Eliza pulls away and wipes her face, the panic attack subsiding. "Use me as bait."

"Absolutely not," I snap.

"That's too risky," Elijah adds.

"I agree." Michael crosses his arms.

"I don't." She mimics his stance. "We've been playing by his rules this entire time. Reacting to the situations he puts me in. So let's turn it around. Let's give him a reason to come out of hiding. If we can trap him, we can catch him."

"Only if he doesn't get to you first," I reply, fear icing my veins.

"He won't because none of you will let him."

"Eliza. As much as I love to toot my own horn, this hasn't exactly been a walk-in-the-park type of case for us," Michael says. "The guy has had the upper hand from the beginning."

"Only because we had no idea who he was. Now, we have a face and a name. Which means you can spot him coming for me before he gets to me."

"There's too many variables." I turn away, shaking my head.

"Lance, she's got a point."

I whirl on Elijah. "What about it being too risky ten seconds ago?"

"I agree that it's risky," he replies. "But so is not doing anything. He's almost killed you three times, Michael once, succeeded in killing her ex-husband and nearly managed to take out his mistress, too. Then there's the fact that he blew up our office and burned down her house. How much more is going to happen because we are too afraid to make the risky move?"

"It's Eliza's life on the line," I growl.

"My life is already on the line."

I turn to her. "You're not a carrot."

"In this instance, I am. You have to let me do something, Lance. I refuse to sit around any longer, waiting for this guy to kill someone else. You can help set the rules, but you know this is our best bet to catch him."

"And if it goes wrong?" I demand. "If he manages to take you somewhere we can't find him?"

She places her hand on my arm, and the mere touch calms the storm in me. "Despite the way I treated you from the moment we met, you've spent every second of the last couple of weeks risking your life for mine. Let me do the same."

CHAPTER 30
Eliza

R ain drizzles from the sky above, and I'm transfixed by the droplets sliding down the windowpane as I stare out at the ocean. Likely because focusing on them means I'm less likely to spiral, knowing that in less than an hour, I'll be leaving this house alone for the first time since I came here.

Today, everything changes. One way or another.

Unless, of course, Randall doesn't show up.

We waited two days before setting the trap, giving him time to return to Hope Springs. Truth is, though, we have no idea if he came back at all. Today could be a total bust. But the pit in my stomach tells me that's unlikely.

"You okay?"

I turn my gaze to Lance. Clad in dark jeans, a dark blue flannel with a white undershirt, he steals my breath. So handsome. So kind. Strong. It's a potent combination. "I'm okay."

"You sure? It's not too late to call this off." He moves into the kitchen and leans back against the counter, crossing both muscled arms. "We could come up with another way."

Shaking my head, I draw the curtains over the kitchen window closed then turn to face him. "We have to at least try, Lance."

"This is your life on the line, Eliza."

It's the same argument we had last night and the night before that. Which led to us hardly speaking at all ever since I first made the suggestion. "Exactly. My life. Which means I'm allowed to make the conscious decision to risk it if it means putting someone like Randall away. He has to be stopped."

Even with the short beard on his face, I can see him clench his jaw. "I know."

"And you'll be there. Every step of the way."

"If we miscalculate, even a second—" He trails off, the worry in his expression telling me everything I need to know. Randall has managed to evade these men for weeks now. Something they clearly are not accustomed to.

One mistake and I could end up in his clutches for who knows how long.

"You won't." I start to move closer then hesitate. We haven't had the chance to talk about what is happening between us. More than likely, it's fleeting. A direct result of being crammed in this space together for as long as we have.

I keep trying to convince myself that, when this is all

over, we'll go our separate ways. He will move forward with his company, and I'll find somewhere else to live and work on my book. We'll run into each other from time to time—small town and all—but that'll be it.

Casual friendship.

My stomach twists.

It doesn't matter that I left Erick over a year ago; my divorce was not finalized until a month ago. Which means that everything I'm feeling for Lance is wrong. Attachment born of fear for my life. It has to be. Because the alternative is much too frightening a concept.

"Stop pulling away from me," he says as he reaches for me, taking my hand and pulling me toward him. "Please." He cups my face, tilting it up so he can stare into my eyes.

"This isn't going to last," I tell him.

"What?"

"This attachment between us. It's not lasting."

"Why can't it be?" He's unoffended, completely, and utterly unbothered by what I said, which only helps me believe it more.

"Because we both have our own lives, Lance. And I just got out of a marriage. My entire adult life has been lived under the thumb of someone else."

Lance is quiet for a few minutes, though he does not stop holding my face. His touch is gentle, serene, and it takes everything in me not to lean into it. "One day you're going to realize that not all men want you under their thumb." He leans down and presses his lips to mine.

I grip his wrists, trying to hold him there for as long as possible.

But, too soon, he's pulling back and grabbing a jacket from the back of his dining room chair. "Elijah will be right behind you," he assures me. "You won't be alone."

And before I can respond, Lance shrugs into his jacket.

"Lance—"

"Let me go, Eliza. If you say anything else, I'm likely to lock you in a room somewhere until this is all over."

I swallow hard. "Just—be careful."

He doesn't respond, just nods and continues out the door and into the rainy afternoon.

Watching him leave is far harder than it should be, like a piece of me has gone with him. A shred of what soul I had left after Erick was done with it. Wrapping my arms around myself, I stare at the door, half-expecting him to walk back through it and make good on his promise.

When he doesn't, I wait for the ding of my cell phone.

Minutes tick by as I stand in the kitchen. Still, I wait. This plan hinges on everyone being in the right place at the right time. Michael was picking up Lance, and the two of them were going to head into town. Once there, they were going to park and sneak around the back of the library while Elijah followed me from a distance. Jaxson will already be inside the library, somewhere in the back where he will remain unseen.

There are safeguards everywhere.

Yet, I still feel completely and utterly alone.

My gaze lands on Lance's Bible where it sits on the

coffee table. Before I can fully comprehend what I'm doing, I cross the room and sit down, gathering the soft leather book in my hands.

I open it to a random page, letting my gaze scan the text written there. And as I take into what is written there, in black and white, an understanding settles over me that, while I may feel alone, perhaps I am not.

"Have I not commanded you?" I read Joshua 1:9 aloud. "Be strong and courageous. Do not be frightened, and do not be dismayed, for the Lord your God is with you wherever you go." Closing the book and my eyes, I let myself feel the message in the Bible, absorbing it as though it were spoken aloud to me.

Why else would I have opened to that particular page? It has to mean something, right?

"God, I'm not sure if You're listening, but I need help. Strength. Please keep Lance, Michael, Elijah, and Jaxson safe. Please, above all else, protect them. Whatever happens to me will happen, but please, please, protect them. Amen." I swallow hard and open my eyes before quickly wiping away my tears.

The relief I feel at simply asking for help is something I was not expecting. But before I can focus too intently on it, my phone dings. I jump up and rush into the kitchen, grabbing it to read the text from Lance.

Lance: We're in place. Be careful, Eliza. We still have a conversation to finish.

I smile despite my fear then take a deep, steadying breath, grab my laptop, Lance's keys, and slip into the garage. I'm meant to look like I'm sneaking out, so as I leave the security of Lance's house, I make a show of checking my surroundings from behind the wheel before slowly creeping out onto the street.

The drive to the library might as well have taken days rather than minutes, for the heavy thundering of my heart.

But soon, I'm pulling into the parking lot right as Mrs. McGinley is locking the door. *Right on time.*

I jump out and rush forward. "Oh no, are you leaving for the day?"

She turns and smiles. "I am. Early bunco game with the ladies." Her gaze lands on my laptop, her expression friendly despite knowing exactly what all of this is about, thanks to Jaxson filling her in earlier.

"Oh, okay." I force myself to look disappointed.

"Were you looking for something?"

"I was hoping to get some writing in. I'm not getting much done at Lance's."

She smiles. "I am happy to let you in as long as you promise to lock up behind you."

"Really?" I shove my fear down and focus on relief. "That would be great! Thank you!"

"Of course." She chuckles and unlocks the door. "Just don't tell anyone." With a wink, she pushes it open and hands me the keys. "You can have Lance bring them by later."

"Will do. Thank you so much. You are a lifesaver."

She gives me a look that nearly borders on worry but flashes a smile anyway. "Good luck." With one final squeeze of my arm, she crosses toward her car and climbs inside. I watch her leave before slipping inside, leaving the door unlocked on purpose.

I toss the keys on the table and head straight for the break room, fighting every urge I have to look for Jaxson hiding somewhere in the place.

Joshua 1:9. I repeat the verse number over and over again as I take my seat at the table. My hands shake, nerves churning in my belly as I fight against every instinct I have and turn my back to the door.

Do not be frightened.

I need to look vulnerable.

Do not be dismayed.

Approachable.

For the Lord your God is with you wherever you go.

And just like that, the trap has been set.

Please, let them survive.

"I LOVE WATCHING YOU WORK. YOUR FOCUS IS ONE OF THE things I love most about you."

I stiffen, every muscle in my body going rigid as I slowly turn and face Randall Frasier for the first time.

He looks older than his passport photo, though I know he's only in his mid-forties. There are bags beneath his eyes, and he's shaved his short beard and gelled his hair. He holds a single red rose.

The sweatshirt he wears has holes in it, but his slacks

look relatively new. Until I note the dark stain near the pocket.

"Those were Erick's. I know because he was furious I couldn't get that stain out."

Randall looks down at the stain then back at me and visibly cringes. "Stupid. It was stupid to wear them." He hits the palm of his hand against his forehead. "So stupid. I thought you would think they looked nice since he wore them. But they have bad memories." He's frantic, gaze furious as he continues to hit his palm against his head.

It's then I note the blood splatter on his hand.

"Not stupid," I say quickly, just to gather his attention.

He has no visible wounds, but the blood is fresh enough it smears on his face when he brushes the back of his hand against his forehead. His dark gaze levels on me once more. "You are so beautiful. Like sunshine." He takes a step closer, and I'm forced to remain where I am, pinned with the table at my back.

"Where are you hurt?"

He stops his advance and looks at me curiously. "What do you mean?"

"Your hand."

Randall turns it over then looks back at me, a proud smile on his face. "Someone was here waiting when I arrived. He was difficult to take care of. But I did it. I was sneakier than the detective." He looks proud. "He thought he was smarter than me, but he wasn't. None of them are."

Dread coils in my stomach. "What did you do to him?"

"I stopped him. He would have hurt you. They all

will." He takes a step closer. "Don't you understand? Don't you see? I am the only one who can protect you. I have spent my life learning how to be invisible. I can teach you. I can keep you from ever being seen again."

My gaze flits to the door.

Randal's cheeks flush with color. "They're not coming for you. They can't get in."

I swallow hard and lunge to the side. Randall grabs me, yanking me against him. A stale stench fills my lungs as he leans in and breathes deeply, inhaling my scent as though he were an animal.

Honestly, maybe he is.

"You cannot keep running from me, Eliza. The game must end now. You are mine. And I am *always yours*."

"No." I struggle against him, but something sharp presses against my throat, and I freeze as a sting of pain steals my attention.

The door bursts open, and Lance and Michael rush in, weapons drawn.

Lance's gaze turns murderous when he sees me. "Let her go, Randal. You're not getting out of here."

"She's mine," he growls. "Mine. Mine. Mine. And you cannot have her!"

"Jaxon," I say.

"Elijah is getting him help. He'll survive," Michael assures me, his gaze never straying from Randal.

"You can't have her," Lance tells him. "But you are going to hurt her if you don't stop."

"If I can't have her, no one can." He raises the blade,

and I slam my foot down onto the top of his then drive my elbow into his gut. The knife slices against the side of my throat and I fall forward, pain searing the side of my neck.

Randall reaches for me, and a gun goes off.

He falls to the ground with an agonized cry as Lance reaches forward and rips me away from him.

I fall into his arms, my entire body shaking. He grips my face, turning my head from side to side to study the cut. "It's just a scratch." Lance lets out a breath and crushes me against his chest. "Just a scratch. Thank God. You're all right."

Sherrif Vick rushes in, weapon drawn, deputies behind him. Then, he sees Randall groaning on the floor, a gunshot wound to his shoulder.

Michael stands over him, weapon trained down, then grins at the Sherrif. "We did all the hard work, Vick, but you can have all the credit."

CHAPTER 31

Lance

T he image of Eliza, a knife to her throat, haunted me all night.

I stare out at the ocean from my balcony now, a mug of hot coffee in my hand, and it still feels so surreal that we managed to catch the guy. That our plan worked with minimal damage. Though, I imagine Jaxson wouldn't consider his head wound minimal.

Randall had managed to sneak up behind Jaxson as he focused in on Eliza while she was coming through the door. Apparently, a lifetime of sneaking in the shadows was enough to teach Randall how to move silently enough even a trained Marine couldn't hear him.

We'd come so close to losing. To being too late because, once again, we'd underestimated the type of person we were up against.

"You sure you should be out there?"

I turn to see Eliza framed in the door, wearing my old

Army PT sweatshirt. The grey fabric would have drowned anyone else out, but she somehow manages to look just as beautiful wearing it as she did in that first photograph I saw of her, body draped in gold. Maybe even more so. "We got the guy, remember?"

"It still feels weird." She steps out to join me, a fresh mug of coffee in her hand.

My gaze lands on the gauzy bandage over her cut. It had been a bit deeper than a scratch, but thankfully, she'd needed no stitches. "How's your neck?"

"Not too bad. Have you heard from Jaxon?"

"He was complaining loudly about Michael's lack of caretaking skills last I heard."

She laughs, a lighthearted sound that might as well be a melody to my ears. "Michael doesn't seem overly maternal."

I laugh. "Understatement."

We stand in silence, listening to waves crash into the rocks below. I'm not even sure where we should go from here. The last two weeks, our lives have been one defensive move after another, and now that we're free of Eliza's stalker, will she even remain in Hope Springs?

Or will she leave just as she left L.A.?

How do I convince her to stay?

"I was thinking it might be nice to go to church today."

Surprised, I turn to face her. "Really?"

She nods, keeping her gaze straight ahead. "Really. I'd like to go. And the dance, too, if that's still on the table."

"Absolutely."

Excitement thrums through me, making me feel like a giddy teenager about to go on his first date rather than someone who has seen everything the ugliness of war has to offer.

"Unless you don't want to go?"

"No, I want to go—to both. That would be great."

She smiles, but it fades quickly, and she sets her mug on the patio table before folding both hands in front of her. "I want to thank you for everything you've done, Lance. Seriously. I can't even begin to offer you any form of repayment because I'm not sure what would even be appropriate."

"I don't need repayment."

"You took a bullet for me. Were blown up. Let me into your home, helped me when I lost everything." Tears fill the corners of her eyes. "No one has ever done anything like that. In my world, it was always tit for tat. Nothing came without strings."

"That's a sad world to live in."

"I agree." She closes her eyes and takes a deep breath then refocuses on me. "I treated you horribly when I got here because you scared me. There was something there, even from that first moment, that let me understand you could hurt me."

"I would never hurt you."

"I know that now. And I'm sorry for behaving the way I did when we first met. I've never had a man in my life who treated me the way you do. Who took care of me without expecting something in return. And it caught me off guard. I was focused on protecting myself and keeping my distance."

She doesn't have to get into the details for me to understand just what it was they expected. And it angers me that she was treated as though she had no worth aside from what pleasure she could offer.

"I just—I don't know if what happened between us was more than just being trapped in the same house together, and I know I just got out of a marriage, but Erick and I were separated for over a year before the divorce was finalized. So, I guess what I'm trying to say is that I—if you are okay with it—I would like to spend time together when our lives are not on the line."

Her cheeks are flushed, her eyes wide as she stares back at me, waiting for a response. I try to put it into words, how I feel, but nothing comes out. So, instead, I reach forward and pull her toward me, crushing my mouth to hers.

Eliza leans into me, melting against my body as though we were made for each other. She fits against me so perfectly that I cannot help but wonder how I ever managed to live without her.

Even as I want to devour her, letting her taste the promises I so freely offer, I pull back and rest my forehead against hers.

"I am in love with you, Eliza Pierce. Head over heels. Madly. Soul-soaring. Spend-the-rest-of-my-life-with-you love."

She pulls back and stares up at me, shock painting her expression. "What?"

"I'm not expecting you to feel it. I know it's early and you've been through far more than any one person should, but I needed to say it so you know where I stand. This isn't casual for me. You aren't casual." I brush the hair from her face. "You're exactly who I've been waiting for."

"Love. Lance, I—" She swallows hard. "I thought I loved Erick. Thought he was my soulmate. And it wasn't until I spent all this time with you that I realized I never loved him. Because if this feeling I have now is love, then I've never felt it before. Not with anyone else."

I grin like an idiot, staring down at her.

"I love you, too, Lance Knight. I'm scared—terrified even—of what that means because I've already been broken, and I've barely begun putting the pieces back together."

"Then let me help." I press a kiss to her temple. She sighs. "Let me be your support while you navigate everything you've been through." Another kiss to her other temple.

"What if you don't like what you see?"

I pull back, still holding her face. "I *see* you, Eliza. And I love every piece of you. You are the strongest woman I've ever met, and I promise you, I'm not going anywhere."

———

I'M CLOSER TO FORTY THAN THIRTY, AND YET I FEEL absolutely sick as I stand at the entrance to the high school gymnasium, waiting for Eliza to arrive. After church, she'd gone to Lilly's to get ready, insisting that she'd meet me here, and even though the threat has been neutralized, there's a pit in my stomach that just won't go away.

"You look like a mess."

"Thanks," I tell Elijah as he comes to stand beside me.

He chuckles. "Well, if you're looking for a distraction, Michael has already started arguing with Reyna."

I look over my shoulder to find him glaring at a short, dark-haired beauty while she points her finger at him. They were high school sweethearts, best friends, and he'd left without a word.

She's treated him with the silent treatment ever since—until moments like these where he goes out of his way to rile her up just so she'll speak with him. In this case, he volunteered to help with setup and likely did something she specifically asked him not to do.

"He hasn't even been here ten minutes."

"I know. Record time," Elijah says as he sips the fruit punch in his plastic cup. "Something about the decorations needing work."

"She's going to make him regret it one of these days."

"Probably." Elijah turns his attention back to the parking lot. "Still no word?"

I stare down at my phone and the text message that has not yet arrived. She was supposed to text me when they were headed this way, and they were due five minutes ago. "No."

"Maybe they just lost track of time."

"Maybe." But something in my gut is telling me that there's something wrong.

Alex's truck pulls into the parking lot, and I relax slightly, though I know nothing but the sight of Eliza will fully calm my nerves.

He climbs out and waves then walks around to the other side and opens the door. Lilly steps out wearing a pink dress, a wide smile on her face. They shut the door, lock the truck, and head this way.

"Where is Eliza?" I demand.

Both of them look at me curiously. "She said she was going to text you. Birdie came by to bring her a pair of shoes she thought Eliza might like. They were right behind us." She turns around and studies the parking lot. "They should have been here already."

"Elijah," I say as I tap on Eliza's contact.

"Already on it." He moves away from me, his own phone out.

"Hi, this is Eliza. Sorry I couldn't get to my phone, but if you leave a—" I end the call.

"Lance, I'm sorry, I don't understand. What's happening?" Lilly asks. She looks completely confused, and while I would love to put her mind at ease, I can't.

"Were they in Birdie's minivan?" I question.

"Yes."

"Lance, what's wrong?" Alex questions. "What can I do?"

"Go get Michael. Tell him that Eliza is missing."

Without another word, both Alex and Lilly rush inside the gymnasium, all while my world comes crashing in around me.

It's possible they could just be running late.

But even as I try to make myself consider that possibility, I shove it out. Something is wrong.

I feel it in my gut.

Eliza is missing, and I have no clue where she could be.

CHAPTER 32
Eliza

My head is *pounding.*

Arms tied around my back, I'm immobilized, but even if I hadn't been restrained, I don't know that I could move much anyway. Every muscle in my body feels as though it's made of lead. My mouth is dry, my throat hoarse.

Every breath is labored.

I try to study the room around me, scanning for anything that I might recognize, but there's nothing. My chair is toward the back, and I'm surrounded by shelves holding document boxes labeled with years in black marker.

It could be any storage room anywhere, for all I know. And I have no idea how long I've even been here.

Is Lance looking for me?

Does he even know I'm gone?

I test the restraints again but run out of breath before I

can make any actual headway. I'd been talking to Birdie—
trying on the shoes she'd given me—and then everything
went dark. Or, at least, that's all I can remember before
waking up here who knows how long ago.

There's no one else here.

No one to tell me where I am or what happened to
Birdie, but with every passing moment, the fog clears, and
my fear continues to grow.

The door opens and a red-haired woman strolls in
wearing khaki pants and a blue shirt.

"You?" I choke out, betrayal hitting me square in the
chest as I try to piece together just what she has to do with
any of this.

Birdie crosses over to me and undoes the lid of a water
bottle. She offers it to me, but I turn my head, refusing to
drink anything. "Stubborn woman. Fine. Suit yourself."
She caps the water and sets it on a shelf then pulls a fold-
up chair from behind the shelf and sets it up before sitting
in it.

"I don't understand."

"You wouldn't. So self-centered. I'd noticed it the first
time we met in person. If I'd known what you were before,
I wouldn't have told my brother about you."

"Brother?"

She glares at me. "Try to keep up, will you?"

"You'll forgive me if I'm a little groggy," I snap back.
"I'm pretty sure I was drugged."

"It's your fault things had to be this way," Birdie says.
"You could have just done what you were supposed to,

and you both could have been happy. Now, he is in prison, and you're walking around, flaunting yourself."

"Randall? This is about him?"

"My brother deserved better," she spits out.

"Your brother. He is your brother?" The background checks showed he had no family, no close friends. I know they couldn't have missed it, so why wasn't it recorded somewhere? Unless, of course, she's just as delusional as he is.

"We grew up in the same foster home. Randall was there for me when no one else was. He treasured me, cared for me, and I wanted to make him happy. Like he did for me."

It's twisted. And her expression shows a madness I hadn't ever noticed before. "Sounds like you were in love with him."

"In love with him?" she glares at me. "Of course, I was in love with him!"

"Then why didn't you marry him? If you weren't actually related."

Her expression remains stone-cold. "Because we were siblings in everything but blood. It would have been wrong."

"But kidnapping me and serving me to him on a platter isn't?"

"You were made for him," she says simply. "You are his."

"He's in *prison*. So care to explain what your brilliant plan is now?"

"He'll get out. One way or another. And when he does, you will be waiting for him. Ready and compliant."

"There is absolutely no world in which I will *ever* be compliant. You'll have to kill me." Fear burns in my gut as I try to rationalize everything she's telling me. "And he's not getting out. So, what are you going to do? Keep me tied to this chair forever?"

"As long as it takes," she replies. "My brother will be happy. He will have what he wants." Her phone rings, and she pulls it out of her pocket. "This will be fun." She crosses over to me and rips off some fresh duct tape from a roll I hadn't seen then covers my mouth with it before answering her phone. "Lance, what can I do for you?"

My stomach plummets, heart racing. I try to make noise. Try to scream and scrape my chair against the floor.

Birdie glares at me and gets up, walking just far enough that I know my attempts at being heard won't be successful. "No, I'm sorry. I was going to drive her, but she seemed to have a bit of a panic attack and asked me to take her to the bus stop."

I swallow hard, tears burning in my eyes.

"I know. I'm so sorry, Lance. I was just on my way to tell you. It's not something I wanted to do over the phone. No, I have no idea where she went. Back to L.A. maybe?"

I try to scream against the tape covering my mouth. I squirm in my seat, ignoring the throbbing in my head. What if he believes her? What if he thinks I left voluntarily? No one will come for me.

Not a single person will realize I'm gone.

Please, God. Please let him see through it. Let him find me.

"I am so sorry, Lance. I know you two were close. Yes, of course. I will let you know if I hear from her. Have fun at the dance. Bye." She ends the call and crosses over to me as she shoves the phone back into her pocket. "That was easier than I thought it would be. Seems your white knight believed you to be a flight risk, too."

Please don't let me die here.

Before I can fully comprehend what's coming, she rears her fist back and slams it into my jaw. Pain explodes along the side of my face, searing me from the outside in. But where physical violence used to make me cower, now it only angers me, burning straight through the fear.

Strength surges through me, and I look up at Birdie even as I feel blood trickling down the side of my face from the ring on her finger.

She reaches up and rips the duct tape from my mouth. "You should know better than to not do what you're told. I would have thought your ex would have beaten that out of you. You. Will. Be. Compliant. You. Will. Be. Willing."

I grin. Not even on purpose, but before I can stop myself, a smile is spreading over my face despite the pain.

Everything I've ever been through. Every broken bone, bruise, grief-stricken moment, has made me stronger. And I don't think I ever realized just how much until right now. Erick put me through hell. I walked through the fires of my own personal nightmare and came out the other side a stronger version of myself.

Apparently, it took being kidnapped to realize it.

I will make it through this.

I will survive.

Because it's what I do. It's who I am.

And because, for the first time, I know I am not alone.

Joshua 1:9, I say in my head.

He was there when Lance was shot.

He was there when Randall came for me in the library.

He was there in times when I didn't even fully believe.

And my God is with me now.

Birdie rears back and hits me again. More blinding pain, thanks to the ring tearing at my flesh, but I do not cower.

I do not whimper.

Hot blood trickles down the side of my face.

"My brother won't care if your pretty face is scarred," Birdie snaps.

"Then go on. Scar me. Beat me. I don't care what you do. I will *never* submit to either of you."

Birdie audibly growls then turns on her heel and stalks toward the door. Once she's slammed it behind her, I let my head fall forward, giving myself a moment to try and blink away the hot tears in the corners of my eyes, forming thanks to the pain.

One. Two. Three. Four. Five.

Breathing a bit more regularly, I sit up and start tugging at the tape holding my wrists together. I rub it against the back of the chair, hoping to catch something—anything sharp enough to slice through the thick strips.

It begins to stretch. To pull.

I move faster.

Please, God. Please. I need You.

The tape snaps, and I reach down to rip it free from my ankles. But I'm not fast enough. The door opens, and Birdie stalks through.

I rush forward, but she whips out a gun and fires. Pain explodes through my shoulder, and I fall to the ground. My blood is on fire, my body ablaze. I stare up at her, ready to meet my end if this is how I will go out.

But I refuse to do it on my knees.

I start to stand. She slams the pistol into the side of my head, and I fall over, vision wavering.

"You will stay down!" she screams.

Another gunshot.

Birdie stiffens then turns slowly. Lance stands behind her, his weapon raised. Elijah is with him, Jaxson on his other side. She tilts her head to the side. Then the gun falls to the ground. I scramble for it, yanking it out of her vicinity right as she begins to fall.

Blood blossoms on her chest, soaking through the blue fabric.

"I got her. Get Eliza." Jaxson rushes for Birdie while Lance sprints toward me, closing the distance between us in three long strides. He lays me back and tears the fabric covering my shoulder away, then shrugs out of his sweatshirt and presses it against my wound.

"Ambulance is on the way," Elijah says. "How you doing, Eliza?" His half-smile tells me I look far worse than I probably realize.

"Alive," I tell him then focus on Lance, who kneels at my side. "I'm sorry. I didn't think—"

"You have nothing to apologize for." He brushes the hair from my head, so I close my eyes. My body begins to shake, a chill overtaking me as the adrenaline begins to wane.

"She's dead," Jaxson says.

It's the last thing I hear before I drift, exhaustion pulling me under.

CHAPTER 33

Lance

The beeping of the machines hooked up to Eliza as she sleeps in bed fills my ears. She looks peaceful now, thanks to the pain medication given to her when we arrived.

Her shoulder has been sutured and bandaged as have the gashes on her face. Three of them—ripped open by the large ring Birdie had been wearing. Then there's the concussion from the weapon slammed into the side of her head.

Anger churns in my gut, and I close my eyes, trying desperately to block out the image of Eliza's blood all over Birdie's hand; as well as the image of the woman I love crouched on the floor, prepared to meet her death.

She'd looked so strong and vulnerable at the same time.

"How's she doing?"

I glance over as Doc strolls into the room, carrying his

jacket. He's off rotation tonight but had insisted on coming as soon as Michael called him. "Still sleeping," I reply, keeping my tone low.

"Good. She needs the rest." Doc's crystal blue gaze travels from Eliza to me. Lines that tell his age crinkle as he narrows his eyes. "How are you?"

"Fine. I'm not the one who got shot."

"Not tonight, you weren't." He takes a seat in a chair and lays his jacket over his lap. "But you did the shooting."

"Birdie would have shot her again if I'd only injured her. That or she would have taken a shot at one of us." Even as I know that the guilt over taking a life is a heavy one to carry. It doesn't matter whether it was in self-defense of yourself or another; that burden is one you hold for the rest of your days.

If I had to do it all over again, though, I'd make the same exact choice.

"Still not easy. Birdie was your friend."

"Some choice of friend," I reply then run my hands over my face. "I'm not sure how we didn't see that one coming. How could we have missed the signs?"

"From what I understand, there were none," he replies. "Everyone in town is pretty shaken up over it. No one would have ever taken her for someone capable of kidnapping and assault. Her husband is beside himself."

Eliza groans, and I lean forward, taking her hand in mine.

Doc pushes up from his seat. "I'm going to go check in

with my colleagues, see if I can get an update." He squeezes my shoulder on his way out, shutting the door right as Eliza's eyes flutter open.

"Lance?" Her voice is hoarse, throat dry from sleep and the medicine they gave her.

"I'm here. How are you feeling?"

"Groggy," she replies. "But otherwise, okay. There's no pain."

"They gave you medicine."

She turns her head to look at me, eyes glossy from the pain medicine, and smiles. "You found me."

"Of course I found you."

"You didn't believe Birdie when she said I left town."

There was a single blip of a moment where I'd wondered if Birdie was telling the truth. But I had this overwhelming feeling of mistrust the moment the woman answered her phone. I can't quite explain it, but I knew she was the way to finding Eliza. "I assumed you wouldn't leave without saying goodbye." I try to smile, but I know it looks forced.

Eliza squeezes my hand gently. "I'm not going anywhere. There are dates to be had between us." Her speech is slurred, but her words mean everything to me.

I let loose the breath I hadn't realized I'd been holding. "Good." Leaning forward, I run my free hand over the uninjured side of her face while keeping my other firmly wrapped around hers. "I was terrified I wouldn't find you."

"How did you know it was Birdie?"

"We didn't. At least, not at first. Lilly said Birdie had brought you some shoes and you were riding with her. At first, we'd assumed somehow Randall had gotten out and grabbed the both of you. Then I tried her cell. There was this feeling I couldn't shake, telling me that I would find you where she was. The real estate office was the second place we checked. We went to her house first."

Eliza smiles once more then closes her eyes for a few moments before opening them. "I asked God to bring you to me, and He did."

My heart warms, joy filling me completely.

Her expression darkens. "She said she was going to keep me for Randall. That she would make me compliant."

The joy vanishes, replaced by anger. "We completely missed their connection because their records were sealed. Elijah called in a favor and found out they'd spent time together in the same foster home, but we still can't find any communication between them since he turned eighteen."

"They must have used letters," she replies.

"That's our thought."

"Water?" she chokes out.

"Here." I grab the hospital cup the nurse brought in with ice water and offer it to Eliza. She drinks greedily then leans back and takes a few deep breaths.

"Thanks."

"Of course. Does anything hurt? I can get the nurse."

She squeezes my hand. "Please don't go. I'm fine."

I remain where I am, not speaking, hoping she will continue to tell me everything Birdie said to her.

"She told me I was made for her brother. And that he wouldn't care if my face was scarred." Eliza pales and tries to sit up quickly; then hisses through her teeth and lies back down.

"Easy, you need to stay where you are."

"My face. Is it bad? I didn't care when I was there, but—"

"Eliza," I say softly. She stills and looks up at me. "You are beautiful."

"But did she scar me?"

"We won't know," I tell her honestly. "But if she did, you'll be in good company." I point to my chest, my attempt to remind her of the scars I still carry.

She relaxes ever so slightly. "I guess I shouldn't care. It doesn't matter, not really. I'm alive, and that's what counts."

"It is. And even if she did scar you, you're still beautiful."

Eliza offers me a smile, though it doesn't reach her eyes. "My house is still gone."

"Yes."

"I don't have anywhere to live."

"You can stay with me."

She laughs softly. "Lance, you've already done too much."

The idea of her leaving, of not waking up and sharing a cup of coffee, or saying goodnight right before bed is far more suffocating than it should have been. After all, I had a life before she showed up. I could have one after.

But I don't want one unless Eliza is in it.

"Stay with me until you get back on your feet, please. You'll really be doing me a favor, I'm not a fan of my own company anymore."

Eliza smiles and shakes her head. "I won't stay long."

"You can stay as long as you need. That guest room isn't going anywhere." I lift her hand and press my lips to the top.

Eliza's breath catches. It's slight, but it makes my heart soar. "Thank you."

"Anytime."

She takes a deep breath and stares up at the ceiling. "What do we do now?"

"We go back to our lives. Our routines."

"How are things ever going to be the same? I feel like I've been fighting for my life since I was born."

"You're not fighting alone anymore," I remind her. "And we take it day by day. Eventually, things will go back to normal."

"You promise?"

"Absolutely," I reply, even though I am going to make it my mission to ensure things are even better for her than they were before.

CHAPTER 34

Eliza

"Stop making a fuss, I'm fine," I laugh as Lance carries my dinner over to where I'm sitting on the couch. It's been three months since I was shot, and Birdie was killed. Three months of being waited on hand and foot by the man who rescued me.

"I don't mind." He grins and sits down beside me, his own plate in his hand.

"I do. You don't have to wait on me."

"But I want to. You would deprive me of what I want?" He leans in, passion sparking in his gaze, then presses his lips to mine.

Desire sears me, igniting my blood and setting my soul ablaze. "I would if it's for your own good. I'm selfless like that."

Lance chuckles and leans back, settling against the couch. "That you are." He sets the plate in his lap and folds his hands. I do the same. "Dear God, we thank you for this meal, and for the chance to share it. Amen."

"Amen," I repeat, then take my first bite of the chicken parmesan he's been working on for hours. "This is delicious."

"Yeah?" His crooked grin makes me smile.

"Absolutely."

He takes a bite and nods in agreement, then gestures to the open laptop on the coffee table. "How's the book coming along?"

"Good. Hit chapter seven today, so I'm making progress. Seems nearly dying and finding myself engulfed in violence was relatively good inspiration."

His smile fades ever so slightly. No matter how many times I tell him that it wasn't his fault, that none of us even began to guess that Birdie was involved, he still carries the guilt of what happened to me.

The seventeen stitches in my face to the three wounds she left, as well as stitches in my shoulder, were a constant reminder to him. Even if they're all gone by now. The scars they left behind—physical and mental—will remain for the rest of my life.

Even Birdie's husband was completely caught off guard. He'd had no idea that she lived in a foster home at all, since she'd told him her parents died after she'd been an adult. It was a shock to everyone here, and even though what she did to me was horrible, I can't help but feel slightly sad for her.

What trauma must she have suffered to behave the way

she did? What happened to form her into the person she was?

Lance's phone rings, so he sets his plate aside and jumps up to grab it.

I continue eating, my thoughts on tomorrow's impending job hunt, so I can afford to rent a place until the light house is livable again. While Lance was gracious enough to offer for me to stay in his guest room, I'd moved into Mrs. McGinley's spare bedroom the week after I'd been let out of the hospital.

I'd wanted to sort out my feelings for Lance, so I could decide whether they were simply a byproduct of the fear and physical proximity, or something deeper. Doing that while living under the same roof with him seemed impossible, so I'd taken the woman up on her offer. I've found that in our moments apart, my feelings for Lance have only grown.

He's the first person on my mind when I wake, and the one I fall asleep thinking of.

Lance returns to the living room, a wide grin on his face. It momentarily steals my breath—seeing him so happy. "So, I know we just sat down, but I have something I need to show you."

"What is it?" His excitement is palatable, and I set the food aside before pushing up off the couch.

"If I tell you, it won't be a surprise." He reaches out and grabs my arm, then pulls me toward the door.

"But, what about dinner?" I look back lovingly at the chicken parm I'm abandoning.

"We'll stop at the diner for tonight and I'll make chicken parm again tomorrow." He hands me my jacket and pulls me out into the garage. After opening the passenger side door for me, he comes around and climbs behind the wheel.

"Can I get a hint?"

"Nope." He turns toward me. "Can you promise to keep your eyes closed?" I do and he leans in to kiss me gently. "Keep them closed, Eliza."

"No promises."

He chuckles and the car begins to move.

We ride in silence, all the while my mind reeling over what he could possibly be trying to show me. Lance has been the picture of attentive over the past few months, cooking and caring for me like we've known each other for years.

Even the rest of the town has helped, too. The times when Lance had to be somewhere else and I wasn't quite up to the task of moving around, Lilly would come over, or Mrs. McGinley would sit and watch TV with me.

The pastor has come by to talk to me, and I've had the opportunity to ask him a lot of questions regarding God and my faith. Last week, he brought over a Bible that he'd purchased for me, something I've been working to read every night since, given the one I had from my foster mom was in the lighthouse when it went up in flames.

There's so much more to faith than I ever realized. It's more than showing up on Sunday mornings and spending an hour singing. It's a soul-deep connection that fills you with peace unlike anything I ever thought possible.

And while I still have so much to learn, I'm feeling more and more like the person I could have been had Erick not gotten ahold of me when I'd been so young.

Lance stops the car. "I'm going to come around and get you, okay? But please, keep your eyes closed."

"I promise," I reply with a light laugh.

The door shuts and a few seconds later, mine opens. Cool air brushes across the skin of my hands and face. Lance takes my hands and guides me out of the car. The sound of the ocean fills my ears as the scent of saltwater brings a smile to my face.

"Okay. Open."

I open my eyes and gasp. The lighthouse stands before me, a pillar of perfection. Where there was rubble, now stands white stucco sides and red stripes that climb all the way to the top. Tears burn in my eyes, and I sprint toward the front door, passing by Elijah, Michael, Jaxson, and a man and woman I don't recognize.

Shoving the door open, I stare at a fully renovated home. Kitchen, flooring—all of it brand new. It's even been decorated, with a soft white leather sofa, a patterned high back chair, and a television that is far newer than anything I could have afforded.

And even as grateful as I am, it's too much.

Way too much.

I turn toward the door. Lance stands just inside, hands in both pockets. "Well?"

"Lance. This is—amazing."

He breathes a sigh of relief. "Good. I am so glad."

"But it's too much, right? It seems like too much."

"No, it's not."

"You re-built my house."

"Actually, I re-built it, Lance just offered notes." The man I didn't recognize steps into the living room, a dark-haired beauty at his side. "Everett Dorsey," he says as he holds out his hand. "I built his house, too."

Lance chuckles and shakes his head. "Always taking credit."

"Fine. Lance helped."

The woman gently slaps his arm, then reaches out to take my hand. "Nova, I'm this one's better half."

Everett smiles down at her like she's the only thing that matters in his entire world. It's then I notice her swollen belly.

"It's so nice to meet you both. I can't—I don't know how to thank you."

"You don't need to. I enjoy working on places that have a lot of history. It was fun to re-store this place to its former glory."

"I think you made it better than it was when I bought it," I comment, turning in a slow circle to study the inside.

"I hope you like the furniture and décor. If you don't, let me know and I can swap it out for you." Nova offers me a business card.

"Contractor and interior designer," I comment. "Power couple."

Nova laughs. "I like you. If you're ever in Boston, look me up. We can grab some coffee."

"I will definitely do that."

Nova and Everett exchange a look. "Well, I'm in the mood for pie. Lots of pie." Nova pats her stomach.

"Then let's go get you some pie. It was nice to meet you, Eliza."

"You, too, I—" Tears blur my vision. "Thank you both so much."

"You're welcome." Nova smiles, then squeezes Lance's arm as she passes. They shut the door behind them, leaving just Lance and I inside.

"There's one more thing," Lance says as he heads into the kitchen.

"Rebuilding my house wasn't enough?" Tears burn in the corners of my eyes as he carries a white box over toward me.

"This isn't from me." He smiles and holds it out.

I remove the lid and choke on a sob as every emotion I'd been trying to hold back comes pouring out of me. With shaking hands, I reach in and pull out the Bible my foster mom had given me all those years ago. "Where?"

"We found it buried beneath some rubble of the second floor. Seems it fell through when the flooring collapsed. It's the only thing that survived from your room."

I run my fingers over the gold lettering, completely amazed at the fact this Bible survived not just the fire, but the water used to put it out. Then again, I'm not entirely sure why I'm surprised. If I've learned anything over the last few months, it's that God works in ways we can't always understand.

He moves things when we believe them to be immovable.

Heals hearts we believe long past repair.

So it makes sense this Bible would have survived the fire.

I hold it against my chest, hugging it to me as I survey the space. Sniffling, I smile and meet Lance's gaze as he sets the white box aside. "Why did you do this?" I ask.

Lance reaches out to brush some strands of hair behind my ears. "I am in love with you, Eliza Pierce. And I know you've been trying to find a way to make this happen and now you don't have to."

"I can't pay you back right now. Not anytime soon."

"I don't want you to pay me back. Ever." Lance takes the Bible from me and sets it on the counter, then reaches into his pocket and withdraws a small, velvet box.

I gasp and step back, afraid and elated at what might be inside. He opens it, revealing a key. Relief shoots through me. Not that spending a lifetime with Lance would be so bad, but I am not anywhere near ready to get married again.

"For the new lock." He grins at me because he knows exactly what that did to me.

"I don't know how to thank you, Lance. Seriously. I—"

"There is nothing I want more than to see you happy, Eliza. And if this makes you happy, it's all I need."

Emotion burns in my throat and tightens my chest. "You take my breath away."

"Good." Leaning in, Lance presses his lips to mine. I wind both arms around his neck and tug him closer, losing myself in the kiss. Every moment of every day, I am grateful that God put us together. That Lance and I, two completely different people, managed to find our way to each other.

"I installed the water heater myself," Lance says as he pulls back.

Arching my brow, I press a hand to my chest, just above my heart. "You mean, a real plumber didn't install it?"

"No," he replies. "Though I was a plumber once upon a time."

I click my tongue and shake my head. "I'll have to get a practicing plumber in here. Someone who really knows what they're doing."

Lance throws his head back and laughs, then grips the front of my jacket and yanks me toward him again. He captures my lips in a quick kiss, then pulls back and rests his forehead against mine.

"I love you, Mr. Knight."

Lance pulls back and grins at me. "That's a good thing, because I love you, too, Big City."

———

THANK YOU SO MUCH FOR READING! I HOPE YOU LOVED ELIZA and Lance as much as I do! There was so much to adore about these two together, from Eliza's hesitance to Lance's steadfast faith, and I am so grateful you came on this journey with me! Please consider leaving a review for them!

If you're ready for more enemies to lovers, faith-filled suspense, then turn the page for the first two chapters of Elijah's book, SEARCHING FOR PEACE!

And, if you join me on my newsletter, you get a free novella featuring your favorite diner owners! Get Lily and Alex's story, PICTURES OF HOPE for free today!

CHAPTER 35
Searching for Peace: Elijah

I hate funerals.

As an Army Ranger, I've unfortunately attended my fair share, and if I can go the rest of my life without seeing another flag-draped coffin, I'd be more than happy.

Then again, the dark wooden box before me is adorned with flowers rather than red, white, and blue. Still, it doesn't make it any easier. In a lot of ways, this might be even harder. After all, Edna wasn't a soldier on the battlefield. She was an elderly woman—a grandmother who'd been in her home.

The lump in my throat grows.

An aged woman smiles back at me from a large, framed photograph, her silver hair pulled up in a bun, her green eyes bright with joy. She looks so happy, so completely thrilled to be staring back at whoever took that photograph.

All I feel is pain.

Grief.

We may not have been family by blood, and I may not have known her more than a few years, but Edna Montgomery was as good a woman as they come. After the first time I helped her carry groceries into her house, she'd practically adopted me as a surrogate grandson. I'd been surly when we first met, jaded by the horrors I'd seen on deployment, and she'd refused to let me continue to be bitter.

I spent three Easters, Thanksgivings, and Christmas afternoons with her. We'd sipped lemonade on her porch on lazy Sunday afternoons when I didn't have to work, and I'd listened to her stories about her late husband and the joy he'd brought into her life before being stolen far too soon.

Now she's gone. Heaven has gained an angel, but I lost mine.

"Mrs. Montgomery was a staple in this town," Pastor Redding says sadly as he grips each side of the podium, his own eyes misty. His wife, one of Edna's close friends, sniffles in a front pew. "She was a shining light, the kindest woman any of us have ever met. She'd never met a stranger and welcomed everyone as though they'd been a part of her life for as long as anyone can remember."

All around me, people cry. Mrs. McGinley—the town's librarian and Edna's best friend—sniffs beside me. Reaching out, I cover her wrinkled hand with mine. She sets her other one over it and leans against my shoulder.

"Edna never had a negative thing to say about anyone, and I think we can all agree that her s'more cookies were the best ones around."

"Best in the world!" Michael, my co-worker and brother in everything but blood, calls out.

People mutter in agreement. A few laugh softly. One woman lets out a choked sob.

"I know we're all hurting," the pastor says, "but take solace in knowing this is not the last time we will see our sister. For, one day, we will walk alongside her in heaven." He bows his head. "Let us pray. Dear God, thank You for the time we were blessed to know Edna here on Earth. Thank You for blessing us with every moment spent. Every laugh shared. Please, God, be with her family and close friends as they mourn, and comfort us all in our pain by reminding us that she is with You. Amen."

"Amen," I murmur alongside everyone else in the pews.

The pastor smiles softly as his gaze travels over the congregation. "There will be another service at the gravesite, and we hope to see you there. Thank you all for coming." He steps down, and everyone stands, lining up on the side of the church to greet the dark-haired beauty standing near the coffin.

Andie Montgomery—Edna's granddaughter. She grew up here, living with Edna after her parents got divorced. Her father left town, and her mother dropped her at Edna's then never came back.

According to what Edna said over the years, Andie was

a quiet girl. Kind. But ended up leaving town with a man almost two times her age. It was a scandal though, in true Hope Springs fashion, no one will openly talk about it.

I do know that Edna gave her every penny in her savings account so Andie could start her own business. Which is exactly what she did as soon as she graduated from design school. The fashion company she started in New York has grown substantially in the last couple of years. It would be impressive if I weren't so disgusted by her refusal to come visit the woman who'd raised her.

While I've never met Andie, Edna spoke about her nonstop. Raving about her brilliant granddaughter. Frankly, I don't care much for a woman who couldn't even be bothered to visit her grandmother on Christmas.

As far as I know, Andie Montgomery has not stepped foot in Hope Springs since the day she shook the dust off her fancy heels.

Even when Edna had been lying in the hospital bed, so weak she could hardly keep her eyes open, she'd begged me to watch over Andie. Urged me to reach out and make friends. Despite the fact that the woman never answered the dozen phone calls I made to her when I'd arrived at the hospital and discovered Edna would likely never leave her bed.

I should go up and introduce myself now, but the memory of Edna's tear-stained cheek as she drew her last breath makes me think better of it. Better that I am not in the same room with Miss Montgomery longer than necessary.

My temper is already something I struggle with. And I've got more than a few unkind things to say to the woman.

"How are you doing?" Eliza Knight asks as she steps into my path, Lance—her husband and my boss—right beside her. Her blond hair is wavy and falls to her shoulders, and her eyes are red and swollen. She'd loved Edna too. We all did.

"Fine," I reply. It's far from the truth, but I'll get there. It's not like death is a stranger to me. First, my parents. Then, my grandmother. Over a dozen of my comrades. Now Edna. Nope, death and I are practically old friends, aren't we?

"Edna was an amazing woman," Eliza says as she brushes her hair behind her ear. "She sat front row at the library when Mrs. McGinley brought me in for a signing after my book released." Her eyes mist. "I'll never forget how she'd smiled at me when I'd been so nervous."

Lance wraps an arm around her shoulders, and she leans into him.

"She was great," I reply with a smile then turn to Lance. "I'm going to head home and check on a few things, then I'm headed to the office. You going to be in today?"

"Later," he replies. "We're going to head to the cemetery then the wake. You're not coming?" His brows draw together, likely in surprise.

"Nope. No need to. I said my goodbyes when she was in the hospital." Edna had a heart attack and had fallen in the shower. The paramedics called me first since I was her emergency contact, so I was with her right before she died. I was the one who called Andie over a dozen times to let her know she needed to fly out. And I was the one she hung up on when I'd finally gotten ahold of her and offered to help plan the service.

So, no. Spending any time with Andie Montgomery in any capacity is something I am just not interested in. Not now. Not ever.

"Are you sure?" Eliza questions. "You can ride with us."

Because I can see that she's worried about me, I plaster on a smile then lean in and kiss her noisily on the cheek. "I'm fine, I promise. See you both at the diner later?"

"Absolutely." Lance waves, and he and Eliza head toward the line while I slip outside.

Early June rain drizzles down on me, but I pay it little notice as I head to the parking lot. The moment I turn the corner though, I stop, practically freezing in place. Andie is leaning against a black sedan parked directly next to my truck, eyes closed, face tilted up toward the sky.

Great. Fantastic.

Hoping she doesn't notice as I slip by, I slide the key into my truck door and pull it open. The aged door groans in protest, and I cringe, silently scolding myself for not oiling the hinges this morning when I'd remembered I should. I'd nearly driven my car over instead, but Edna loved this truck.

It had been her husband's, and I've been in the never-ending process of restoring it ever since she'd insisted I take it out of her garage.

"You're Elijah Breeth."

Here we go. Taking a deep breath, I turn. "Yes."

"We spoke on the phone." Very cut and dried, matter of fact.

"We did."

"My grandmother adored you."

"I felt the same for her."

"She talked about you all the time." Her gaze flicks to the truck. "Told me about how you were restoring my grandfather's old truck."

I cross my arms, unease prickling my spine. If she's planning on taking this truck from me, she'll have a fight. I have the title, a bill of sale, and enough money to take even her to court.

"Is there something you need?"

She narrows her gaze on me, piercing green eyes that might as well be emeralds for the color and lack of emotion. "You don't like me." Once again, it's a statement rather than a question.

"I don't know you," I reply. "Difficult to not like someone when you don't know anything about them."

"According to my gran, you knew everything about everyone." Her tone leaves no room for a rebuttal. "She said you made it your job."

She wants to play ball? Fine. "Miss Andie Montgomery. Twenty-seven. Fashion icon out of New York. Never been married. No long-term relationships to speak of. Couldn't be bothered to visit her grandmother once in the few years that I knew the woman. How am I doing?"

Most people will look at least mildly uncomfortable when you spout out facts about their lives. But this woman doesn't even flinch.

"Congratulations on being a fantastic cyber stalker, Mr. Breeth. My grandmother undersold you." Her tone drips with sarcasm. "As for not visiting, I've been busy building a business. My gran knew that. And our visitation schedule is none of your business."

Her cool tone infuriates me. "You're right. My mistake. Though it seems as though the woman who raised you dying alone in a hospital bed is the right time to set your business on hold."

If looks could kill, I'd be joining Edna right about now. "My gran knew I loved her."

"Sure she did." I climb into the truck, but before I can close the door, Andie wraps slender fingers around the side of the door. Nails tipped with black, they're nearly a perfect match for the dark hair cut to her shoulders.

"Are you going to the cemetery?"

"No," I reply.

"Now who's not making time?" she asks, releasing the door. "Have a good day, Mr. Breeth."

Before I can say something I'll need to seek repentance for later, I slam the door and pull out of the parking lot. Fury burns in my veins, and I know going home to check emails is just not going to do the trick.

I need the gym.

First home to change. Then straight to the gym to work off some steam.

Everything about Andie is in contrast to her grandmother.

She's cold. Unfeeling.

Edna was the warmest, most loving woman I've ever known.

And as much as it pains me to admit it, I hope to never, ever have to cross paths with her granddaughter again. Edna's final request echoes in my mind.

"Please watch over her, Elijah. She's not as tough as she seems. She needs someone to watch out for her. You will, won't you?"

I'd promised. How could I not? Edna had died a few heartbeats later, a smile on her face because I'd agreed to always watch over Andie.

Taking a deep breath, I whip into the parking lot of the lighthouse that now serves as our office building and my apartment.

Sorry, Edna, I think this might just be the one promise I have to break.

CHAPTER 36

Searching for Peace: Andie

It's been nearly a decade since I was last in Hope Springs, Maine. Truthfully, I'd never meant to stay away from my gran this long. Even though coming back to this place felt like an unattainable task.

The house I grew up in still looks the same. A simple white cottage with bright green shutters and a door the color of the ocean. Sea glass wind chimes my gran made hang on nearly every eve of the wraparound porch. Fresh paint adorns the handrails, and I know that it was Elijah who painted them.

Elijah. My gran told me he was attractive, that he had kind eyes that reminded her of my grandfather. But now that I've met him, I can admit she undersold the looks department. Even if she did oversell his personality. He's strong, built like a fighter, sharp jaw coated with stubble, hazel eyes that shine even in the overcast afternoon.

Every time we'd spoken, and we talked quite a lot, my

gran spent more time talking about him than she had about what was going on in her life. Maybe, if she'd focused on herself rather than him, she would have remembered to tell me about the heart problems she'd been having. I could have gotten her to New York, found her good doctors, gotten her on some sort of medication.

I close my eyes and take a deep breath, urging the tears to disappear. I do not cry. It's my rule. Tears do nothing but make things worse.

"Keep it together, Andrea," my mother would have sneered. *"Tears are for the weak, girl. Are you weak?"*

No. I'm not.

"Get it together, Andie," I whisper to myself as I start up the cobblestone walkway, my suitcase in hand. I have one month to get everything in order here before I need to go home and prep for the spring show. One month, and I'll leave this town behind and never look back.

After all, there's nothing left for me here anymore. Just bad memories and heartache.

I push open the door and am hit with the delicate floral aroma of freshly cut flowers. It's like a knife to the gut when I move into the living room and see two vases of wildflowers. Who put them there? Given that they look fresh, it wasn't Gran who chose them. It wasn't her who carefully picked every bloom from her garden.

A soft meow fills my ears, and I turn as the largest black and white cat I've ever seen steps out of her bedroom and pads down the hall. After carefully setting my bag on the floor, I lean toward him and hold my hand out.

"Hey. You must be Aggie," I say as the cat touches its cool nose to my fingers then arches up under my hand. "Gran told me all about you." Hesitantly, I pick the cat up. He rubs against me some more, and I smile.

I've never been much of an animal person, but my gran always had a cat. And now, I suppose, I do too.

"I hope you'll be okay with New York," I say as I carry him into the living room and set him on the cat tower. Large picture windows make up the back wall of the house, and outside, Gran's garden is in full bloom. Flowers, rows of lettuce, green beans, and what looks like carrots sticking up from wooden garden beds that have been completely re-done since the last time I saw them.

Elijah again, no doubt.

He apparently made it his personal mission over the last three years to make sure my gran had everything she needed. While the town would pitch in here and there when they could, he'd gone through and polished off her entire to-do list in a matter of months, then meticulously maintained the yard, bushes, and even helped her upgrade a few things throughout the house.

The master bathroom remodeled.

The carpet replaced.

When she'd first told me about him, I'd thought it was sweet. Kind gestures from a kind man. Until she'd told me she'd given him my grandfather's truck. That was the first time I'd realized that there was probably more to his intentions than simply helping an elderly woman.

A wave of anger rushes through me at the image of him

sitting in the front seat. Even if he had looked good behind the wheel.

The moment she told me she'd deeded it to him, I'd realized just what kind of man he was. I've seen plenty of them during my time in New York. Elijah Breeth is the type of man who uses older women, offering them kindness and a shoulder until he drains them of everything they have.

What else did he take from her?

With that in mind, and knowing he has a key, I head straight for her bedroom. Seeing her bed carefully made, her slippers waiting for her feet the moment they touch the floor, is a stab to the heart, but I have a reason for being here, so I focus.

Turning, I reach for the free-standing jewelry cabinet my grandfather made for their fifteenth wedding anniversary. It was the last one they'd shared before the accident, and my gran treasured it. I open it, mentally prepared to see it completely cleaned out.

But when I see the glittering diamonds of her wedding ring sitting beside diamond stud earrings, pearls, and other pieces of expensive jewelry, I breathe a sigh of relief. Had he not taken these because they'd be so obvious? Because I would have noticed right away?

Someone knocks on the door, so I shut the cabinet and turn toward the living room, pausing by a mirror to make sure I look relatively put together. My dark hair could use some time with a straightener, thanks to the humidity, but other than that I look relatively put together.

So I reach for the door and pull it open.

Lilly, one of my oldest friends. stands on the other side, still wearing the black dress she'd been in for the funeral. Her hair, nearly the same color as her outfit, is up in a tight bun, and her bright blue eyes are rimmed with red from tears shed for a woman who was practically a second grandmother to her.

"Hey," I greet, plastering a smile on my face. "Come in."

"Thanks." She smiles tightly and steps into the house.

"How are you doing?" Lilly asks as she sets her purse on the floral-printed couch.

"I'm okay. It's just weird being back here."

"I can imagine." She looks around the room. "It's been a long time."

Nine years, seven months, and three days. But who's counting? "It has."

"I remember being so shocked that the town still looked exactly the same as I'd left it." Like me, Lilly had bailed on Hope Springs the second she could. Of course, her reasons had been quite different than mine. While I was following a man who I had no business following, she was running from one. Her high school sweetheart and fiancé, Alex, had joined the military. Without any warning, he'd broken things off and left town.

We'd caught up a few times when she'd been in New York or I'd been traveling for work, but three years ago, Gran told me that she'd returned and gotten back together with her Alex, who is now the owner of our small town's diner.

They got married a few years ago and had a daughter.

Sarah, I think, is her name.

"Can I get you something to drink?" I ask as Lilly takes a seat on my gran's couch.

"No, I'm okay." Her gaze drifts to the garden, and I wonder if she's thinking of all the times we'd played tea party when we'd been kids. Sitting out amidst the floral blooms, speaking in fake accents, all while Gran delivered us tiny peanut butter and jelly sandwiches cut into various shapes. "I can't believe she's gone."

"It seems surreal," I agree.

Lilly smiles sadly, tears in her eyes, and I fight to control my own.

I do not cry, I remind myself.

"Do you remember when I'd tried to pierce my nose and it—of course—went *horribly* wrong?" She laughs, reaching up to touch the side she'd shoved a needle through when we'd been sixteen. She'd been furious with her mother for something—I don't even recall what now— and she'd jammed that needle through her nose, then came running here before her mother or stepdad had been able to see it.

"Gran gave you a washcloth and told you to make better life choices." I snort, recalling the way she'd tried to hide her own laughter.

"She did." Lilly shakes her head, a smile still on her face. "And Felix hadn't even been mad," she recalls. "He'd told my mother—who had been furious—that sometimes we have to do dumb stuff in order to avoid doing dumber stuff when we get older."

"That's absolutely Felix," I muse. Lilly and her mom had come to Hope Springs after her mother met and fell in love with Felix during the town's children's toy drive. Held every Christmas, a group of volunteers takes presents to the shelters in Boston. She and her mother had been living in one of those shelters, and according to Lilly, it had been love at first sight for the hardware store owner and her mom.

Love.

I'd once believed in such things. Honestly, it was their love story that put stars in my eyes in the first place.

That and the romance novels I'd snuck out of Gran's home library as a teen.

Now I know better.

"How are things? How's your daughter?" I ask, trying my best to change the subject.

"Sarah is good. Getting big. She just turned two." She shakes her head. "They say terrible twos will start any day now, but I'm not seeing it yet."

I smile. "Then you're lucky. My assistant a few years back had a toddler. He was a menace."

Lilly scrunches her nose. "Yikes."

I shrug. "I thought he was cute, but I didn't have to deal with the meltdowns." She'd quit shortly after she'd found out she was pregnant with number two. As far as I know, she's now on four, and they're happily living in

New Jersey. Occasionally, I still beg her to come back in some capacity since everyone I've hired since hasn't lasted more than two months.

Except this last girl. Mia has potential, thankfully.

"How about you? Any prospects where you're at?"

It takes me a minute to realize she's talking about men. "Hardly." I snort. "I have zero interest in relationships."

Her expression turns serious. "Have you heard from him since—"

"You mean since he took off with one of his students and left me a sticky note on the refrigerator of the four-thousand-dollar-a-month apartment he saddled me with? No." Honestly, some would say it was bound to happen, given the history between the two of us. But I hadn't seen it coming. I'd been young and naïve.

"Yikes." She visibly winces. "I still can't believe—" She stops talking, and I know what she would have said.

Because I am the girl who ran off with her history teacher. An eighteen-year-old who'd left everything she'd ever known behind to follow the divorced thirty-seven-year-old she'd been too stupid to realize had been grooming her from the moment they met.

The entire town knew it even if they didn't talk about it. While secrets spread like wildfire in most small towns, gossip is not tolerated in Hope Springs. If it's good, they'll share. If it's bad, it gets buried.

And a troubled teen chasing her high school history teacher is pretty bad.

He'd left me a year later. Saddled me with an apartment I couldn't afford and a credit card I'd been unable to pay down. My credit took a hit, and I'd been homeless for the better part of a year, sleeping on the couches of my college friends and an occasional park bench. Doing whatever I had to in order to survive. Gran never knew that though.

When I told her I was leaving, she'd voiced her concerns, her disgust, then let me make my own choice. If I'd told her how much trouble I'd been in, she would have sent me more money. But I hadn't had the heart to tell her I'd blown every penny of her savings not wrapped up in my tuition on the apartment and a car for George.

There are so many things I wish I could take back. It's too bad you can't bury your past in a pine box, six feet down.

I clear my throat. "How is Alex?"

"Great," she says, her cheeks turning pink. "He's playing softball this season with the guys from Knight Security. Pastor Redding is on the team too."

"Knight Security?"

She cocks her head to the side. "I was sure your gran would have told you about Elijah. He was with her all the time."

"She told me about him," I say. "Just not Knight Security."

"He works there. They're a private firm, run out of the old lighthouse. Well, they were above the bakery before it got blown up."

"I'm sorry, *what?* The bakery got blown up?"

Lilly throws her head back and laughs. "We have so much to catch up on."

"Apparently." Though I desperately want to know what would have led to Pastor Redding's wife's bakery being blown up, there's one person on my mind. As he has been since I saw him in that parking lot. "Tell me about Elijah."

"He's nice. Helpful. Keeps to himself most of the time, aside from when he was with your gran."

"How long have you known him?"

"Since I got back into town. They'd just opened the firm, and he came into the diner with Lance Knight and Michael Anderson."

"Anderson? Wasn't he with—"

"Reyna Acker," she finishes.

"Gotcha. He's a few years older than us."

She nods.

"I don't know a Lance though."

"Lance moved his security company here. Both he and Elijah served with Michael."

"He's military." Which makes complete sense now that I've seen the man. He looks every bit a soldier.

"Your gran didn't tell you that? I'm surprised. They were close."

"She didn't mention that he'd served. She told me that he helped her. That he fixed things around the house and sat with her on Sundays. She'd tell me about things he said, conversations they had, but that was it."

"And you didn't ask the backstory of the man hanging with your gran?" She doesn't mean it as a jab, and I don't take it as one. Lilly has always been blunt. To the point, no sugar coating. Which is something I really appreciate about her.

"I was busy." But it's a weak excuse, and we both know it. "Our phone calls were brief. Often, but brief." And how much am I regretting that now that she's gone?

"Gotcha. Well, he was an Army Ranger, and while I don't know the details, I do know that all three were involved in some incident that nearly got them killed when they'd been overseas. He's single though. As far as I know." She wiggles her eyebrows.

"Hard pass," I reply. "The two minutes I spent with him in the parking lot of the church were long enough."

"Not a good impression, huh?"

"You could say that." I push to my feet and cross into the kitchen. In pure Gran fashion, the large glass jar on her counter is full of cookies. Reaching in, I pull one out. "I need to get started going through her things. The will reading is tomorrow, and I only have a month to get this place cleaned out and sold."

"You're not staying?" Lilly stands.

"No. My life is in New York," I reply.

"You're not even going to keep the house?" When I don't respond, she holds up both hands. "Sorry, not my business."

"No problem. Thanks for coming by."

"Of course." Lilly grabs her purse and stops just short

of opening the front door. "Come by the diner, okay? We'll make you some dinner. Best coffee around."

I smile. "Will do."

GET YOUR COPY OF SEARCHING FOR PEACE TODAY!

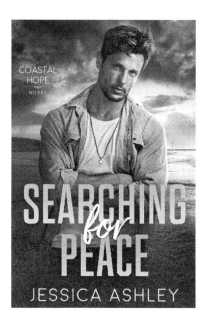

A woman with a harrowing past. The wounded veteran who never breaks a promise.

After the sudden death of her grandmother, Andie Montgomery finally returns home. It's the last place she wants to be, especially when she discovers her grandmother has left her house not just to Andie–but to a handsome, yet grumpy former Army Ranger.

Dealing with him is the last thing she wants to do, but when someone tries to kill her, he risks his life to save hers.

After making a deathbed promise, former Army Ranger Elijah Breeth is pulled into danger alongside the cold, unfeeling woman he swore to protect.

And the only clue they have as to who is after Andie, is a box of letters left beneath her grandmother's bed.

As Elijah digs deeper into Andie's past, he begins to realize that the dark-haired beauty is more than what she seems...and her secrets might just be enough to bury them both.

Get your copy!

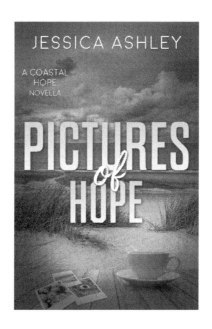

Get your hands on Alex and Lilly's story for free today!

As a travel photographer, my life has been one adventure after the next.

Every location I visit a far cry from the small town I grew up in.

A place I'd been desperate to escape after my ex broke off our engagement and joined the military.

However, home has a way of calling you back.

Three years after my mother's death, I find myself returning to Hope Springs.

But I'm not the only one who came home.

The man who practically left me at the alter is here, too.

And he's determined to heal what he shattered all those years ago: me.

Grab your free copy today!

SECURITY

Founded by veterans, Knight Private Security is your best bet when it comes to safety.

God blessed us with a desire to help others, which is precisely what we do.

Whether you want to ensure your loved ones are safe at home, protect your business, or need security for an event, we are just what you are looking for.

Highly trained and ready to protect you at all costs, our team will risk everything to ensure you are shielded from whatever danger you face.

MEET THE TEAM

Lance Knight (*Founder/Private Security Specialist*): Captain. Army Ranger. His career in the military ended when he was shot multiple times and a bullet fractured his spine.

Elijah Breeth (*Tech Specialist*): Staff Sergeant. Army Ranger. After an IED nearly ended his life, he left the military behind, but still wanted to serve the community.

Michael Anderson (*Private Security Specialist*): Staff Sergeant. Army Ranger. Grew up in Hope Springs, and after getting out of the military, he began working as a bouncer in various night clubs. Now, he's returned to his home town, though travels as his position as a private security specialist demands.

About the Author

Jessica Ashley started her career writing romance novels for the secular world, before deciding she wanted to use her love of storytelling to help bring people closer to God.

She is an Army veteran, who now resides in Texas with her husband and their three children (whom she home-schools).

You can find out more about her and her books by visiting her website: www.authorjessicaashley.com or by joining her Facebook group, Coastal Hope Book Corner.

Also by Jessica Ashley

<u>Coastal Hope Series</u>

Pages of Promise: Lance Knight

Searching for Peace: Elijah Pierce

Second Chance Serenity: Michael Anderson

More coming soon…